Quantum

Truth Devour

www.truthdevour.com

Published in 2018
by Truth Devour
www.truthdevour.com

Interior layout and design
by Publicious Pty Ltd
www.publicious.com.au

Book cover design by:
Artist: Diana Toma
Email: diana@artbydianatoma.com
Facebook: facebook.com/ArtByDianaToma

Prepublication Data Service details available
from the National Library of Australia

ISBN: 978-0-6480905-0-2 (pbk)

Also available in ebook
ISBN: 978-0-6480905-1-9 (ebk)

Hush the voices,
Still the sirens sumptuous calls,
Righteous front for witness,
Alignment to normality,
Bow now,
Cut to the curtain as it falls,
The world,
Our stage,
See how we are compelled to conform.

Who are we when none are watching?
Imaginations run rife,
Debauchery behind closed quarters,
Saints and sinners in high demand,
Lovers choose wisely,
Mutuality shared,
Smorgasbord of flavors,
Race, creed and color,
No bounds,
Woman to Man,
Man to Man,
Woman to Woman,
Consensual expression,
Any which way,
That we can.

How heinous they cry!

Nay,
Judge ye not,
For things, we fail to relate to,
Or understand,
Celebrate thy own choices,
And
        Let
            Love
Reign by thy own command.

Truth Devour

ALSO BY TRUTH DEVOUR

<u>Soliloquy's Labyrinth Series</u>

Adult Contemporary Fantasy / Paranormal
with a psychological edge

Illuminarium
(1st Book)

Insurrection
(2nd Book)

<u>Enigma Series</u>

Adult Contemporary Fantasy Trilogy
with sensual erotic undertones
and a dash of paranormal

Wantin
(1st book)

Unrequited
(2nd book)

Sated
(3rd book)

www.truthdevour.com

DIRECT
DEVOUR

Contents

Discord 1

Reciprocity 29

Longanimity 59

Jay Bird Blue 88

Duplicity 114

Family 146

Decree 169

Dominion 191

Sibling Rivalry 233

Farewell 256

Dhyāna 287

Discord

As I entered the room, I could feel a chill wash over my body. They enthrallingly looked like zombies to me, zoned out, traversing the open space in rows of diagonals with no detectable purpose. The dullness in their eyes, coupled with the drool escaping their swollen chapped lips made me question what was the point of keeping them alive at all? Their state appeared almost catatonic, if not for their aimless amble from point to point. Roaming among them, I could feel the heat generated from their bodies. I imagined their inner turmoil swelling as I felt the intrusion of their blank stares. After all I had been through, this place was the one that was triggering my sense of fear to rise to the surface. The vacancy in their eyes held a familiarity, even the smell of the room invoked a reaction that made my skin crawl. I wanted to get out of there, but I also knew that this was precisely where I needed to be. My hunch was that some of the crucial answers I required to connect missing links resided within him.

"Digby is over there sitting by the window."

I looked in the direction to where the orderly was pointing. "I see him, thanks."

"No problems. I'll be right over here if you need me."

I knew I must have looked concerned as I glanced at the him.

"I'm just giving you some space. There's nothing to worry about, these savage beasts are doped to the eyeballs and docile as lambs. Hell, most of them have frontal lobotomies, so you are in zombie town girl."

"Okay." I said wiping the sweat from my brow.

Internally, I was trying to squelch my rising compulsion to turn and run out of the room. I methodically placed one foot in front of the other, completely focused on navigating a clear path through the wasteland of zombies, heading straight toward my destination, while being avidly tuned in to the sound of the orderlies fading footsteps. My heart began pumping at speed as I placed my final step before the ominous Digby Mangonel. His right leg was crossed over his left with his hands neatly placed in his lap. I watched the rise and fall of his chest as his shallow breath made his loose off white t-shirt rhythmically dance. The protruding veins on the surface of his hands coupled with his drawn facial features indicated that he was most definitely underweight. My eyes gravitated to focus on the crown of his head, where the flecks of dandruff on his side part spread outward from his hairline. It was akin to a random splatter of twinkling stars against a blackened night sky.

"Please take a seat Ms Perelle." He diverted his gaze from the window to confidently stare at my crotch. "I'm assuming you have remained…. unmarried."

I pulled out the plastic chair and took my position across from Digby. Cautiously, I placed my sweaty palms flat on the table's surface and released my breath.

Digby smiled, "Welcome to Houghton House, the institution devoted to the barbaric experimentation on the criminally insane." He paused for a moment to gaze into my eyes. "It's been quite a while since I've had the pleasure of your company my dear."

"You remember me? I wasn't expecting that." I said feeling the tension in my body begin to slightly dissipate.

"How could I forget such a rare beauty?"

"You seem rather cheerful and oddly alert in comparison to your," I glanced around momentarily, "inmates."

Digby's leg jerked causing it to bounce. He maintained eye contact with me as he casually moved his left hand to still the muscle spasm. "Nothing is ever as it seems, you of all people should know that."

I chose not to respond.

A wry smile appeared on his patchy shaved face, "Life is a series of choices. The mystery is that no matter the choice made, in the end you wind up exactly where you need to be at the time that you need to be there."

I felt my lips purse, as I acknowledged his words, "You were expecting me then?"

"Of course. I knew it was only a matter of time before you connected the dots. It's a decade later than I had anticipated. I guess it goes to show that I don't know everything, either."

I glanced at the reflection in the window to check on where the orderly was positioned. When my eyes adjusted to the light's glare, I could see he was leaning against the wall near the doorway with his arms folded, staring up at the television.

"May I call you Harper or do you prefer something more formal Ms Perelle?"

I looked at Digby and smiled, "Sure, Harper is fine."

"What did you tell the powers that be in the institution in order to convince them to give you access to visit me?"

I looked down at my fingernails for a moment. "Given our history, I told them that I was considering an offer to do my doctorate and wanted to explore the possibility of basing it around you."

"Hmm." Digby stroked the air under his chin as though there was a beard.

"Our history, imagine that. Harper Perelle openly admitting we are connected."

"I have nothing to hide. You were my first, Digby."

He leant forward and calmly placed his cold hand on mine. "Are you flirting with me?"

I slowly recoiled back in my chair, "Let me assure you, it's the furthest thing from my mind. I would appreciate if you respected my boundaries and refrain from openly leering at my crotch while you're at it."

Digby snickered, "Playing hard to get. I can work with that."

"I've re-read the session notes I had taken while you were in Dr Crude's care. I was hoping that we could talk about what you believe was happening back then. I'm looking for your retrospective insight and current position on the events."

Digby sat back in his chair defaulting to mimic my body language. "Ah yes. You were so young, fresh out of university, absorbing my every word. Unlike that ignorant text book joke of a psychiatrist Crude who was campaigning for me to be locked up."

"Can you go back to what had been happening and talk me through it?"

"I know what you are looking for Harper and more importantly what you need to hear. The question is whether you will trust what I have to say after what I did?"

"I'm here aren't I? I don't have time to waste on riddles." I was feeling agitated by his smug demeanor.

Digby leant in and whispered, "On the contrary, you have nothing but time. It doesn't matter the choices you make, you will end up exactly where you are meant to be. The choice only determines the path you navigate. Your destiny has been divined and nothing you can do will ever alter this. Don't be a fool and waste your energy believing otherwise."

"So, I can't influence my fate, only the route in which I travel to it?"

Digby smiled, "Precisely." His expression altered as his eyes surveyed the room. "I know you want to know how to find them. You want access to the Interferon's covern."

I held no intent to correct him and decided to see where the dialogue would lead. I raised my eyebrow as I tilted my head forward, "Do you know how to find them?"

His left hand covered his mouth as his index finger tapped twice on his cheek. "Why did I kill Dr Crude, Harper? What did this woman possibly do to deserve the wrath I unleashed on her?"

I diverted my eyes to gaze out the window, releasing the breath I had been subconsciously holding. "At that point in time, you presented behaviors that would suggest that you were in a heightened state of paranoia. You seemed to struggle with being able to delineate between what was happening around you and what you felt was happening to you. You regularly appeared agitated.

On numerous occasions, you freely expressed your frustration at her inability to understand what you were proposing. I assume you felt alone in your plight to be heard, understood."

"Text book blah, blah. You can do better than that. Why did I kill her?"

I looked into Digby's eyes, "You pose a question only you can provide the answer to. I may be able to surmise, but the truth is yours for the telling."

Digby's face lit up as he readjusted his posture to be more upright in his chair, "Humor me and surmise."

I clamped down on the left side of my bottom lip as I whispered the word, "Safety."

"Go on."

"If everyone thinks you're insane you are no longer deemed a threat because no-one is likely to take what you have to say seriously. You become labeled, institutionalized and forgotten."

Slowly, he raised his hands and clapped them together three times before tucking them tightly underneath his armpits. He stared at me for a few moments, then began rocking back and forth.

"Go on."

"I don't believe what you did was personal, rather Dr Crude was a convenient target. As far as I am aware, this was the first and only time you have taken a life. I suspect you didn't realize the extent of the rage you held within you, nor did you imagine that you were capable of unleashing such ferocity. You may have approached the situation with a premeditated idea of what would take place, but to some degree, I suspect you lost a sense of yourself when you transitioned into an unexpected state of rabid frenzy. The report indicated you were found sitting naked in a welling pool of her blood, thrashing back and forth while screaming an amalgamation of obscenities and gibberish to her severed head."

Digby's right eyebrow raised with a quiver, "Why didn't you attend the clinic that day?"

"I received a message the night before from Dr Crude's personal assistant to say that all sessions were being canceled and I wasn't required to attend."

"Was there a reason given?"

"No, and at the time I never thought to ask."

Digby shifted in his chair, appearing ridgid in his posture. His left leg was beginning to present with a dull tremor.

"Are you suggesting my absence played a role in what happened that day?"

Digby released a muffled laugh, "It was you that I had set my sights on killing that day." He paused for a moment to lick his lips.

"You have no idea how disappointed I was to enter the room and see your corner chair empty."

Digby had released his left hand from the security of his armpit and fanned his fingers as he said the word empty. I felt a cold chill crawl up my spine.

"When I asked whether you would be attending the session, she shook her head and smiled, stating you were no longer assigned to the clinic. She tricked me into believing that you were never coming back. It was like a switch flipped inside me, her incessant jealous behavior, that smug grin invited my rage and I…"

I placed my hand up, "You can spare reciting the details. I saw the photos and read the coroner's report. I'm well aware of what you did."

He tilted his head as he assessed my expression, "You seem ambivalent."

"I can't alter what has transpired nor hold myself responsible for the choices you made."

Digby slammed his hands on the table causing my body to jolt. Through gritted teeth his words seethed, "Do you know what horrors I have had to endure in this malignant place because of you?"

I remained still and glared at him.

He readjusted his posture to lean back in his chair once more, "I can see that we are quickly moving toward arriving at an impasse. Perhaps we best postpone our discussion for another day."

I shook my head slightly, "There won't be another day. It's now or never."

Digby smiled, "I possess the knowledge you need. You will be back, and you will keep returning until I tell you what you hunger to know. I'm going to take pleasure in drip feeding the details to you at my own leisure. It could take days, months, perhaps even years. It will all depend on how compliant you are to my needs."

I slowly rose to my feet, "This isn't a game."

He released a bellowing laugh that immediately encouraged the others to alter their direction. I glanced at the exit.

"That's where you are wrong Harper. It is nothing more than a game and right now they are playing you like a fiddle."

Digby leaned forward as he hissed. "You need me."

His words hit an untapped raw nerve. I curbed my desire to react, deciding the better approach was to maintain a modicum of composure and walk away. "Goodbye Digby."

"See you soon, Harper."

I froze mid step and calmly replied, "No, you won't."

I began to make my way toward the door.

"Very well, an invitational taste then."

Digby's voice carried a tone of desperation. I stopped mid step, to hear his plee.

"It wasn't meant to be like this. It was never part of the plan. You should have been there that day. The motions were set in play for me to die by your hand."

I turned to glance into his eyes, "Free will is the governor. Thou shall not die by my hand."

Digby smiled. "My life was predestined to be taken by the soul key of wills. Harp player." He tapped the side of his head near his temple. "The question 'why' should be posed and sought to be understood. It is within this, that clarity resides." His index finger began making circles in the air in front of him. "Until then you will continue on your merry go round."

A surge of heat shot up from my feet through my body as I tried to navigate passed the sea of zonked inmates who seemed now to be strategically congregating around me. Their haunting stares released the sound of screams in my mind as I struggled to shove my way through them. The orderly was too engrossed in watching the television to notice my struggle and had not acknowledged me as I walked past to exit the room. He too appeared to be in a trance.

As I arrived at the reception desk there was a different attendant behind the counter. She stared at me and then leaned over to watch my hand as I marked the page to sign myself out. Placing the pen down I waited for her to finish inspecting my signature under the lamp. She was closely measuring it against the identification card I had provided upon entry. It felt torturously slow. Eventually she retrieved my personal possessions and flagged the security guard to approach. He openly exchanged glances with her before quietly escorting me out of the building. The moment I reached the car park I bridged my hand on the nearest vehicle to support my balance as I reefed forward gasping for breath. The breeze ran cool against my sweaty brow. I felt a compulsion to run as fast as I could for my senses warned that I had inadvertently avoided a monstrous encounter. The sound of my heart beat rising to my throat heightened the feeling of dread. There was no relief felt as I reached my ride. I fumbled for my keys conscious that the bevvy of security cameras captured my expression of angst. When I got into my car I opened all the windows to receive the welcome rush of brisk air as I drove out of the lot and onto the road that led me to the highway. His words 'You need me,' played on my mind. He set his sights on killing me that day but actually planned to die by my hand. Why?

* * * * *

Against my desire to simply stop, I decided to pull out the few recordings I had taken of Digby's sessions with Dr Crude. During my final year of college, I had been intermittently attending as an observer at the time that Digby was assigned to her. Huckleberry nestled on my chest while I placed the headphones on and clicked play.

Session 202 with Digby Mangonel

"How are you feeling today?"
"Fine."

"Digby, I need you to extrapolate. I'm here to help you and can only do this when you participate. Let's refrain from the single word responses please."

"Sure thing."

"Clever, two word responses are no better. It's been a week since our last session, why don't you give me the highlights of the things that happened."

"I slept, woke, ate, shat, sometimes showered and then slept some more."

"Did you meet anyone interesting? Watch any good movies? I'd like to know more about how you filled your days."

"Did you research the leads I gave you last week?" There was a smugness in his tone.

"Honestly, no."

"Why not?"

"If I am to help you Digby I need to remain impartial and not go down a rabbit warren of conspiracy theories with you. The assistance I offer is about getting you to see how you are blurring the lines between reality and fantasy. I've told you my diagnosis leans towards you being a fit for dissociative disorder with a penchant toward conspiracy theories being your trigger for visceral illusions. No one is watching you. There is no secret organization that controls us through subliminal messaging. These are all concepts your mind created to play tricks on you."

"You are a liar."

Sigh, "What am I lying about?"

"Twenty-two minutes after our session was over you began searching online, looking up the links I gave you. A total of seven calls were made from your personal phone that was related to the leads I provided. Yet, you profess not to go down a rabbit warren 'with' me."

"Have you been spying on me?"

"No Dr Crude. They have, and they took pleasure in ensuring that I was made aware that they are watching your every move right down to the minutest details."

"What does that mean precisely?"

"It means that I know about that cut on your inner right rather fleshy thigh and how you got it shaving in the bath yesterday evening."

Silence ... for a moment only the disturbing crackling noise on the recording could be heard.

"I found your life rather mundane to witness, boarding on pathetic. The highlight of my week was when you masturbated to an old photo of your ex husband. The one who cheated on your sorry ass countless times and then finally mustered the balls to leave you for his receptionist. Every night this week I have watched you console yourself with a nightcap of wine, Valium and tears. Now here you are dressed to impress, preened from head to toe projecting the lie you wish to sell, but you will forever be ... naked to me."

Russle, russle.

Click.

Sitting up I retrieved the tape from the case to inspect the handwriting on the label. This wasn't one of my session recordings. I had never heard this before. My notes were submitted for assessment during the evidence collection period of Digby's trial. When they were returned to me I didn't check to verify it was all mine. Looking in the box I could see two more of the recordings in Crude's penmanship.

I placed the earliest dated tape in next.

Session 189 with Digby Mangonel

"How are you feeling today?"

"Tortured by the watchers who relentlessly observe my every move. They know everything. They are everywhere peering into my psych, trying to get me to do things. Awful, horrible things."

"What kind of things?"

"Where's the girl?"

"I am unsure of whom you are referring to Digby."

"The girl, the one who sat in that chair over there and watched us. Where is she?"

"Oh, you mean Harper. She won't be a regular part of our sessions. Do you recall that I explained to you that she is a graduating student who is attending a variety of my clinical sessions as an observer?"

"There are things she needs to hear. Things they want her to know. The devil is in the details. Plant the seed and let it grow."

"Digby, you seem agitated. Have you been taking the medication I prescribed?"

"Did you hear me? They want HER."

"Who are 'they' Digby?"

"I told you. I told you. I told you. The Interferons are making a move to take over the world through manipulation and mind control. They are using us as pawns to execute their bidding. Mark my words there is no refusing them. You cannot hide when technology, your friends, your family are all channeled into conspiring against you. Comply or die, they are the choices we have."

"You say they want her. Do you know why?"

"No, not yet. My attempts to find more details have been thwarted. She is shielded; people must know she needs protection. They want her but seem to be hesitant to do anything about it. That's why they need me. I'm supposed to do the dirty work. They are telling me things, showing me things, forcing me to understand what should never have been revealed. Can't you see? You, me, it's not a coincidence. They orchestrated this. We are nothing more than puppets on a string. Except her, she's different. She's ... weird."

"I need to know if you have been taking your medication. Can you tell me truthfully?"

"Yes."

"So, you have been taking them?"

"No."

"I'm confused, why did you say yes, if the answer is no?"

"I said yes to being able to answer truthfully."

"So yes, you can answer truthfully but no you haven't been taking your medication. Have I got it right?"

"Yes."

"Digby, I'm concerned about your escalating paranoia. It's clear to me that you aren't sleeping. I can tell by your frequent leg spasms that the anxiety you are feeling is amplifying your ticks. Perhaps it's time to consider spending some time in the safety of a hospital where you can be monitored a little closer."

"No, No, No, No, No, that won't work. They run the institutions; they run all the loony wards in all the hospitals, that's where they have the most leverage.

Psychiatry was their greatest trick ever pulled. I can't. I WON'T. NO, NO, NO, NO, NO, NO, NO, NO."

"Get off the chair and sit back down before you hurt yourself. Calm down, I need you to take your medication. If you promise to do that as prescribed then we can hold off on anymore talk of me admitting you, okay?"

"YES, YESsss, lets do that. Yes, pills, I'll take em. I'll take em."

"Do you have any with you today? I'd like you to take one now if you do."

"No, No, No, No, No, I don't have any."

"You must promise me that you will go straight home and take your medication. It will help you to feel better."

"YES, yes, let's do that. Yes, pills. I'll take em."

"Where are you going Digby?"

"I'm going home now, I'm tired."

"We haven't finished our session. Please come back and sit down."

"Um, no. Will she be here next week?"

"Come sit, so we can talk about it."

"No, I'm tired. I need to go home to take my pills."

The door squeaked open, then closed.

Sigh.

Click.

I inserted the final tape.

Session 208 with Digby Mangonel

"You look like you are feeling better."

"I am."

"I'm pleased."

"What do you think has made the difference this week?"

"I noticed you have a new receptionist."

"That's correct, Nora has taken a few weeks leave to care for her mother, so I called in a temp to cover for the duration of her absence."

"Did you interview her?"

"Yes, of course."

"So, you did a background check then?"

"Don't be paranoid. Let's refocus on you answering my questions for a change."

Muffled laughter.

"What has helped you feel better this week Mr Mangonel?"

"I know what needs to be done, and so... do... you."

"You are beginning to speak in riddles again. Can you extrapolate and remove the assumption that I have the faintest idea of what you are speaking of?"

"The smirk on your face suggests otherwise Ms Crude. You know what needs to happen. Our part in this charade is almost at an end. There is no denying your truth. We make a great team."

Laughter.

Click.

Huckleberry was fast asleep on my lap. I stroked him softly; my little man was all grown up. His presence in my life calmed me. I began fast forwarding the tape, stopping intermittently to check but it appeared that there wasn't anything else captured. This recording was the most disturbing of them all to me. I decided to listen to the session again, this time paying closer attention to the tone in their voices. They were conversing like familiar friends. Dr Crude's words were served in a masked playful manner. It was as though the recording only held purpose to capture the shift in their dynamic.

This morning when I met with Digby, he said that Crude tricked him, yet this recording suggests they were uniting forces in some way. Imagery of Crude and Mangonel having intercourse started to seep into my mind as I tried to make sense of it all. Once she learned that there was complete invasion of her privacy Crude chose to continue to provide sessions to Digby. Any rational psychiatrist would seek immediate intervention and report it to the authorities for further investigation. I can only assume given her choice to continue the sessions that she was doing so willingly.

Huckleberry's ears pricked up as he lifted his head.

Knock, knock.

I placed Huckleberry on the floor, tucked the recordings underneath the coffee table and answered the door.

"Officer Bradlyn."

"Good afternoon Ms Perelle. How are you?"

"I'm okay. What can I do for you?"

"I understand that you made a visit to Houghton House this morning."

"I did." I said feeling cautious about where this might be headed.

"We received a phone call raising some concerns regarding your presence there and thought in light of the recent trauma you experienced that it might be worthwhile dropping past to see how you are managing."

I could see by the way he was fiddling with his fingers that he was feeling some small measure of apprehension.

"I'm not following. What exactly did the staff at Houghton House believe was alarming enough to notify the police and how is it related to me?"

"There was no record of your entry into Houghton House marked in the visitor's book, nor were you captured on their main surveillance cameras arriving or leaving the property. There is however, footage of you inside the institution in a highly restricted area where no visitors are allowed. This raised cause for concern, among other things."

"That's odd. I announced myself upon arrival, signed in, was escorted to the room and the same occurred on the way out. Their cameras might not be working but they only need to double check the guest register to see that I absolutely signed in. I'm still not following what the true cause for concern stems from."

Officer Bradlyn gave me a reassuring smile, "Perhaps its best if you come with me and see for yourself."

I stepped back, "Where are you intending to take me?"

"To Houghton House so you can see the surveillance footage. It might be easier to offer an explanation to the events in order to alleviate any concerns."

I shook my head slightly. "I'll take my own car and meet you there."

"I'd prefer if I took you in my vehicle."

"I don't mean any disrespect Officer Bradlyn, but I must insist upon driving myself. I'll meet you down stairs in five minutes and will follow you there, so we arrive at the same time."

"Okay." He said as he stepped back and turned.

I closed the door, placing my head on it as I shut my eyes for a moment. What on earth was happening now?

* * * * *

Inside the monitoring control room at Houghton House, the security guard offered me his seat in front of the main monitor. "Just click play here to start the footage."

I looked at Officer Bradlyn and the Houghton House staff standing beside him before turning to press the space bar on the computer. I watched as the flickering black and white footage depicted a snippet of me walking across the room toward Mangonel. Then the frame switched to a closer view over the shoulder shot of my back sitting at the table across from Mangonel. The focal point was on him.

"You remember me? I wasn't expecting that."

"You seem rather cheerful and oddly alert in comparison to your, inmates."

"You were expecting me then?"

I slowly pressed the spacebar to stop the video then turned to look directly at the security personnel.

"What's wrong with the sound recording on this?"

The security guard's body stiffened up. He bent down to check the volume, "Nothing, it's operating correctly."

Something was wrong. I could feel the little hairs on the back of my neck start to stand as I recommenced watching the footage. Trying to feign composure I discreetly searched for cues that would help me explain what the hell was going on. It took a brief second before I realized the complimentary oddity to the missing audio. Digby's mouth never moves. His lips were swollen with drool seeping out in globs onto his chest and lap. It was disgusting. The footage had reached the point where my head turned to glance at the reflection in the window to check on where the orderly was positioned and then returned to look at Digby.

"Sure, Harper is fine."

"Given our history, I told them that I was considering an offer to do my doctorate and wanted to explore the possibility of basing it around you."

"I have nothing to hide. You were my first, Digby."

"Let me assure you, it's the furthest thing from my mind. I would appreciate if you respected my boundaries and refrain from openly leering at my crotch while you're at it."

I pressed the spacebar to stop the video. "I've seen enough."

The head of the psychiatry division at Houghton, Dr Spence gave me a gentle smile as he stepped into my view. "We are currently unsure how you gained access to the facility and more so, how you bypassed security to enter a room where there are strictly no visitors allowed."

I stood up so he no longer had the advantage of peering down at me. "I entered the same way I did this time, through the front door. Once I signed in, I handed all my possessions to the reception desk before being escorted by an orderly into that room that you see me in. It was all prearranged two weeks ago through Professor Sutain who I understand is the managing director of Houghton House."

They all looked at one another, "I'm the appointed managing director and the head of psychiatry for this facility. We don't have anyone by the name of Professor Sutain on staff."

"That doesn't make sense. I have email correspondence from him confirming the authority for access to Digby. When I arrived this morning, the receptionist said she was advised to expect me."

A lady stepped forward, "I was on duty this morning and I don't recall seeing you at all."

I looked at her and smiled, "No, you weren't the person at the desk this morning. Perhaps you were on break."

"Actually, I've been the only one here all day."

I looked across at Dr Spence, "I don't understand how that's possible."

"I'd appreciate you forwarding the email correspondence to my security team, so they may investigate further."

"Sure, I'll do that as soon as I'm back home."

Officer Bradlyn cleared his throat. "Ms Perelle, there is also some concern pertaining to the behavior you displayed while in the presence of Digby Mangonel. It appears you were engaging in a one sided conversation with him."

I looked down at my hands for a moment, "Yes, it does appear that way."

"It's the only way it could be given that he has been mute for nearly ten years. I cross-checked our patient records to confirm my understanding of his circumstances. It appears due to his spontaneous violent outbursts there was an order placed for him to be lobotomized. Once he emerged from the procedure, he never spoke a word. He has been since treated with shock therapy, ice water immersion baths and countless other procedures without a noise passing by his lips."

I looked at the monitor and starred at the still image of Mangonel.

"What we observed gives us cause for concern. Officer Bradlyn has confirmed that you have recently been involved in a highly traumatic event. I feel you may need to consider seeking some professional assistance to help you through this challenging time in your life. We are yet to understand how you could enter this highly secure facility undetected, then navigate into a locked down room filled with some of the most dangerous mentally unstable criminals in the world, only to sit down and hold a rather cryptic conversation with a mute."

Nothing I was seeing was making any sense to me. I knew if I tried to explain that Digby was quite lucid and talking to me this morning that I would sound crazy. I needed to buy myself some time to figure this out. I nodded my head. "I appreciate the concern and am aware that there are what seems to be a series of unexplained anomalies that not even I at this point can explain. I will send you the emails when I get home so that you can start your investigations."

"I have a colleague who I can highly recommend to assist you," offered Dr Spence.

"No thank you. I have my own longstanding therapist, Dr Huckleberry. I'll make an appointment to go see him as soon as I get home. I'm sure reciting this event will place him in a tailspin. Would you mind providing me a copy of the footage, please."

The security man looked at Dr Spence to seek approval. When he received his cue, he responded, "Sure. If you can give me ten minutes, I'll provide you with the stream."

"Great, you had mentioned there is no footage of me entering or leaving the building this morning. Is this correct?"

"Yes."

"Then I'd also like to get sample copies of the footage for the camera's that captured my entry with Officer Bradlyn, if that's okay."

Once again, he looked across at Dr Spence for approval before he responded, "Sure."

"Why do you want the footage?" asked Officer Bradlyn.

"It seems curious to me that the only footage captured is limited to that room. I want to evaluate it pane by pane to see if there are any clues that could assist me in explaining what has happened. I know that when I entered the room there were from my count approximately nine cameras. When you look at the footage I am primarily captured from one angle. This seems really odd to me."

"The other cameras were malfunctioning this morning," blurted the security guard.

Office Bradlyn shifted his stance, "Really? Well then it is possible that the cameras in the foyer and out the front enterance were also having issues."

The security guard raised his hand, "No, we cross checked them, we have full length footage on all angles from this morning."

"Dr Spence you mentioned the sector I entered is a highly secure area."

"Yes, it is."

"Can you please explain to me why the security person monitoring the cameras would have allowed a civilian to be present and remain for such a length of time in that locked down room instead of raising an alarm?"

He cleared his throat as he repositioned his arms to be folded tightly across his midriff. "The security guard was questioned in regard to this. He stated that at no point did he observe your presence in the room."

"Why haven't you volunteered this information until now?" asked Officer Bradlyn.

"Well it's clear by the footage that Ms Perelle was present, so we can surmise that the security guard fell asleep during the time she was in attendance, which is the only explanation that can account for her not being detected."

I smiled, "How do you explain the floor staff also not seeing me, especially given the length of time I was in the room? Were there any therapy sessions being held this morning in the common area? Typically, in institutions such as this there are." I knew from previous attendance to psychiatric facilities that open group sessions were often held in the common areas of the building. I was simply backing a hunch.

"Um, yes there was."

I started to feel a sense of relief. "Did they see me in the room or are we assuming that they were asleep on the job too?"

Dr Spence cleared his throat again but this time he shifted his body weight to lean on his left side. "I admit there are some oddities that we cannot explain regarding your presence not being detected, but the video footage is irrefutable. You were here."

"To that point, if my presence wasn't detected while I was here, then how did it get detected after the fact?"

The security guy smiled, "I can answer that. When I came on shift I noticed that the cameras were displaying jitter, then they froze for a couple of minutes before going completely offline for over twenty minutes. I got assistance from tech support to reboot each of the systems and began investigating to identify the issue. It was at this point that we came across some footage, which alerted us to your presence this morning."

"That makes sense. What remains confusing is how you came to learn my name. If there is no record of me entering the building, signing in or out, can you tell me how you managed to determine my identity so quickly?"

Dr Spence jumped in, "I'll answer that. We didn't know who it was when we made the call to the police. The only name we knew for certain was Harper."

"Actually, I was the Officer who received the call and I can assure you that Harper Perelle was named during the discussion, so her question remains valid. How did you know her full name?"

I placed my hand on Officer Bradlyn's arm, "It seems there are a few things that clearly don't add up. This whole situation was angled toward a focus on my presence rather than encompassing the volume of inexplicable anomalies surrounding the events that took place this morning. I'd like to have the footage professionally examined to see if it can provide me with some answers."

"I fail to see how that could be of any use," said Dr Spence.

"Your tone and body language is presenting as defensive Dr Spence," I said as I intentionally stared at his folded arms.

"What do you expect considering you have breached our security, trespassed and now somehow converted this conversation into an investigation of the very institution that I am charged with running?"

"Okay, now place yourself in my position. I liaised with 'someone' whom I believed was a representative of this institution, upon my arrival at reception I was acknowledged; after signing in I was escorted to the room to speak with Digby Mangonel. How do you think it feels to return this afternoon under police escort to be stultified by this video footage that depicts me as mentally compromised? I mean look at this." I pressed the space bar to restart the video.

"I've re-read the session notes I had taken while you were in Dr Crude's care. I was hoping that we could talk about what you believe was happening back then. I'm looking for your retrospective insight and current position on the events."

"Can you go back to what had been happening and talk me through it?"

"I'm here aren't I? I don't have time to waste on riddles."

Quick as a whip I pressed down on the space bar as I saw a blip on the screen. "Wait, can you rewind to the flicker on the screen please."

The security guard sat down in the chair and proceeded to go back frame-by-frame.

"There, stop. Look, the bird outside is flying by but it oddly disappears at the mid point. Hold on a second, can you zoom in to focus on just the window please."

A smile of satisfaction grew. The magnification showed the mesh grate on the side of Digby's frame and clear glass on mine.

"Well I'll be damned," said Officer Bradlyn.

"This confirms the footage has been compromised but it doesn't explain how it's been done or why. It's like I was led to believe that I was here but was actually somewhere else that looked exactly the same. I don't understand it."

Dr Spence lent in to take a closer look at the monitor. "Oh."

Officer Bradlyn glanced at me and nodded his head, "Dr Spence if you have any further insight I would suggest that you share it with us now."

"It seems that Ms Perelle may have been taken to the studio's which are located at the back of this complex. It's the precise replica of this building that was built near on a decade ago when a deal was brokered by the government with some Hollywood types. Loads of crime and thriller themed series have been filmed there. TV shows such as, Missing Linx, The Bancheeto Bro's and more. They wanted a realistic set and decided to model it after Houghton House right down to the fixtures, with the exception of the security meshing outside the windows. They said it compromised the lighting."

I checked my phone, "Is the entry to this facility on Barker Road?"

Dr Spence shook his head, "No that's the studio. This building can only be entered by Falcon Drive."

Officer Bradlyn clapped his hands together, "It seems the good news is that no breach has occurred, but we still need to understand why someone would go to such a length to make it look like there was."

"With no disrespect intended Officer Bradlyn, there must have been a cyber breach that occurred to have the security camera's tampered with and substitute footage loaded to the network. Right now, possibly the biggest concern is that this facilities network has been compromised."

"Yes, of course, I meant it strictly in terms of yourself, Ms Perelle. There is definitely a need for further investigation in regard to the matter overall."

I smiled, "Thanks Officer Bradlyn."

"I'm just glad to be of service," he said as his cheeks flushed crimson.

"I don't think there is anything else we can resolve right now. I would be interested to pay a visit to the studio. Would you mind escorting me?"

"Absolutely, it's where I planned to head to next. Dr Spence can you please have your team send across a copy of all the video feeds to the station. I will also need a full list of the names of the staff that were working today. I'll return with a colleague to begin compiling statements for an official investigation."

"We welcome the assistance Officer Bradlyn. In the meantime, I am going to get the head of security to review all our protocols and have our IT division do a full assessment of the network to try and identify how the breach was executed."

As we both walked out the door I felt an enormous wave of relief wash over me. There was certainly a definite potential for the outcome to be vastly different given the odds were almost all favored against me from the outset. My only advantage was my cognitive reasoning and that, I knew, was only going to get me so far.

Reciprocity

Upon my arrival home, there was a package wrapped in plain brown paper positioned at the foot of my door. It had some twinning around it with a couple of sprigs of fresh lavender secured by a tight bow. I looked up at the ceiling vent and wondered if it had been delivered by mysterious means. There wasn't an address or postmark, so I knew this meant it was hand delivered by someone outside of the standardized postal service. The waft of the fragrant lavender greeted my senses, making me feel safe. I bent down and collected the parcel before entering my apartment.

Huckleberry was waiting on the other side of the door, vigorously wagging his tail. He leapt up as I lowered my hand to scoop him into my free arm. In his usual delectable fashion, I was greeted with frantic licks on my face, causing me to squeal with delight. I'm so grateful to have him in my life.

Carefully I placed the package on the kitchen bench alongside Huckleberry, and then switched on the kettle before proceeding to prepare his dinner. When it was ready I put Huckleberry down so he could eat, then began making myself a cup of tea while quietly deliberating about whether it was too early to head for bed. I opted to migrate to the sofa.

Reflecting on the day's events there was a part of me that felt as though I was trapped within a perpetual spin cycle of a front loader washing machine whereby I was being tossed, pushed and pulled in a repetitive rhythm. The existential position was my feeling that I was equal parts a participant within the washer as well as the witness on the outside, watching it all take place. I could sense that there was a flurry of knowledge that I was on the cusp of obtaining that would provide me with the breakthrough I needed. I knew I was balancing on the edge of something that could be a duality of strength and destruction and it all evolved around me.

I took a sip of my tea while staring at the package on my lap. It was releasing a low frequency vibrational hum. A silent white noise of sorts that felt mildly menacing. Slowly, I unravelled the paper to reveal a penned note and a hand made untitled book that was bound in tapestry.

Harper,

A reflection sought and found. The dark secrets of how they sow and we reap.

Lib

The inside page had a spattering of random formulas some of which I recognized such as Einstein's theory of relativity $E = mc^2$, Euler's equitation $V - E + F = 2$ and the Pythagorean Theorem of $a^2 + b^2 = c^2$. In the center there was a decoratively drawn scroll framing one formula, visually calling it out as a showpiece of sorts.

$$N = R^* \cdot f_p \cdot n_e \cdot f_l \cdot f_i \cdot f_c \cdot L$$

I didn't have the first clue as to what it represented but I did recognize the element symbols cleverly weaved into the frame as part of the scroll. Earth, Water, Air & Fire. There was a faint ghosting outline of the eye of Horus behind the formula with the Ankh just below it, both within the frame. It almost looked as though it was sun bleached to stain the mark into the paper rather than being drawn. The eye of Horus is the watchful all seeing eye of creation and the Ankh is known as the breath of life. I flipped to the next page where there were two words written: Conspirathorium Valedictorian.

Valedictorian I knew was a person noted as a high achiever who as part of their outstanding academic success is assigned the responsibility for delivering the closing statement at a graduation ceremony. I had never heard of the word conspirathorium. Its origin base I'm guessing is derived from the word conspiracy, but the addition of thorium held interest. It's a naturally occurring substance that contains radioactive elements. In chemistry class, it was referred to as Thor due to it originally being named by its discoverer after the Norse god of thunder.

I began flipping through the pages to see if I could gleam anything from the contents to help provide more context. At first glance, it all seemed to contain a bunch of formulas erratically scrunched together. Pages and pages of mathematical strings of madness with the odd commentary such as, electron falls into proton to make hydrogen. The details were way beyond my expertise to decipher. Still, I continued to turn the pages.

The elemental symbols for Earth, Water, Air & Fire were repeated in some sections paired with a singular chemical element.

Earth + $_{90}$Th (Thorium)
Water + F^- (Fluoride)
Air + N_2 (Nitrogen)
Fire + Pm_{61} (Promethium)

The attending note to the book said 'A reflection sought and found. The dark secrets of how they sow and we reap,' which to me meant that this information is dangerous and therefore needs to be restricted. The entire content is hand written and the oddity of the tapestry book cover supported how personal the work seemed to be. I felt the onus was weighted on me to decipher the information. The energy of the book made me adopt a feeling that I couldn't take the risk of involving anyone in case it revealed something of a sinister nature. In reality, I no longer knew who I could trust.

I decided to close the book in order to begin a re-evaluation of my approach to everything. Digby's words, or whomever he was this morning, held a raw truth. To them it is nothing more than a game and right now they are playing me like a fiddle. I needed to step back from all of it to assess my position. While I began to once again ponder the events of the day, I decided it might be worth checking the buildings surveillance cameras to see if I could get an insight into how the package was delivered.

On my way out my front door I checked all the possible entry points of the corridor, including the ceiling vents. There wasn't anything that appeared out of order. I pressed the button to the elevator. When the doors opened I noted the faintest hint of perfume. I selected the ground floor, so I could go to the building's control room.

Inside the security sector, Rolston the technical operator on duty replayed the footage for me during the window of my absence. It only took a few minutes before I spied the person who entered the building through the front door carrying the package. They took the elevator to my floor, placed the parcel on the ground, turned, looked up at the camera, and smiled just before re-entering the elevator to leave. I could see by the way Rolston did a side-glance at me that he was confused as to why I would want to see footage of myself delivering a package to my own apartment. The person was the spitting image of me. She was even wearing the exact same attire and her mannerisms and gait were uncanny. The confidence she possessed to look straight into the camera and smile was warranted given the flawless depiction. I was speechless.

"Thanks," was all I said as I headed out of the room and back to my apartment. I climbed up the spiral staircase to my bedroom and flopped onto the bed face down. This was all so overwhelming. They were relentless, and I was starting to see that I was being manipulated to feel like nothing more than a dispensable pawn in their game.

Huckleberry jumped up to join me. I could hear him sniffing while lightly digging into the pillow near the top of my head. He was looking for my face. Slowly I lifted myself up and turned around, so I was now lying on my back. Satisfied with this he curled up beside me, placing his head on my chest so he could stare into my eyes. I gave him a reassuring pat. It was going to be okay I thought to myself. I just needed to figure things out. There had to be a way to place myself on the front foot of this experience.

I'd grown accustomed to using the energy of the Cintāmani stone to assist me in raising the frequency of my own vibration. I fumbled about in my side draw to retrieve it. As I lay back down I put it on my third eye charkra then quietly stared up at the sky through my glass ceiling. It took a minute to settle as I focussed on the blanket of delicious blue hues, while willing myself to relax. I needed to allow my mind to freely wander the expanse of my thoughts to decipher the experiences. I wanted to understand what it was that I was missing.

"Guide me," I whispered as my surroundings faded away to a saturation of blue.

Pictures slowly started to appear and disappear like a series of blips. Initially I couldn't make out what they were, so I trusted that I wasn't meant to and continued to maintain my inner stillness. When the image of the Houghton House reception attendant's face appeared, the focal point emphasized the exchanged glance between her and the security guard that escorted me out. It replayed in slow motion over and over. With each pass I was being shown I focussed on the little details.

- The partial reveal of a tattoo on her left arm matched the top of a tattoo rising above the collar on his neck.
- Her nails were manicured into oddly sharp points on her two outer most fingers on both hands.

○ In her right ear she had a flesh colored earpiece imbedded.

Images of myself inside the room with Digby presented a split second after I acknowledged the attendant's earpiece. Once again, my mind was showing me frame by frame stills. This time it was the reflection in the window during the moments from when I was trying to check on where the orderly was positioned. To the beat of the image repetition I began breaking down the scene.

○ There was a mirrored window behind the orderly where I could see the faint outline of a moving shadow.

○ The orderly was so fixated on the television that he seemed to be in a state of trance.

○ A fleeting glimpse of Digby's reflection revealed he had something embedded in his left ear.

The point of view immediately switched now to looking at Mangonel face on. His head was twisted away ever so slightly so the right side of his profile was favored, hence I never got to see his left ear.

His words, "How could I forget such a rare beauty?" echoed over and over as the image flashed to Digby's leg jerking slightly, causing it to bounce. Then the words, "Nothing is ever as it seems, you of all people should know that."

I observed the scene several times and was struggling to understand what I was supposed to see.

"Show me," I whispered.

"How could I forget such a rare beauty?"

My leg began to spasm when a ZAP of electrical current released a sharp pain into my limb with a flash of white light appearing from the back of my pupils momentarily blinding my sight.

Huckleberry yelped as he leapt off to the side. I caught the stone in my hand as I sat up and stared at my muscles contracting above my knee. Placing my other hand on the area to calm it down I closed my eyes and said, "I get it." Huckleberry returned to my side to lick my arm.

The person who was playing the role of Digby was being instructed on what to say by the occupants behind the mirrored window. The comment he made about my appearance may have been off script, so a shock was somehow remotely administered to remind him not deviate from the puppet masters command. The whole thing was elaborately orchestrated. The Interferons wanted to depict me as mentally compromised, which is why they had their minions overlay that footage to make it look as though I was holding a one sided conversation with the real Digby Mangonel.

All the spying with drones that has taken place, the discovery of the symbols in the ears of the watchers after they are activated, was set to amp up the pressure I felt about being under constant surveillance. Any normal person would have told their friends and family, perhaps sought the assistance of the authorities. It builds a case for me to be perceived as mad and would thereby discredit anything I said. Dr Crude's key session recordings being planted amongst my things support my theory. They must have expected that I would look through my notes and discover them. Instead, I bundled them up with all my other college items, placed them in the attic and never gave them a second thought. This is possibly why the faux Digby mentioned I was expected ten years prior. They are modeling their moves off psychological profiling of stereotypical behavioral traits.

The extent of their premeditated planning is somewhat outstanding. If I am correct in my line of thinking, Digby was supposed to die by my hand for reasons I am yet to fathom, however, it didn't go to plan. When he was imprisoned in the psychiatric facility for his crime, they had him lobotomized to ensure the secrets remained trapped within. Still the idea of a whole studio being built in waiting for my attendance seems extreme, but to have it function as a viable business along the way to hide the intent, makes it both plausible and genius. Perhaps it is all coincidence but somehow based on everything that has happened, I am beginning to doubt that any of it is. The person who delivered the package, my doppelganger, her appearance made me wonder if this was a silent threat demonstrating that I could be switched, and no-one would be any the wiser. What doesn't seem to make sense is the constant skirting around the act of doing anything definitive. Why show me they can switch me instead of just doing it? Drip-feeding me an insight into their capabilities only makes me wiser. Are they trying to educate me or scare me?

My thoughts were distracted by the sound of the cell buzzing. Tucking Huckleberry under my arm I rose to my feet and headed downstairs to fetch the phone to see who was trying to reach me. While positioning my little man on the sofa I grabbed the phone just as it stopped ringing.

One missed call – Mom.

I clicked on the reply button to autodial.

"Hello."

"Hi Mom, sorry I just missed your call. How are you?"

"I'm great! How are you?"

"I've been pretty busy with work but fine otherwise."

"I was hoping you would be free for dinner tonight. Your father and I were looking to go into town for a bite to eat and were hoping you might join us."

"Tonight?" I said trying to think of a reason not to attend.

"Harper, we haven't seen you since…" She exhaled, "We haven't seen you in a while, so it would be really nice to catch up. Your father and I miss you."

I leaned my head down on the rise of the sofa. "What time?"

"Six thirty at the Majorica. I reserved a booth overlooking the atrium."

I could hear the delight in her voice. "I'll meet you both there just shy of six thirty."

"Your father will be chuffed."

I laughed, "Me too. Bye Mom."

"See you in a few."

Reaching across I placed the phone back on the coffee table before turning to perch myself on the edge of the sofa. There was less than two hours available for me to get ready and head over there. I felt jealous of Huckleberry who was curled up in a ball of contentment resting his sweet eyes. My preference would have been to stay in, but mom was right, I'd been avoiding spending any time with them. I didn't want to confront what might surface when I saw my father for the first time. Knowing he's oblivious to what took place didn't make it any easier for me. From a space of cognitive reasoning I can understand the evil force imposed upon me in the attic was using my dad's body as a vessel. All this insight didn't make what occurred any less palpable.

I picked up the mysterious book and flicked through the pages once more. The image of the girl smiling into the security camera played in the back of my mind. The package was dropped off only minutes before I arrived. If I hadn't managed to keep myself together at Houghton House this afternoon, I may not have unveiled the truth of what was occurring nor held the opportunity to deflect the attention in another direction. There was a very real possibility that I may have been detained for questioning or worse. This book had been delivered so close to the time of my arrival that she may have run the risk of crossing my path. It makes me wonder whether the book was delivered as a result of an assumption that I would be otherwise detained. Alternatively, it may have been a back up plan introduced as a continuance of this elaborate ploy to direct me toward a specific thought process that leads me to their desired destination. My mind was churning with a multitude of angles and ideas. The only clear advantage I seem to have is that my behaviors are mostly unpredictable.

Gently shifting forward, I gave Huckleberry a light kiss, placed the book on the table and headed back upstairs to get ready.

* * * * *

Driving to the restaurant I continued to try to evaluate the situation. It was becoming clearer to me that their actions are motivated to prevent me from having any credibility. If I am perceived as crazy, then I am forced into a position of alienation. The less support provided, in theory, the more vulnerable I become. They either want me to be at their mercy or dependence, perhaps both.

A neon light in the distance caught my eye. I burst out laughing when I read the words, '*Curiosity killed the cat*' all lit up in electric pink with a reflecting lime green billboard as the backdrop. Someone had placed their graffiti mark and spray painted commentary in black directly underneath, '*Jesus loves my pussy. It's heaven scent.*'

"Ha, Oh my Lordy, Lord, yes." I said slapping my hand on the steering wheel. I just had the greatest epiphany, which meant a slight detour was required. The clock on the console was displaying five past six. The restaurant was another eight or so minutes away. This gave me a solid ten minutes spare to find an old fashion phone booth to place my theory to the test. I decided I had the time and veered off the main drag to find a bank of shop fronts.

Pulling into the first convenience store I could find, I parked the vehicle and went inside to try my luck. As I scanned the area I spied one tucked into the far left corner. The outer shell of the booth was intact, but the receiver had been pulverized. The unrecognizable remnants of the receiver was aimlessly hanging by a few threads of frayed cord.

"Excuse me, I'm looking for a public phone. Do you know where I can find one locally?"

The man behind the counter didn't look up as he responded succinctly with a "No."

Another fellow who was stocking the shelves rose to his feet while waving to draw my attention.

"You can try the subway station two blocks down. They have a few."

"Great, thanks."

Just as I was reversing my car out of the parking spot I could see that the person who had been stacking shelves was now standing in front of his colleague at the counter. The frantic motion of his arms indicated he might be telling him off. The counter man didn't seem phased. I just shook my head and proceeded down the road. The world is full of zombies.

It took another four minutes to find the station, then park and walk up the ramp. On the subway platform, just past the ticketing booth, there before me was a bank of phones. Knowing my little experiement needed to be untraceable, I opted to test my theory against a free service. As I dialed the number for the operator I glanced around to ensure I wasn't within earshot of anyone.

"Operator, how may I assist you?"

I cleared my throat before projecting the deepest voice I could muster. "Um yes, I'm looking for the contact number for conspirathorium valedictorian please."

"Can you spell conspirat… rum for me?"

"Sure, C O N S P I R A T H O R I U M VALEDICTORIAN."

"There doesn't seem to be anything listed by that name."

"Um, okay, could you look up conspirathorium on Google to check that I have the right spelling. I've misplaced my phone and need to get in contact with them. I'd really appreciate the help."

"One moment please."

I could hear her tapping away on the keyboard.

"I'm sorry the only thing Google returned was conspiratorium without the h. I ran this through our system and its also drawing a blank. Is there any other name I can try and help you with?"

"Did you check with the full name, conspirathorium valedictorian?"

"Yes, nothing is coming up by that name. Is there any other name I can try and help you with?"

"No, that's fine. I appreciate the assistance. Good night."

"Bye."

I wiped down the receiver before placing it onto the cradle.

Walking back to my car I felt a sense of liberation. Let us see if curiosity does try to kill the cat.

Heading back toward the main road I noticed a couple of the passing vehicles driving suspiciously slow as they went by. I dropped my sunviser to block my face from being in clear view. There seemed to be something out of place about how deserted the area had become.

When I pulled into the Majorica car park there wasn't a clear spot available to be seen. I drove around the rows of stationary vehicles. The one remaining vacant space was near a darkened lane at the furthest point of the lot. A quick survey of the area only had me notice that the streetlight had been blown out. A shadow in the reflection of my rear view mirror revealed yet another vehicle driving by rather slowly, this one didn't have its front beams engaged. Aside from this oddity there didn't seem to be anyone else around.

The console clock shone quarter to seven. I was already fifteen minutes late. There was something about only having this one space available that made me decide I would prefer to park somewhere else. It wasn't my personal safety I was concerned about. I didn't want my vehicle out of view where they could gain access and tamper with it. The technology of tracking and surveillance equipment has come such a long way that something could be easily installed and super hard to detect. I drove out of the restaurants lot and headed down the main street where I decided to park it outside a busy all night gaming arcade. Then I hiked it back to toward the restaurant.

My phone began to buzz just as I entered. I didn't have to look to know it would be mom checking to see how far away I was from arriving. I spotted them both pretty easily and waved so she would disengage the call.

Mom gestured to dad who turned to look in my direction. His face lit up as he rose to his feet spreading his arms wide open, "Beanie Bear."

I wrapped my arms around him for a big squeeze, "Hey dad. You look great."

"I shine best when I'm around you," he said as he planted a kiss on my right cheek.

"Hi mom," I passed across my hand to hold hers as she stood up.

"Let go of her, it's my turn."

Dad started to release me and then re-engaged his arms. He whispered into my hair, "I've missed you so much."

I could feel mom behind me attempting to pry dad's arms apart. I laughed as I began to tickle the sides of dad's rib cage. He weakened his grip enough for me to duck under. This gave mom her opportunity to partake in a welcoming cuddle before we assumed our postitions at the table.

Just as we were seated the waiter arrived with the first course.

Mom leaned over and touched my hand, "I hope you don't mind, we ordered some starters to share."

"Great," I said looking at the antipasto platter and dips now positioned in the center of the table. I reached across and took a sprig of parsley from the garnish, popping it straight into my mouth. Part way through chewing I looked directly into my father's eyes, "How are you really feeling?"

"Honestly, I've never been better. My memory is still foggy around some things, but otherwise, I'm feeling grand."

I turned to mom, "Is he up to his usual antics?"

"Worse, once he was given the all clear from the doctor's he signed himself out of hospital and sent me a text message to pick him up from the ice cream parlor."

We all laughed.

"Have you noticed how popular this place has become? There isn't a vacant table and the waitressing staff seem to have doubled since the last time your father and I were here."

I glanced around, "It is rather busy."

"Beanie Bear, try the white bean dip. It's delicious," said dad in between chomps.

I reached over, broke off a generous piece of the warm rustic bread and placed a scoop of the dip on my plate. He was right, the texture of the pureed white beans, myrtle, thyme with a hint of truffle oil, created a happy marriage of flavors.

"Choice dip, this is yum." I said mid chew.

"How's work?" He asked.

"Its fine, they have been keeping me out of mischief." I was lying. I had resigned from my job months ago but didn't want to have to explain why or how I was now sustaining myself financially. It would draw too much unwanted attention, so I chose to maintain the façade.

"Are you back at work?"

Dad pointed to his mouth full of food to signal he couldn't talk.

"He is Harper, he returned this week."

"You must be relieved to have him out of the house."

Mom lent forward feigning exasperation, "I thought the day would never come. This week is the first opportunity I've had to reclaim some time for myself. Your father has become quite the handful."

I laughed, "Mom is clearly happy to be rid of you. The question remains are the people in the office glad to have you back?"

"Of course, they are. I've been subjecting them to all these tests that I had to endure while being assessed in hospital."

"Really, like what?"

"No Harper, don't get him started, please."

"It's okay, we'll just do a couple," said dad. "They gave me a series of puzzles to solve and brain teasers."

Mom placed her head in her hands and shook it from side to side, "Here we go."

Dad repositioned himself to be sitting more upright as he rubbed his hands together. "Before Mt. Everest was discovered, what was the highest mountain in the world?"

"Ha, really? Mt Everest."

Dad squinted his eyes at my response then licked his bottom lip to collect a rogue crumb.

"Ok, smarty, you are in a running competition and just passed the person in second place. What place are you in?"

"Second place. Really dad? These are so obvious."

He sat back for a moment and looked at me, "In Romania you cannot take a picture of a person with a wooden leg. Why not?"

"It stands to reason, pardon the pun, that you can't do that anywhere in the world. Last I heard you need camera equipment to capture an image."

Mom smirked at dad's annoyance.

"Johnny's mother had three children. The first is called April and the second is called May. What's the name of the third child?"

"Johnny."

Dad slapped his hand on the table, "Oh come on. You must have done these before."

"I promise, hand on heart I haven't. I find it fascinating that these are even remotely challenging for anyone. The answer is presented within the frame of the question, so it seems redundant to ask the question at all, let alone define them as a riddle. The solution simply requires attention to literal details."

Dad folded his arms while sporting a cocky smile, "There are six eggs in the basket. Six people each take one of the eggs. How can it be that one egg is left in the basket?"

I popped a piece of the bread in my mouth; "The last person took the basket with the egg sitting inside. Hence there are only six eggs and six people as stated."

Dad raised his clenched hands in the air while contorting his face to playfully express his frustration. I sat there beaming with a smile of satisfaction.

"Enough you two," snapped mom.

Recomposing himself he gestured to mom indicating there would be one more. "A man is walking in the middle of the road covered from head to toe in black. It is a back street with all the street lamps off. A black car approaches with all his lights off but manages to stop in time to avoid hitting the pedestrian. How did the driver see him?"

I sat up and scratched my head. "Okay, repeat that one again." I closed my eyes to play out the scene as he said the words.

"A man is walking in the middle of the road covered from head to toe in black clothing, including a ski mask. It is a back street with all the street lamps off. A black car approaches with all his lights off but manages to stop in time to avoid hitting the pedestrian. How did the driver see him?"

I ran through the possible scenarios depicting them like flash cards in my mind then opened my eyes, "It occurred during the day. Ta Daa." I said doing jazz hands in celebration.

"Well I'll be dammed," he said sitting back in his chair, "I spawned a genius."

"Ha, I love how you managed to divert the credit to yourself. Let's order some wine. Mom will you have some?"

"Please," she said in a tone that indicated to me that she wasn't enjoying herself.

I gestured to the waiter standing closest to our table to come across.

"Can we get a bottle of the Idyll Estate cabernet please?"

"Absolutely, I will be back in a moment."

Just as the waiter was walking away I noticed a person hovering in the background that was intermittently looking in our direction.

"We should consider placing an order for our mains," I said reaching for the menu.

"We've hardly touched the entrée with the exception of your father." Mom leaned across to poke his protruding belly.

My eyes scanned the menu, "I feel like having something warm. A nice soup or lightly dressed pasta with seasoned vegetables."

"That's sounds nice. I'll probably have the same."

I nodded to acknowledge my mom. "Dad, is there any space left in that rather rotund belly for a main meal?"

"Sure, Beanie Bear, it's all compartmentalized. I have a quadrant in here for entrée, over here is where the main will be stored and this final sector is reserved for dessert, then the final one is for a cheese platter."

I laughed, "You really have developed an obsession with food."

"That I have." He said while rubbing his belly.

The waiter returned with our wine and three glasses. He served a sample portion to me first. I smiled as I waved to suggest pouring the rest. I held no intention of trying the wine. The Idyll Estate range of reds and in particular this cabernet and I were already pleasantly acquainted.

As the waiter walked away mom waved her hand to grab my attention. "Have you noticed that gentleman over there is looking at you?"

"I think he is glancing this way in general, not at me specifically."

"No, I'm certain it's you that he is focussed on."

I raised my glass, "Who cares, let's just ignore the world around us and enjoy our time together."

Mom and dad joined in the toast.

"Are you ready to order your mains?"

I turned in the direction of where the voice was coming from. The waiter stepped across when he recognized from my gesture that I would begin with placing the order, "Sure. I'd like the linguine please."

He nodded at me and then immediatley looked at my mom. "Something for you?"

"I'll have the broccoli soup thanks."

"Would you like a serve of hot buns with your soup?"

I noticed mom blushed as he spoke to her.

"No thank you. A portion of the soup will be fine."

"Very well, and for you sir?"

"I'll have the twice cooked lamb shanks please."

"Excellent choices. I will return with your meals." On his way toward the kitchen the waiter gestured to another staff member. That person came promptly to our table to clear the food then returned to reset the table in accordance with our meal selection. Just as he was finished the stranger from across the way decided to make his approach.

Mom raised her eyebrows as she sipped on her glass of wine.

"Hello." He said glancing at my parents.

"Hello."

"Hi."

"I hope you don't mind the intrusion." He looked directly into my eyes. "Harper, I was wondering if I could have a word."

"I'm unsure of who you are."

Furrows appeared on his brow. "Perhaps the confusion is mine. I thought we had a date tonight. I've been patiently waiting at my table while watching you over here, well, how can I put it? Ah yes, ignoring me. I'm not sure what's going on, but it appears that you have double booked or this is some kind of psychological power play?"

"Oh," exclaimed mom.

I released a sigh as I assessed his demeanor. His visual cues indicated that he was genuine.

"I'm unaware of who you are or how you know my name, but I can assure you that I've made no plans outside of this one."

He scratched his head.

I paused for a moment as I studied him.

"I tell you what, pull up a seat and join us for dinner. It appears that you have an interesting story to tell and my parents and I are destined to be your captive audience."

He seemed surprised when I mentioned my parents.

"I don't wish to impose."

I used my foot to push the empty chair out, "Join us. I insist."

He released a nervous laugh as he sat down. "I'm Ross, pleased to meet you."

"How do you know my daughter?' Asked dad.

Ross looked at me.

"I can't help you because I don't recall ever meeting you. In fact, given my rather exceptional memory, I could bank on the fact that we haven't met."

He leaned in slightly toward me and whispered, "Are you joking right now?"

I shook my head, "No, honestly I am clueless about who you are and why you feel you know me."

His cheeks turned a lovely shade of crimson, "Last night?"

I shrugged my shoulders.

Mom placed her hand on his arm. "Are you okay?"

He looked at her and smiled, "Yes, thank you. I'm just a little confused about the mixed messages I feel I am getting."

I took a sip of my wine. "Tell me what I don't know about 'us'?"

"We randomly met yesterday evening at the SoHo lounge. I was sitting at the bar quietly having a drink while listening to the musician playing the piano. You came in, chose to sit beside me, I ordered you a drink and then we spoke for a while."

I could see through my peripheral vision that my father was getting agitated. He was tearing small strips of bread, rolling it between his fingers until they became tiny dough balls that he insisted on flicking onto his plate.

"Is there anything else Ross?" I could see his pupils dilate at the mention of his name.

"What was it that you were just thinking about? You're withholding something. What is it?"

He glanced at my parents and then back at me.

In a reassuring tone I said, "It's alright. Tell me."

He hesitated, dropping his gaze to focus on my wine glass. "We went back to my house and, um, spent the night."

"This is preposterous," said dad throwing the rest of the bread down.

I placed my hand on my father's arm, "Its okay, I believe him."

"What?"

"Everything he has said so far is true. He isn't lying. The only catch being that it wasn't me he shared the experience with."

Ross shuffled in his seat, "I don't understand. Of course, it was with you."

I shook my head, "It wasn't. There is a woman who looks exactly like me roaming about town. Our mutual appearance is uncanny. When I saw her, I had to do a double take to check I wasn't looking in the mirror. She was caught on my apartment building CCTV leaving a parcel out the front of my apartment today."

Mom placed her hand across her mouth as she gasped.

I looked at her, "Don't tell me I have a secret twin sibling."

"No, of course not."

Dad's eye twitched.

"Dad, what is it?"

He cleared his throat, "Nothing. Now's not the time Beanie Bear."

I nodded my head and released a sigh. "Ross, what you are suggesting is that she is using my name which is identity theft. When did she request that you meet her here for dinner?"

"I received a text saying she wanted to do it all again and to meet her at Majorica. I have a place a few blocks away, so I walked over. There was a booth reserved under your name."

"I'm interested in the precise time. Can you show me the text message please?"

"Sure."

While he was retrieving his phone from his pocket I observed my mom in my peripheral vision. She was blankly staring at her hands while dad remained silent.

"Here, you can see it was received at 5:45 pm."

I pulled out my phone and took a picture of the text. It appeared to have been issued by my number. "Do you mind?" I asked as I raised the camera to take an image of him too.

"Err, no I guess not," he said coyly.

I took two images. One captured the details of his face and the other incorporated his body. As I placed my phone down I re-engaged with his eyes, "Show me."

Ross subconsciously gripped his phone tighter. "Show you what?"

"The pictures you took of last night. Don't bother trying to deny it. I know you have pictures. Show me."

He glanced at my parents and pursed his lips, "They aren't really appropriate to display." He turned to me and muttered, "Is this some weird fantasy role play thing that I'm not following?"

"Your pasta madam." The waiter placed the piping hot dish in front of me.

"Soup for you," he said as he winked at mom, who responded by once again blushing.

He passed the lamb shanks my dad ordered over to him with a nod.

"Would anyone like some cracked pepper on their meal?"

"No, thanks. Ross, would you like to order something?"

"No, I really should be going."

I placed my hand on his arm, "Not a chance, we still have a lot of catching up to do." I glanced at the waiter, "Thank you." He acknowledged his cue to leave and did so swiftly.

"I can't," said Ross.

"Sure, you can. Just unlock your phone and I'll do the rest."

"Please show her," said my mom encouragingly.

"It's a video," he said cringing.

"Then press play. I need to see it."

He brought up the video before passing the phone to me. I could instantly see that the footage was taken in the thick of their explicit exchange. I looked up at him, "Where is the volume on this phone? I want to turn it down for obvious reasons."

Ross released a nervous chuckle as he pressed the button to reduce the audio output to minimal volume. "So, you do remember."

I didn't bother to correct his suggestion, being defensive only made me look guilty. I pressed play fully conscious that my parents were awaiting a reaction. There she was on her knees sucking on the end of his knob as she looked up at him filming her. I switched the audio to mute the moment I began to hear the expletives being ushered between his gasps resulting from her firm grasp of his ridged penis. I viewed the three minute extravaganza hoping to identify any tangible physical delineation between us. This Jane Doe appeared to be my exact replica. When the video was complete, I selected the forward option, sending it to my phone. Once I heard the buzz confirming receipt I deleted it off his device. "Is this it?"

"Yes."

I squinted my eyes as I assessed his response. I knew he was telling the truth, but I needed to buy myself some time. "Let me check," I said as I navigated to the settings area and pressed the request for full factory reset.

"Are you okay Beanie Bear?"

"I'm fine." I passed the phone back to Ross when it was complete. "Let's eat before our food gets cold."

"Perhaps I should go."

I smiled, "Thanks for stopping by."

Ross stood up slowly, "I'm not sure what tonight was about, but yesterday was amazing."

I focussed on twirling my pasta onto my fork. "Bye Ross."

"Is there a chance we could ..."

My father dropped his fork rather loudly against his plate. "She said goodbye, Ross."

"Of course, sorry. Enjoy your meal."

"Thank you. Bye," said mom politely.

Dad waited for him to exit the restaurant, "The nerve of that guy."

"Yes, Harper it was all very strange. I'm concerned, do you think he is mentally unstable?"

Lifting my fork in an exaggerated manner I shoved the pasta into my mouth and began to chew as I watched them both. Mom couldn't hold my gaze and dad was fidgeting. When I washed down the remaining pasta with some wine I cleared my throat before speaking.

"Spill it dad. You said now is not the time but clearly it is. What don't I know? Do I have a rogue sibling roaming out there?"

"No, don't be silly. It's just at one point a very, very long time ago there was a government branch sponsoring genealogical preventative biomedical research that called for volunteers to donate DNA samples to science. Families, who were accepted, as candidates into the program were required to donate fingernail clippings, hair follicles, skin cells, saliva, and blood samples. There were also a suite of health and psychological tests run. Your mother and I signed up through the ballot system, as did hundreds of thousands of other US citizens. Each family selected received five thousand dollars tax free for their contribution. Some of us were later notified that we qualified to be target candidates for what they called the upper echelon biometrics program. Your mother and I signed an authority for them to harvest some eggs from her fallopian tubes and I supplied a deposit of my sperm. Later when Dylan arrived on the scene they swooped in to take the placenta, the umbilical cord and some non-invasive DNA samples. When you were born we had already been paid, so we were obliged to follow through with the same. In exchange for our contribution to science we received a staggering fifty thousand tax free dollars. It was such a large sum of money back then. We used it to buy our first home."

I was dumb founded at what I was hearing. "You never thought to consider what the ramifications were in doing this?"

Mom chimed in, "You have to appreciate this was all done during a time where they didn't have the advances of today. It was all very innocent I can assure you."

"I'm surprised at how naïve that statement is coming from a woman who spent her life hyper vigilant about researching and scrutinizing everything. Who is this government group? What has become of the program?"

Dad reached out and held moms hand. "Its not your mothers fault, she was very reluctant to do it, but I campaigned pretty hard to get her on board to participate because it was an awful lot of money Beanie Bear. It set us up for the life we have."

I was aggitated at learning that the Interferons possibly knew me on a cellular level.

"What is the name of the group?" I asked releasing a sigh.

My dad shook his head, "It doesn't matter, they don't exist anymore. A few years into the programme they lost their funding, so the project was disbanded shortly after you were born. We received a letter confirming that all genetic material collected was properly discarded through their bio hazard protocols."

I felt sick.

"Are you enjoying your meals? Is there anything else I can get you?"

I looked up at the waiter whose stealth approach caught me by surprise. There was something about his confidence that irked me. "Actually, I was curious about how it is that you are already acquainted with my mother?"

He shifted his posture into a mode of deflection, "We have crossed paths a few times. Loraine frequents the coffee house where I am the part time barista."

I glanced at mom, "Did you know that, wait," I re-engaged with the waiter's stare. "Sorry what is your name?"

"Devon."

I slowly turned my head to glare at my mom. "Did you know that Devon works at the Majorica or is this just a happy coincidence?"

Mom pushed a strand of hair behind her left ear. "I don't recall, he may have said something."

Devon smirked, "Would you like to see the dessert that is on offer?"

"No thanks," said dad pushing his partially eaten lamb shank away.

I wondered if he understood the waiter's cocksure statement or was he reacting off the surface of what was being discussed.

"Very well, I will leave you to enjoy the rest of your meal." Devon walked off with a notable strut and slight skip in his step.

"I don't know what has gotten into you Harper, and I don't appreciate the insinuation," snipped mom.

"What is it that you don't appreciate Loraine?"

Dad turned to me, "Harper, stop."

I looked down at the wisps of steam still rising from my main meal. "I've lost my appetite. It's clearly been a strange night and a very tiresome day for me, so I am going to head off."

Dad rose from his position, "We had best be going too. I'll settle the bill."

Mom was struggling to hold back her tears. There wasn't much left to say without everything falling apart in a potentially dramatic public display. I stood up and gestured that she does the same.

"Bye mom." I said giving her a cuddle.

She squeezed me tight, "You have no right to judge without understanding what I"

I pressed my lips close to her right ear, "Life is about choices and chances. You make a choice and you take a chance. You do as you wish and embrace the consequences accordingly. Live with no regrets."

"Can I get in on this action?" asked dad as he wrapped his arms around both of us. His vice grip locked in forcing us to join in his gentle sway.

"Grrrroup hug." He said as he squeezed tighter.

I inhaled their scent and held on for as long as I could to savor the few moments of our remaining time. I now recognized this evening marked the beginning of the end of my family. Everything was geared toward our binds falling asunder; there would be little I could do to change the path they had chosen to take.

Longanimity

The media reports were in a frenzy covering the events relating to the swat team take down of the Telco operator service division called Point to Point. The coverage stated there was confirmed evidence of a breach to government security and threats to the nation that warranted immediate action. One report suggested that Point to Point was a profitable cover for a fee for hire black ops underground hacking syndicate. A week into the ordeal has already seen the cease of their business with all the corporate documents seized. Night show interviews with some of the employees alluded to full interrogation tactics being applied while Myer Riggs who was currently labeled the suspected king pin of the operation is believed to be under house arrest.

It confirmed my suspicions about the book I received from my twin Jane Doe. Although the information contained within the book appeared to be authentic, it was so complex that it would have naturally forced my hand at either seeking help to interpret the contents or to go online myself to find some answers. Then it dawned on me when I saw the neon sign '*Curiosity killed the cat,'* that the idea of looking up the word conspirathorium valedictorian via an online search engine might have been a hacker's tracer bait calling card to sniff out my networkof resources. After all, it was the obvious thing to do. If you don't know something you look it up. That's why I decided to test the theory by using the telephone service operator as my guinea pig. I had no idea it would lead to this takeover circus. At least this would have them fishing for weeks on a false path. What I wondered now was whether the rabbit warren was so deep that it involved the government or were they like the rest of us, just dispensible puppets manipulated with Interferon mastery. There was no immediate way for me to tell.

The noise of Huckleberry scampering as he ran toward the door pulled me from my thoughts. When I looked in his direction and smiled he began spinning in circles, wagging his tail. I grabbed my phone and keys from the bench before joining him. He squirmed with excitement as I placed his body harness on. Finally, I reached for my hat, then headed out the door for our morning walk. Each day I try to take a new route to make our venture interesting, while also being less predictable for the watchers who still seemed to be present to observe my every move. It was ingenious that no matter which direction I chose, Huckleberry found a way to navigate to his favorite haunt.

When we arrived at the dog park some of Huckleberry's best furry friends were out playing in the contained area. He looked at me wagging his tail vigorously as though asking for permission to go join in the fun. I picked him up, unhooked the leash from his harness and placed him over the fence. He swiftly ran to the team of dogs releasing a series of high pitched barks while spinning in the air. They welcomed him with wagging tails, licks and sniffs and then proceeded to once again be immersed in play. I loved watching them interact. They exuded such joy it delighted my heart.

"May I join you?"

I turned to see a lovely old lady approaching my left side. She adorned a classic straw hat with a fresh but withered single white daisy poking from the brim.

"You are welcome to, yes." I said politely stepping across, so she could lean on the fence for support.

Huckleberry unexpectedly turned and ran up to us with zeal. He scaled the length of the meshing fence using his hind legs to propel himself into my arms. I laughed as I caught him. "This is Huckleberry," I said trying to shift my face away from his frantic licks.

"Oh my, he is a sweet one. He truly loves you."

"Yes. Settle Huck's." I said as I released him back into the enclosure. He took one glance at the both of us, released a bark and returned to join the others.

"May I be a bother and suggest we take a seat on that bench over there?"

I looked at the empty seat, "It's no bother at all."

She graciously accepted the offer of my arm. Slowly we walked to the bench, then I supported her until she was safely seated before positioning myself beside her.

"Do you live near by?" I asked.

"No, no, dear. I don't live here at all."

"Well, it's a lovely day for a walk and this park has some glorious patches of garden. All you need to do is meandor down toward where that treed area is," I said pointing in the direction she would need to go.

She looked at me nodding her head in acknowledgement. The thick dark ring around each iris created the illusion of depth in her hazel eyes.

"I'd like to tell you a story if I may."

I continued to gaze into her eyes while she patiently waited for a cue to start.

"Sure, I'd like to hear your story."

Her cheeks plumped as she smiled. "There is a little known fable that is built on the premise of truth that I feel would be of value to share."

I quickly glanced over to locate Huckleberry to check that he was all right. When I spied the tip of his wagging tail among the sea of swishing hind quarters I returned my focus to the old lady. "You have my undivided attention, please go ahead."

"Once upon a lifetime or so ago there was a little bird thought to be the only one of its kind. No one had been able to catch it, so its gender was unknown. They assumed that it was male because of the beautiful hues of blue plumage adorned from the crest of its head, along its back, right through to the tip of its elongated tail. To the uneducated eye, he was often mistaken for a common Blue Jay but was nothing of the sort. This bird for a myriad of reasons was unique and somewhat extraordinary."

The old lady paused for a moment to look deep into my eyes. She silently nodded her head at the precise moment my heart skipped a beat. The leaves in the surrounding trees began to rustle to the command of a cool light breeze that pleasantly caused goosebumps to dance upon my skin.

"He was known by the locals as Jay Bird Blue. During the cycle of the full moon he could be seen romancing the skyline by calling out to the darkness in dulcet tones. There was something in the way his pitch was raised during those nights. Each time he sang a different unique tune. It made people who were listening feel a sense of whimsy. We shared a sweet notion that perhaps one day he would receive the reply he undoubtedly yearned for. Month upon month, year upon year he was observed during the full moon doing his dance and singing the most complex of songs in a way that made your heart ache for love. I'm unsure if you are aware dear but once every couple of years there is a month when the full moon is set to appear twice. You must have heard of the phrase, once in a blue moon."

"Yes, I've heard of it."

"Well, what is lesser known is the fact that there is a special event that takes place in the month of December once every one hundred and thirty one years. During this time, the full moon mysteriously appears in the sky three times consecutively. It is a rare phenomenon. No scientific explanation has been provided about why the moon stills at this juncture."

I shuffled back deeper onto the width of the park bench, so I could cross my legs. "That's a new one. Is this really true or part of the story you are telling me?"

The old lady placed her hand on my knee, "No, no my dear, everything I am telling you is true. I swear it on my own life."

I glanced across to check on Huckleberry again. He was playing what looked like a version of tig chasy along with a Whippet, and a Jack Russell who were using the Great Dane as an obstacle course of sorts. The Whippet brazenly weaved between the Great Dane's legs as Huckleberry and the Jack Russell followed in pursuit.

The Dane was wildly wagging its tail while bobbing its head down playfully snapping at their feet with its slobbering mouth. My attention was drawn back to the lady as she gently patted my leg.

"I was just checking on my dog. Please continue. I'm fascinated to hear where this story will lead."

"On the month in question the little Jay Bird Blue was seen building a nest up high in a sycamore tree. It had all the neighborhood talking. Little was known at the time about this particular month of December being auspicious due to the inexplicable tri full moon cycle. The idea of this little bird instinctively creating a nest in what was deemed out of synch of the typical 'spring time' breeding season was a curiosity. Our tiny community set it upon ourselves to assist our Jay Bird Blue by leaving bits and bobs that we thought might be of use to our feathered friend. Things like strands of yarn, straw and hair from our brushes. Each day he would happily frolic through the new pile to select some items to build out his rather elaborate nest. By the time he had completed its construction he had cleverly woven the materials into a kaleidoscope of colors. The most impressive portion of the nest for me was the underside, which had strings of crystal from an old chandelier; a small dream catcher and half a wind chime dangling down. It was a masterpiece."

"Wow, that sounds incredible. I would love to have seen it." I said.

"Yes, anyone who took the time to watch and appreciate this little creature fell in love with him. As I said, he was extraordinary."

I readjusted my posture to lean forward so my head could rest on my hands, "What happened to him?"

"Well during the first full moon of this month he did his dance upon the horizon, cleverly singing yet another new song. This time in the distance a corresponding call could be heard. The tonal range delivered a complimentary variant of tune to the one being sung by Jay Bird Blue. Across the length of the night they exchanged verse upon verse. I didn't sleep a wink as I celebrated the sounds of hope in the air. Now at the time I never saw another bird appear, but I was certain it was getting closer as I heard the replies to his song grow louder. Before the morning sun greeted the skies, my weary eyes betrayed me as I drifted off to sleep, only to be awoken by the noise being generated from the whole neighborhood, who were congregated outside projecting a buzz of excitement. Together we searched for him everywhere, but he was no-where to be seen. It wasn't until much later that afternoon he returned to roost on his nest. He remained there for the duration of the day, only venturing off from time to time to feed.

Upon the eve of the second moon his conduct had changed. He was flying up high into the sky to begin his song before the sun had set and was diving down toward the sycamore tree and then swooping up into a loop heading back toward the far reaches of the sky to call out again. His zealous acrobatic display, I suspected, was designed to impress. Once more, against the light of the full moon his silhouette could be seen dancing while bellowing his song. It was this night when no return call was made but a presence of another bird was witnessed circling about him. He furiously danced while the bird jutted around to inspect him from all angles. By the morning, they were once again gone."

Huckleberry startled me as he jumped onto my lap, immediately propping himself on his hind quarters to lick my face. I picked him up and repositioned him, then began gently patting him. "He's obviously had enough play time." I said with a chuckle.

"He is a sweet one indeed. May I?"

"Sure, he loves attention."

I watched the old ladies wrinkled hand extend to slowly stroke his back. Huckleberry closed his eyes, placing his head down to relax. The skin on her hand was so pale I could follow the lines of protruding blue veins up the length of her arm. I wondered how old she was.

"Age is only a number my dear. There will come a time when you will stop counting because you realise it no longer matters. Now, where was I?" She said leaning back on the bench.

"You had just told me that the second moon had just come to pass, and the birds were no-where to be seen."

"Oh yes, of course. Well the same again, by the afternoon Jay Bird Blue returned to roost on the nest but his little night caller however was no-where to be seen during the day. We were curious to know whether it was the same species or another breed. It was only joining our Jay Bird Blue in the late evenings, so it was too dark for us to tell. In truth, it didn't matter. We were all so chuffed at the idea that our little friend might have found a companion. Everyone kept an eager eye out, but the mystery bird was never sighted in the sunlit hours.

Upon the eve of the third full moon without a peep exchanged they were together again. The two of them were synchronized to perfection, both intertwined in a dance that made me shed tears of joy. She was visually quite ordinary in comparison to him, yet together they shone brighter than the sun that was setting in the backdrop. What I witnessed was the purity of true loves greet. He had longed for her and waited his whole life to be united. It felt as though the timing of the tri moon month signified the opening of a window whereby they could finally hear one another's call. They remained together from that night forward, never leaving one another's side. They raised their children in the nest he had built and lived a happy, song fulfilled life."

"That is a beautiful story. Thank you for sharing it with me."

She reached across and started patting Huckleberry again.

"You know, they say now during a tri moon if you call out to your one true love that they can hear you from across the planes. They attribute it to the ebb and flow of the moons energy building to a frequency that penetrates the barrier of time. Past, future and present are briefly aligned to the core essence of oneness. If your love exists within your lifetime they will find you, but if they are in another plane, they will simply hear you."

"To hear them, I imagine would be a perpetual tease and a confirmation that you are alone. I find the idea of this really sad."

"All is not lost if they are across the planes because the gift of connectedness will replenish their hope thus giving them the strength to complete their journey in preparation for the time when you are ready to find one another."

A tear unexpectedly escaped the side of my left eye.

"We call it once in a blue bird moon and, my dear, it begins the day after tomorrow."

"The tri moons?"

"Yes. Miracles are set to happen on a blue bird moon." She collected my teardrop onto the tip of her finger then leaned in and whispered, "speak so your true love may hear you. The other half of your soul yearns for you too."

I felt a slight shiver run gently up my spine as I bowed my head slightly to acknowledge her words. "Thank you. That story was incredible, and you are such a generous person for taking the time to share it with me."

She braced the back of the bench seat as she slowly rose to her feet. "It is you who has shown me the kindness. Thank you for listening. I must be off now."

"I'm Harper." I said as she began to slowly walk away.

She turned and smiled, "I know, my angel."

I looked at her feeling slightly puzzled by her words, "Do I know you?"

She nodded her head ever so slightly. "You did once, and fate will do so again soon."

"Can you tell me your name?"

"You know who I am, Harper."

There was a glint in her eye that shone like the fleeting sparkle of a shooting star just before it fades into the distance. I watched her place one foot then the other down the pathway while feeling the growing build of urgency to know more. Unconsciously I blurted out, "Mable?"

She turned once more, smiled, and nodded her head to acknowledge the name before vanishing. I stared at where she had once stood for a while, almost expecting her to reappear. I hadn't a clue where the name Mable came from or for that matter who Mable was supposed to be. Huckleberry was fast asleep on my lap, oblivious to what had happened. I gently propped him up, kissed him on the head before placing his royal sleepiness on the ground. I reattached the leash onto his harness, and then set off to head home. Out of curiosity I walked the same route Mable had just taken, pausing at the spot where she had dissappeared. There lay the withered daisy from the brim of her hat. I picked it up, placed it between my fingers and twirled it as we walked along the path while wondering how this beautiful soul was connected to me. I felt glad that I had met her and inexplicably also experienced a little saddness that she was gone.

On the way home, I noted that most of the streets were eerily empty. I had grown so accustomed to having watchers everywhere. Today, even in the park there was a distinct absence of random people walking by. I wondered if it had anything to do with the upcoming tri moon.

My first point of call when we arrived home was preparing a snack for Huckleberry, although I feared he might not hold any room for it judging by the volume of water he was lapping up from his bowl. I had a collapsible container in my pocket at the park but with all that was happening, it completely slipped my mind to offer him a drink. Once he had a few bites of his meal he settled into his bedding. I could always tell when he was exhausted because of the location he chose to sleep. If he wanted to be completely undisturbed he slept in his own bed, all other times he located himself as close to me as possible. In fact, there isn't a part of me he hasn't slept on or next to. The wriggly worm would find a way to nuzzle into the crook of my neck all day if he could.

The term once in a blue bird moon played on my mind. The story Mable told wasn't familiar, but the phrase was most definitely resonating with me. It kept dancing upon my thoughts until I realized the link. It had been referenced in one of the birthday messages

I had received from my anonymous friend across the years. I retrieved the pile of cards and began opening each one. I'd forgotten how beautiful the detailed engraving on the cover of the card was. There stood Maat the goddess of truth and justice with Ammit the devourer to her right. After my immersive encounter with her in my parent's attic, I now felt them both to be my friends. There were dreams that I have had since that seemed to teleport me to the time of her influential ruling in Egypt. It was as though she was showing me her life in a way that allowed me to be a conscious witness. The oddity is that it always seemed to be me experiencing it directly through her eyes. I was certain a portion of her empowering essence was still coursing through my veins.

I flipped open each of the cards in sequence. Upon arriving at the seventh card I found myself looking once again at the tattered edges. I recalled previously pondering why this of all the cards seemed to be the one worn the most. It's not like anyone else was able to read the message.

Control is an illusion. It is advantageous to feed their need to lull them into a false sense of security. Watch the puppeteers feast in their false bounty of manipulation using their leverage of trias. They are heaven's keys bound.

The reality does not alter but perception shifts when you strike to tend to the needful once in a blue bird moon.

Free will is always the true governor of thy soul.

From me to you, happy birthday.

P.S: The phases of a blue bird moon hold a unique frequency for you.

Trias means three in Latin. The traditional representation is symbolized by the triangle and the word triad in current terms is associated to organized crime. I recall initially thinking that this message suggested that the Interferon's held access to the utilization of established corrupt organizations or at the very least hold associations to them. In light of now hearing Mable's recount of the Jay Bird Blue story I think I was off the mark. Bahrain had told me that all souls were split and roamed to find their other half. The universal energies are replenished and at their highest when twin flames unite. The flames of two combined are a miracle of creation and produce love and light in the form of vibrations, which provide regenerating sustenance to life. He also said the Interferons are unseen warriors set to the path of destruction, born with an eternal desire to conquer and control. It makes sense that the knowledge of the significance of the tri moon phase has been suppressed from the public. The Interferons don't want twin flames calling out to one another. To do so would create an insurgence of hope, thus replenishing their strength to complete the journey. They want to irrevocably break people's sense of free will. If our will is broken, then there is no connection to our soul and therefore no further reincarnation to the flesh is sought to complete the cycle of lessons. We become lost, which weakens our universal position.

They are heaven's keys bound.

Bahrain said that there are fourteen unique souls who, when paired as twin flames, form the seven keys. Each possesses a unique ability, which when united, will shift the universal energy to one power, thus opening the realm of possibilities to Equanon. It means that the Interferons are most likely trying to suppress any connection between the fourteen souls during the tri moon phase.

I glanced at the clock on the wall. According to Mable I had two days before the cycle began. How was I supposed to track down the other six pairing of twin souls?

"Arf, arf."

I turned to look for Huckleberry, but his bed was empty. As I glanced up toward my bedroom I could see him peering down at me. His tail wagged when we locked eyes.

"Arf, arf."

I headed up the stairs to my room to find Huckleberry had repositioned himself to have his head poking out from underneath the bed. I dropped to my knees and bent forward so I could get to his level. He immedialetly backed up slightly before turning to sit beside the old trunk, then pawed at the side a few times while looking at me.

"Arf, arf, arf, arf. Mmmm, Mmmm. Mmmm. Arf."

"Okay, I get it." I said laughing. I felt my hands twitch as I reached for the trunk containing the mythological artefacts. Once I dragged it out I scooped Huckleberry into my arms, gave him a loving squeeze and then placed him on top of the bed. I took a deep breath as I began to release the latch. Any normal person would have gone insane with curiosity about the collection of oddities contained within. I however, felt a sense of resistance toward the contents. It wasn't due to fear but rather an awareness that I couldn't be certain about their origins. I held an underlying suspicion that not everything here had an application for good. What if in a rage I was tempted to use such a tool? Even with the best of intentions I could unleash something that works against me, inadvertently aiding the Inteferon's cause.

Huckleberry began whimpering again.

I looked at him as I released a sigh. "I don't know little buddy. I'm psyching myself out of it again."

He waved his right paw in the air.

"At least one of us is certain." I positioned my hands on either side of the lid. "Let's do this."

I pulled back slightly as the dust particles floated upward with a gush. A faint scent of frankinsence and myrrh rose to tickle my nostrils with its perfume from the moment the lid was lifted. Initially I glanced at the folders placed in there by my mother. She had merticulously catalogued what she believed the items were.

"Sorry mom." I whispered as I began collecting the wad of material to remove them from the trunk. These would need to be burnt to abolish any temptation I might conjure to read her research. In order to discover the capability of each artefact I would need to trust my instints and ensure that I'm not mislead by any external influence. The Interferon's proved they had easy access to everyone, so I knew the probability of them sending my mom down tainted paths while doing her investigation was highly plausible. The only way to proceed is on my own.

Placing my hand methodically over each of the items I could feel their unique vibrations warming the center of my palm. Once I truly settled into a semi meditative state the vibrations adjusted to a series of waves of energy that seemed to be communicating something. Each item I hovered over had a unique story to tell that was translating in a match of hues gliding upon my eyelids that were timed to perfection with the wafts of energy concentrated within my left palm. It was extraordinary, but I found myself struggling not to break my focus as I wanted to peer down at the items that seemed to feel as though they were a close match to my own.

I persisted with trying to read the energy of the contents while recognizing that the sphere contained within a tightly bound deep purple velvet cloth continued to draw my attention. Initially, I tried to resist its calling but found each time I allowed my hand to relax it would naturally gravitate toward it. I released a deep breath and settled on choosing to explore this item.

Upon removing it from the oddly shaped trunk I closed the lid, then for a moment glanced up to check on Huckleberry. He was curled in a delicious little ball fast asleep. Comforted by the sight of him resting I returned my focus to the sphere. As I untied the tightly wound knot I realized it was a beautiful shawl with a hand stitched motif of orange flowers on one section, the inside seemed to be made of raw silk. Carefully I began releasing the contents from the shawl, which revealed the underside of an ornately designed three legged stand. It had the mythological God Pan cast in different positions playing the flute. His thick hairy goat like legs complete with cloved hooves formed the feet, while his naked upper torso was designed to retain a clear crystal sphere in position. The stand was rather heavy and extremely detailed in its craftsmanship. Even the tiny flutes appeared to be hollowed. I wondered if it had been originally fashioned for this purpose or whether it was designed to hold something else entirely different.

Although it nested perfectly within the stand, it seemed out of place to me.

My legs were beginning to ache from being pressed against the hard floor. Not wanting to disturb Huckleberry I opted to gather everything and head downstairs. The dining table was the obvious place to sit but I decided to get comfortable in the reclining chair and used the lap table I had tucked away on the side as my platform to perch the ornate stand on. Up until now it hadn't occurred to me that I didn't know what to do next. I used the silk side of the shawl to wipe away my finger prints from the surface then stared at it for a while.

I could feel myself losing focus with my mind drifting toward reciting the events of the day. Allowing the daydreaming to draw me in I felt my body jolt to attention when my eyes unexpectedly spied something whiz by in a flash aross the spehere. Whatever it was that had entered, moved across the length of the sphere then disappear in a super fast fashion. I could feel my breathing change as I witnessed it happened again. It took a few more times for it to occur before I gathered my senses to piece together that it was a bird flying overhead. Its image was being reflected upside down in the crystal. I felt a little silly but tried not to allow that to take over my need to focus. As an aid to the reduction of further distractions, I chose to drape the purple velvet shawl over my head and then covered myself and the ball completely with Huckleberries sofa blanket. There in the darkness with only the faint aroma of Huckleberry's scent to calm me, I allowed my hands to cup the side of the ball and began to stare into the abyss.

"Show me," I whispered.

There was a warmth that palpatated at the center point of my palms. I could almost here the slight hint of a gentle humming noise. It made me feel a sense of comfort. As it grew in strength I wasn't certain if it was being generated by me or the crystal. Slowly an effect of ripples, like you see when disturbing the surface of water, appeared. I could only identify from the delta between the dark and light shimmer that it was indeed a liquid substance that I was seeing. Shapes began to form, thousands of hands reaching out, grasping at nothing. People on their knees, hands clasped praying. A significant number of individuals flashed as animated millisecond snippets layered over each other before fading away. There wasn't anything distinguishable about the pattern that was emerging, with the exception of all of them holding the commonality of being human. Most of them were speaking. I wondered what they were saying.

"Let me hear them."

I immediately reached to cup my ears as an onslaught of words and thoughts saturated my drums with a cocophony of expressed desires that made me want to instantly implode.

"STOP the sound."

It ceased on command and provided a sensory relief. I now appreciated the silence and was only left with having to contend with the noise generated from my own head thumping in protest of the experience. It was hard to settle my nerves to refocus on the multitude of people that were still being presented. Annoyed with the unnerving sensation I felt from the intrusive gaggle of people's voices, I could feel a build of tension in my body. I was starting to convince myself that this was a bad idea and fought to hold myself present to the experience.

Closing my eyes to clear my thoughts I inhaled and released deeply three times before placing my hands around the crystal ball once more. I did my utmost to align my mind to discard the distractions and to commit to paying attention. When I felt I was ready I reopened by eyes to be greeted by the darkness once more.

"What are you showing me?"

A wave of forms appeared to once again mold into the shape of humans. The volume of imagery of people quickly escalated to present at a speed that was so fast it was becoming a melting pot of blurred psychedelic colours. I shook my head to deter the build of queeziness I felt watching the mottle of patterns. Suddenly, I gasped as I struggled to breath. My hands fumbled to find the edges of the blanket to pull it off me, while my head automatically reefed back to draw in some fresh air.

A solid ten minutes must have passed by before I allowed myself to open my eyes. I didn't want to look at the crystal ball anymore. The intensity of how it felt to have everything amplified made me feel slightly insane. Slowly, I grabbed the left side of the shawl that had fallen onto my shoulders. I dragged it off my neck, then placed it over the ball before lifting it up to put it on the coffee table.

Conscious that I was experiencing light headedness, I tucked away the lap top table and eased myself up from the chair. Carefully I took slow measured steps, making my way into the kitchen to grab a drink. I put my hand under the cold running water to remove the sting of the heat in my left palm. Dampening a clean tea towel, I washed my face before resoaking the cloth to drape it on my neck. I grabbed a small glass that was within reach and filled it half way before placing it to my lips. With my first sip, I swished the liquid around my mouth. This made my senses heightened to the pleasure of feeling moisture. The cool of the water maintained its presence down the length of my throat. I wanted more and began to refill the glass over and over gulping the water until my stomach visibly swelled. It disturbed me that the images wouldn't stop flashing about in my mind. After I removed the damp cloth from my neck, I glanced over at the crystal ball once more. The shawl had fallen off. Sitting there on the table it seemed innocent enough and could be easily mistaken for a decorative paperweight, but I now knew better. The energy that flowed from it was too much for me to manage. I decided it was time to return it to the trunk, then I could have a quick shower before finally joining Huckleberry in bed. Perhaps in the morning after some rest I would be able to quietly step through what had happened to try to decipher the message. For now, my mind was muddled, and I was zonked from the weirdness of the experience.

I drank the last remaining drops of water and then placed the glass in the sink before returning to the crystal ball. When I was standing over it I could hear its distinct hum. I shifted the shawl, spreading it out flat on the coffee table, hesitated for a moment, and then picked up the ball to ... BAM a white blinding light shot up in a continuous stream as my hands became suctioned to the sides of the ball. My head was held back, forced to gaze at the imagery projected on the evening clouds. There were people everywhere, hands reaching overlayed onto a mash of people from different era's all doing the same thing in distinctly different ways. I released my body from struggle and gazed at them all as a tear rolled down my cheek. The evolution of the imagery switched to couples dancing, holding hands, laughing, it profoundly moved me. I had been compelled to see them from an altered perspective. The intensity of the pattern so evident in a non-linear way that it was now hard for me to accept that I missed it. As the overlay of manic imagery reinfused with the raw beauty of couples intertwined I observed in awe of the possibilities.

"I finally get it." I whispered.

The stream of light went out leaving my body to slump. My knees gave way making the weight of my body too difficult to hold. I dropped to the floor instinctually lifting the ball above my head to protect it from harm. The warmth resonanting from it now generated a sense of comfort. I layed down on the floor on my back then placed it on my chest. Closing my eyes to listen to the gentle hum.

It made sense to me now. Each human possesses an insatiable hunger for connection to their counter part twin flame. The tri moon phase holds an opportunity for all who yearn to be reunited. Our global unity could become the platform to launch a hieghtened universal vibration. This mission was far greater than just myself and the other six pairing of twin souls. This was the time to ensue self empowerment for the masses to take charge of their own destinies.

The clock had just struck one am. I had less than twenty-four hours remaining to convince the world that a tri moon would not only occur but could also provide people with a chance to connect with their loved one's, whether it be in this life or across the planes. This was an opportunity to shift the axis in our favor on a metaphysical scale. I recognized it was no easy plight but then nothing worthwhile ever seemed to be.

* * * * *

By the time midnight had arrived the following day the word was starting to spread. My underground team of hackers seeded the message through their networks to increase the magnitude of the threads that needed to be layered across the internet. Initially, we targeted esoteric groups by creating notification pop up windows on sites that were frequented in significant volumes. The hackers co-ordinated an expansive team to join on forums posting chat threads that linked to a custom made website, which we backdated to appear as though it was created fifty years prior. This was to provide readers with a level of confidence of its authenticity. It covered the phases of the moon cycles across the last ten decades then segued into full moon trivia, which intermixed common knowledge material with lesser-known facts. A full detailed page was assigned to describing the phenomena of the tri full moon neatly looping into a fable about twin flame union. Globally millions of people were being targeted. A specific thread of customized campaigns were developed to engage healers, hippies and pagan ritualizers. This proved to be an invaluable way to gain momentum. There were a range of links that began to have a life of their own with self-proclaimed experts making statements across a variety of social media platforms. Even the people who were spruiking against the idea were contributing to rapidly spreading the word. The team were set to remain vigilant on the task at hand for the duration of the time we had remaining. I could only hope the phenomina of the back to back full moons would cause enough of a stir; thereby encouraging individuals to take a chance at calling out to their twin flame when they witnessed the miracle event occur once more on the third evening.

I felt like I hadn't slept a wink for over forty-eight hours and was now finally lying in the warmth of my bed with my trusty Huckster snuggled under the sheets in a tight ball. I positioned my hands behind my head with some pillows to partially prop myself up in an attempt to remain awake for a tad longer. The brilliance of the lunar night sky helped build the anticipation of the moon making an appearance across my skyline view.

* * * * *

My body jerked forcing me to wake as I felt Huckleberry scurry from underneath the bedding to rise to the surface. In a daze, I stared at his snout poking out from the layer of blankets and wondered if he was overheated. Lifting my head off the pillow I looked around feeling discombobulated by my surrounds. I sat up and then spun around to prop myself onto my knees while trying to get my bearings. The bed had moved one hundred and eighty degrees. Jumping out from underneath my duvet I walked the perimeter. Still half asleep I scratched my head while trying to comprehend how it was possible that my bed had changed position. I peered down to check the legs to confirm my four-poster king sized bed was still bolted to the floor. It was. Tilting my head up I could see the moon was shining over me. The luminescence provided clear visibility. Huckleberry was enthusiastically jumping about the bed in play, pouncing on the shadows cast by the clouds passing by the moon. The stone feature wall in the family room area below was aglow with colors refracting from the light of the moon traveling through the ornate backboard of my bed. It had been hand made by the architect who gifted me the piece when

I purchased the property. The design was an eclectic mix of some fantasy scape pollination between Dr Seuss and Alice in wonderland. Watching the picture projecting on the uneven surface of the stone wall made me feel that the light was enabling it to posses a life of its own. I sat on the edge of my bed to stare at the picture slowly forming on the wall. Intermittently I could see a flicker of what appeared to be a blood red shimmer almost blinking in the center of the imagery. As the clouds cleared leaving the moonbeams uninhibited the outline became solidified. It was a magnificent classical depiction of the tree of life. The way the light fell onto the wall there were shadows cast beneath the stone that naturally jutted out from the wall. I smiled as I realized it looked like hidden steps leading up to the trunk of the tree.

Huckleberry barked as a clicking noise presented. I looked around to identify where it was coming from suspecting it might be a cricket. The echo was throwing my hearing out but Huckleberry was fixated on barking at the wall. Just as I stood up the clicking changed to a musical tune, the kind you hear when you open a little girl's jewellery box to find a dancing ballerina inside. It caused Huckleberry to switch from barking to spinning in circles as though he assumed the twirling ballerina's role. It lasted for no more than a minute before being replaced by a loud THUD, which released the latch to a secret door. I watched in amazement as it creaked open on the wall.

"Wait here boy," I said, patting Huckleberry before heading to the fireman's pole. I grabbed on and slid down while smiling. As I reached the bottom I laughed, I never tired of being able to do that. After straightening out my bunched up pyjama pants I walked across to survey the area in the hope of identifying the best way to climb the wall. Thoughtfully I wandered back and forth to assess it from all angles before settling on my route. I grabbed a shopping bag and torch from the kitchen to ensure that if there was something to retrieve that I was prepared. I held no desire in me to attempt this lofty height more than once.

Huckleberry had jumped off the bed and was now hanging his head between the balustrades, so he could see me better. The initial few steps were easier than I had anticipated. I did have an underlying concern that the structure may not be sturdy enough to hold my weight, but it didn't seem to budge. Steadily I made my way closer to the center point of the wall. Beads of sweat were forming across my brow and my hands were beginning to shake. I wasn't scared of heights, but I still held no desire to look down. I used my toes to grip the rock it was perched on. It took the better part of twenty minutes to navigate my way to the upper portion of the wall. Positioning myself to align my head with the door I readjusted my body, so I was able to lean into the rock to allow my left hand to be free. When I shone the torch inside the open cavity I could immediately see a single sealed envelope. Shining the torch carefully I inspected the space inch by inch to ensure that I didn't miss anything. I could see the musical machinery on the back of the door was part of an elaborate locking mechanism. The red shimmer I had noticed from my bedroom was a stone the color of ruby that allowed for concentrated light beams to enter the door from specific angles. It was an amazing piece of artistry. Satisfied that there was nothing else remaining, I took the envelope and placed it and the torch in the bag. Just as I closed the secret door, the latch clicked locking it in place once more. The seal of the edges were so perfectly created I could no longer detect the outline of the door.

When I finally placed my feet back on the ground, Huckleberry was there to greet me with his tongue franticly licking my toes. I had heard him pacing the floor while intermittently releasing a whimper as I had made my decent. Bending down I swooped him up to give him a cuddle. He tried to squirm his way toward my face as I laughed. He settled into licking my arm instead as I walked across to the sofa to take a seat. Propping up a pillow beside me I placed him down, so he could settle. When he calmed, I reached into the bag to retrieve the letter. My hands were still shaking from the climb. Feeling plum tired from the unexpected exertion of energy, I couldn't be bothered with getting up to switch on the light, so I opted to use the torch. I shone it on the outside of the envelope, flipping it around to inspect its plain outer layer. It felt like it was made from cheap quality recycled paper. I opened the unaddressed envelope and peered inside. There was a single key and a letter. I took out the single folded piece of paper to read the hand written message addressing me.

Dearest Harper,

I find myself struggling to encapsulate all that is required to be known. I sit here with a pile of failed attempts covering my desk and wonder if I will ever be satisfied with my choice of words. It amazes me that twenty-six singular characters when combined provide us with a mechanism to channel our thoughts in a manner that others can understand, yet still the complexity of communication is in being able to issue a sentence that is read and interpreted in alignment with the writer's intent. Even in this version of my letter I once again find myself attempting to preface my writing with an insight into my struggle to articulate the preciseness of my thoughts. It leads me to wonder whether my best approach is to say less than initially desired. This way we will have little to misunderstand between us.

When I was in college I met a woman who, within an instant, I knew was the person I wanted to spend the rest of my life with. Post graduation we married. Saying 'I do' to her is still one of the happiest moments of my life.

My wife was sixty-one when she passed away from terminal cancer. In the last few months of her life she revealed to me her deepest regrets. I as her supporting husband listened. It was in essence a devastating realization for myself to become aware that the person I love so deeply was still someone who I was yet to truly know. She had harbored the burden of many secrets.

It is not my place to justify the choices she made, nor do I wish to place judgement on her. She is and always will be first and foremost my wife. This is not to suggest that I condone what had taken place. In truth, it is hard for me to comprehend why such atrocities in human behavior exist, none the less they do.

The day you and I met I was filled with awe. I'm not sure that you are even aware of how captivating you are, which makes you all the more beautiful. I treasured the little time we spent together. There is no doubt in my mind that you are significant and thus your journey is riddled with the diversity of the broadest of spectrums between life's joy and correspondingly it's pain. To that end, my wife was an unwitting contributor to the latter.

In the envelope, you will note there is a key. It opens the safety deposit box I created for you at the Renkin Bank located on Carpel Street. Contained within is the deed to this building. All the monies accrued from the rental of the apartments from its outset has been placed in a trust that only you have access to. I have supplemented the funds equal to the amounts you have paid for your own apartment to ensure you are fully compensated.

Harper, I spent a decade post my wife's death creating this safe haven for you, as an apology from us. This was my wife's last wish. It is not my place to ask you for forgiveness and I appreciate given what little I have divulged that you will not possess enough context yet to comprehend the magnitude of what occurred, that indeed drove my wife to despair.

This apartment was designed to protect you. It holds many secrets, synchronized to unveil when the time holds true for you to know more.

Stay Vigilant & Keep Strong
Elon Braymer

Releasing a deep exhale as I reread the words, stay vigilant and keep strong. My thoughts flashed back to the day I was introduced by the realtor to Elon. Its an easy recall for me because I found him to be such a visually interesting character. I was at the realtor's office sitting on a rather uncomfortable leather sofa. Elon was nestled into a large arm chair and was watching me closely while he sipped his coffee. I bantered on answering his questions completely oblivious that the meeting had been orchestrated. There was a definite aura of sadness around him. His parting words as he held my hands were, 'I wish my wife was here to have met you.' I considered it peculiar but never really held a reason to give it a second thought.

Carefully I lifted sleeping Huckleberry into my arms and returned to bed. I placed him under the sheets next to me to give him some warmth. The little tacker didn't stir further than releasing an adorable yawn and giving me a single lick while his eyes remained shut. I gently gave him a pat and then dropped the sheet to leave him to his slumber. Once again, I found myself staring up at the night sky, this time wondering what it was that this woman who was a complete stranger to me could have done that was so heinous.

Jay Bird Blue

Greeted by the warmth of the late midday sun I could hear Huckleberry panting before he poked his head out from under the sheets. My eyelashes were clagged shut with a thin layer of crust. Releasing three consecutive yawns I knew if I allowed myself to I could easily drift off to sleep again, so I shuffled my way out of the bed then fumbled toward the bathroom. The muck on my eyelashes scratched at my skin as I washed my face. I had not been this gunged up since I was a child. Leaning forward I stared into the mirror, forcing my eyes to blink until my blurred vision dissipated. I paused for a moment as I observed the crinkles in my skin. I couldn't recall the last time I had a proper look at myself. After pulling a few faces, inspecting my teeth and checking for any rogue hairs, I stripped off and headed for the shower.

The warmth of the water was comforting. I closed my eyes to amplify my enjoyment of the droplets landing and rolling down my body. I got a fright as I felt something touch the surface of my foot. Gasping I reefed my leg up while simultaneously looking down. I burst out laughing when I realized it was Huckleberry looking like a drowned rat. In his wisdom, he must have decided he was due for a wash. He did that from time to time.

Huckleberry raised himself up on his hindquarters as a queue for me to pick him up. I perched him on top of the fold out bench. Just as I started shampooing his coat he placed his front paw on my shoulder, so he could lean forward to collect the falling water onto his pink tongue. Once he was teaming with suds I focussed on washing my own hair. We took turns in rinsing. When I propped him up on the bathroom counter to get him ready to be dried he automatically assumed the position on his back with his legs up. The little scamp loved the warmth of the dryer on his belly. I was smiling as I fulfilled his wish to be pampered. I made sure he was sufficiently dry before giving my own hair a blast to get it to the point that it was semi dry. Huckleberry headed down stairs, while I fumbled about in my wardrobe to settle on what I would wear for the day. As soon as I was dressed, I headed for the kitchen.

My stomach rumbled while I made myself some porridge for breakfast. Huckleberry was happily tucking into his meal with his tail wagging. In the back of my mind I wondered whether the spirit I met in the park whom I called Mable was in fact Elon's wife. Without knowing what she looked like I wouldn't be able to confirm. Although, in light of what had just been revealed to me, it would make sense to reconnect with Elon, however, the feel of my stomach churning at the very thought of this, suggested that my instincts were telling me not to.

Thinking back to the time my settlement of the apartment came through, I recalled the relator mentioning that Elon had ventured overseas with the intent of retiring. No specifics were provided about the locale. It seemed from what I could glean from his note that he was genuinely struggling with whatever he held the burden of knowing. Elon's extension of small insight to me was perhaps his creative way of connecting without dredging up the history of how and why this all came to pass. I could hear the words, 'leave it be' whisper in my mind when I entertained the idea of finding him.

I took my steaming porridge with me to the dining area, so I could stare up at the wall. The massive stone face cascading from the roofline of the cathedral ceiling all the way down to the floor was basking in sunlight. The ominous, raw, uneven surface was a fine representation of nature's imperfect, yet perfect beauty. I held a new appreciation for the way it had been constructed. Each piece was filled with character that was enhanced by the streams of light that bounced off its edges. I pulled out a dining chair and sat down to eat while I visually explored the wall.

Just as I was set to indulge in another piping hot mouthful of porridge, I heard my cell buzzing. Enthusiastically I ran across to the lounge and began tossing the sofa pillows about. Lodged between the cushions, I just managed to grab it to answer as the call diverted to my automated call service. I saw that it was my mom, so I pressed redial.

"Hello."

"Hi mom, sorry I couldn't get to the phone in time to answer. How are you?"

"Oh. I'm fine. We haven't spoken in a while, so I thought I might check to see how you are."

"I'm okay. Huckleberry has been his usual demanding self, so I've been rather busy catering to his every need." I said trying to keep things light.

"Have you heard any more from that strange man?"

I had to think for a moment.

"Harper, are you there?"

"Yes, sorry I was just trying to figure out who you were referring to. I am assuming its Ross, the man who appeared at dinner the other week."

"Ross, yes that was his name. I've been really concerned and decided if I didn't hear from you by today then I would call."

"There's no reason to worry. It was a case of mistaken identity. Have you heard from Dylan?"

"He called a couple of days ago. He and Kichiro are planning to come for a visit as soon as he gets his clearance for his holiday leave."

"Great. It feels like forever since I've seen him. I can't wait to meet Kichiro."

"He sounded excited on the phone and said that Kichiro was using the trip as extra incentive to practice his English. Dylan said he really wants to make a good first impression."

"In Japanese culture family is so important. I can only imagine the amount of pressure he's probably placing on himself."

"Yes, it does sound like he is trying very hard."

"Oh well, that's something to look forward to. How is dad?"

"He returned to work fulltime from last week. There is such a backlog for him to catch up on. He has been working extended hours, leaving early and staying late. We haven't really seen much of each other."

I knew there was more to the story, but I chose not to delve. "Okay, well hopefully he is being sensible and will pace himself, so he doesn't get run down. How are you?"

"To tell you the truth I'm a bit of a nervous wreck. I thought I was able to hold it all together, but it seems that I am becoming more and more emotionally unstable. I cry at a whim, there is something driving me toward making huge changes that at this late stage in my life quite frankly I'm terrified to do."

"Mom, I can't talk to you about this. Its not that I don't wish to support you in your choices, if you believe it will make you happy. I'm your daughter; so, it's unreasonable to expect me to be your confidant or councillor. My suggestion is to find someone you can trust to be your sounding board or hire a professional."

"I know." She said with a sad voice.

"How long has it been since you went and got a full check up. The whole shebang of bloods, smears, breast exam, you know, the works?"

"It's been a while."

"I'd suggest you assess your physical wellbeing first to ensure there isn't something underlying that is affecting you. Hormone imbalances, absence of the right levels of, Iron, Folic acid, and Vitamin D are all contributors to healthy brain function and mood stability. While you're waiting for the results it wouldn't hurt for you to get back into a routine of meditation, yoga and perhaps consider re-joining that Himalayan singing bowl class you use to rave about. I'm not sure what reasons you have for feeling the need to diverge but what I do understand from observing your recent behavior is that you aren't certain either. Your whole adult life has been devoted to family, perhaps now is the time to work on reconnecting and replenishing yourself so you feel balanced and whole again."

"I have felt lost for quite some time. You're right, I should try and focus on reclaiming a sense of myself. I've been so out of sorts that I hardly recognize who I am anymore."

"Yes, the stunt you pulled the other night with Devon is completely out of character. It was reckless and cruel. I'm not sure if dad figured it out and, in a way, I hope he is still blissfully ignorant. I just can't understand what you were thinking."

I could hear her trying to muffle the sound of her crying.

"Mom, if you and dad are drifting apart, or you feel that you have reached the end of your journey together, that's your choice and between you both to manage. Regardless of what has transpired to drive the circumstances to where they are today, dad doesn't deserve to be disrespected. To have us attend a family dinner and be served by your lover or would be lover is really poor form, and I simply can't understand what you were hoping to achieve by doing it."

"I'm so ashamed," she whispered.

"You knew I would see it for what it is, so I can only conclude that you wanted to be caught."

"Honestly Harper, I don't know what I was thinking."

"Mom, I love you and want you to be happy. The kind of happiness I'm referring to is the contentment that can only be derived from within you. I'm not sure how serious you are with this Devon fellow, but I can tell you that he cannot fix whatever is causing you to feel broken. He is a distraction from whatever it is that you're choosing not to address. That's all I am going to say on the matter. It's your life mom. You are welcome to live it in any way you wish. All I ask is that you look inward to find what makes you truly happy and then honor that."

"You are so level headed and clever. Thank you for not hating me."

A tear escaped from my eye as I blinked. "There is no reason I could possibly imagine that would warrant me ever hating you mom. I just want you to be happy, truly happy."

"I want that for you too Harper."

"I know you do but in essence we are both charged with the responsibility of making ourselves happy. Its time that you focussed on you."

"I will."

"Mom."

"Yes, Harper."

"I know that this might sound like a strange request, however, I want to ask you to do something."

"What is it?"

"I'm not sure if you've heard the buzz regarding the phenomenon of a tri full moon that's happening. Last night was number one of three. It is set to occur in succession so tonight and tomorrow the full moon will once again be present."

"There was something mentioned in the paper this morning. I didn't read the whole article."

"There is a belief that during a tri full moon you can call out to your one true love and no matter where they are in the universe they will be able to hear you."

"That's a very romantic notion."

"It is. My request is that you clear your mind tonight and tomorrow evening, stare out at the moon and speak from your heart to your true love. Let it be carried to them so they may respond in kind."

"I don't think it's your father," she whispered.

"I'm not suggesting that it is. What I want is for you to create the energy and opportunity to reconnect with the love of your life so that hope is instilled, and you can find your way back to each other's arms, when the time is set to do so. Call me a hopeless romantic but I've decided that I want to believe in fairy tales. Will you, do it?"

"Sure, I'll do it for you."

"No mom, do it for you."

"Okay, yes you're right. I'll do it for me."

"Good." I said feeling relieved.

"I love you Harper."

"I love you too mom. Let me know when Dylan confirms his travel dates."

"Will do, bye."

"Bye."

As I placed the phone down Huckleberry jumped onto the sofa to snuggle next to me. I looked across at where I had left my porridge. I knew it would be warm, possibly even cold by now. I despised the idea of reheating food and I couldn't be bothered making another batch. I was too hungry to try and ignore my pangs, so my only remaining option was to head out for a late lunch. I ran upstairs to grab a jacket, feeling strangely energised from the raw honesty of the conversation I managed to have with my mother.

Huckleberry was waiting at the door intently staring at my hands as I approached. I knew he was looking for his harness. I showed him my empty hands, then bent down to give him a pat. His beautiful little face stared up at me. He was only providing a partial wag of the tail, still watching where my hands were. I could tell he was hopeful as his eyes jutted between glancing at my left and right hand. When I whipped out the harness and leash from my side pocket he twirled around with excitement only temporarily containing his expression of joy long enough for me to put it on him. Grabbing my keys and phone I locked the door behind us and headed out toward the main drag where all the hip coffee houses were positioned.

Café Aurora was the third place I paused at to glance at their menu. On the list of specials for the day the roasted peppers topped with baked goats cheese on sour dough took my fancy. Huckleberry curled in a ball under my chair as I sat down. My favorite part about this strip of eateries is that they are mostly all pet friendly.

"Good afternoon,"

"Hello."

I watched as the waiter bent down and placed a complementary, size appropriate raw bone in front of Huckleberry along with a fresh container of water.

"He's a cutie."

"Huckleberry's a heart breaker for sure."

"I love his name, Huckleberry." He looked down at him for a moment and smiled. "It really does suit him."

I bent forward to look at him and then glanced back at the waiter smiling. "It truly does."

"What can I get for you today?"

"I'd like to order the roasted pepper and goat cheese on sour dough please."

"Great choice, can I get you a beverage?"

"I'll have some sparking water thanks."

"Sure, I'll bring that out right away." The waiter gave Huckleberry a little wave as he walked off. I could tell he was smitten.

On the seat next to me was a folded up newspaper. I placed it on the table and began flipping through the pages. Seven turns in I spied a single full length column that was devoted to the topic of the tri full moon. It was good to see that my team of hackers were building enough hype to get the mainstream channels to jump on board and report on the current social media buzz. The gist of the article was suggesting that the concept was a load of tripe and that the next two evenings would provide the required proof that it was just a hoax. This brought a smile to my face, there was no doubt in my mind that what Mable had told me was true.

"Here is your sparkling water." The waiter poured the contents of the bottle into my glass and then added a slice of lemon.

"Thank you."

"I'll return in a few moments with your meal."

I watched him walk away and noted that he seemed to have a slight limp on his left as he stepped. The front of the café wasn't over crowded. The weather was putting on a show with a cloudless blue sky. Judging by the noise I imagined that most of the patrons were seated in the garden at the back of the property. My preference was to be positioned at the front where I could be entertained by the passing foot traffic.

The waiter was true to his word and had returned quickly with my meal.

"Here is your roasted pepper medley. Is there anything else I can get you?"

"Wow this looks amazing. I didn't realize that peppers came in such a variety of colors." I said as he placed it in front of me.

"It's a popular dish. Would you like some freshly cracked pepper on top?"

"No thanks. This will do me just fine."

"Very well. Enjoy your meal."

The smell of the peppers had my stomach doing flips. The first bite of the meal graced my taste buds with the full flavor of the peppers coupled with a hint of rosemary and garlic oil and the distinctive tang of the goat's cheese. I was in heaven. Between bites I washed it down with small sips of the refreshing sparking water, while watching the world pass on by. It was nice to have a moment of normalcy.

On the return journey home, I opted to take the long route with a deviation to the dog park so that Huckleberry could have a play. There were only a few dogs present so I joined Huckleberry in the cordoned off section. I helped him climb the ladder to the slide and then watched as he hesitated at the top before bravely coming down with a wagging tail and smile on his face. Quickly he ran straight back to the ladder to get assistance again. Placing my palm open on the back of his neck, he pushed against it to get the support he needed to climb up each rung of the almost vertical steps. Much to my surprise the other dogs started to assemble near the ladder, patiently waiting for my assistance. An old St Bernard positioned himself at the bottom of the slide. He watched over the dogs as they came down, licking them and when required assisting with their dismount.

"You've made some friends."

I turned to the direction of the voice, "Yes, it would seem that way."

"I'm Grady, the St Bernard is mine or I'm his, sometimes the lines get crossed." He said releasing a hearty laugh.

"He's a dear soul. I've been admiring his protective nature. Eagerly watching over the dogs as they race down the slide. Its adorable."

"Yes, he once found a box filled with abandoned kittens. I wanted to pass them to the local animal shelter, but he wouldn't have a bar of it. In the end, I caved and let him raise the litter. He was the proudest daddy and very vigilant in teaching them how to fetch a ball."

"Really?"

"Absolutely. I have six cats that all think that this St Bernard is their father. They sit, roll over, fetch. Here, I have a photo."

He reached into his back pocket, pulling out his wallet.

"Take a look."

I finished helping a beagle up the ladder before stepping forward to glance at the photo. "Oh my, that is heart melting."

"Two Christmas's ago we had it as our greeting card. The photographer was amazed at how well behaved the clan were. Especially when they were fitting the cats with their little elves costumes."

"Its clear that you have a special bond."

"We do."

"Which one of these tail waggers is yours?"

Huckleberry came running toward me almost on cue, leaping off the ground for me to catch him. I swung him up in the air and then dropped him into my arms for a cuddle. "This is my little scamp, Huckleberry."

"He's a lively fellow."

I laughed, "He has his moments."

Grady reached across and patted Huckleberry, then looked at me and smiled.

"I'd best be going." I said. "It was nice to meet you."

"Yes, I hope to see you again."

I nodded my head, "I'm sure we will." I gave his St Bernard a pat as I walked by. When I was back over the fence I placed Huckleberry down to walk the rest of the way home.

It was nearing dusk as we entered the apartment. With a satisfied tummy, the exhaustion from the adventures of the evening prior began to creep up on me. I knew that this evening was significant, as it would prove the tri moon phenomenon isn't a hoax. Still, I needed to rest. It would occur regardless, so I didn't feel the need to be a witness to its occurrence. I picked up the letter from Elon off the coffee table on the way up to my room. Huckleberry took the lead. When he reached the top of the spiral staircase he turned to watch me approach, while releasing a big adorable yawn. I picked him up, gave him a kiss on the top of his head and placed him under the blankets so he could find his spot as I slid into some pyjamas. Climbing into the bed I put one of the pillows over my head to block out the light. It wasn't long before I felt the warmth of my duvet lull me into slumber.

* * * * *

I woke to the sensation of Huckleberry frantically licking my face. Using my hand as a shield to block his tongue lashing, I turned to my side. This instigated his need to dig at the base of my back as if he was going to tunnel his way under me to get to the other side. I shook my head and laughed. Without warning I turned, grabbed him with both hands placing him above me as I repositioned onto my back.

"What is going on with you?"

He was vigorously wagging his tail as he used his paws to emulate walking in the air. I placed him on my chest and held him in position because I knew the moment I let go my face was going to be bathed in saliva. He tried to squirm free as he happily panted.

"What?" I said laughing.

He lifted his head to look up toward the sky. I followed his gaze and was greeted by the glory of the full moon shining through. The beams of light were angled in a way that made the air above me seem to possess a haze. I watched as the dust particles floated serenely about.

Huckleberry released a bark, while his outstretched paw landed gently on my throat. This time he was staring at something behind me. Shifting him off my chest I turned to prop myself up on my knees. I gasped as I saw that the colorful picture on the wall of the tree was present again. It was a cloudless night sky, so the detail projected from the bedframe was depicted with crystal clarity. I had not seen anything quite so beautiful. As my eyes scanned over every inch of the detail I realized the secret door had re-opened.

I leapt out of bed and in the same fashion as the night before chose to slide down the fireman's pole. This time when I approached the wall, I didn't hesitate to begin my climb. I made my way up feeling the immediate activation of my muscles as they twitched.

The slow burning sensation that was building was a sure sign that my arms would be super sore tomorrow. Still, I persisted until I was hovering over the open cavity. My chosen route placed me in a better position than it had the previous eve. As I peered in I switched hands so that I could brace myself securely. I positioned my body to be flush against the wall, while my right hand was freed to retrieve the object sitting inside the cavity. I wasn't expecting to find anything given it had already been emptied by me the night prior. My objective for climbing up was merely to close the door. Inside the secret panel there laid a book that was leather bound and wrapped with a brown leather belt. I readjusted my footing to release the pressure tension I was feeling. I inspected the book from different angles to determine if it might contain something breakable. Surmising it was paper, I quickly glanced down to see where Huckleberry was before deciding to take a punt by letting it go.

THWACK. It landed on the floor below me.

I reached in and felt the surrounding walls of the cavity to see if I could detect the presence of trap doors that might reveal other hidden treasures. I wasn't completely satisfied before resealing the space but knew by the cramp developing in my left leg that I was fast approaching my body's limit. I carefully made my way down the wall and jumped to the ground when I was at a safe enough distance. A small sharp sting of pain ran up my ankles through to my shinbones as I landed.

Picking up the book, I made my way to the kitchen, placing it on the bench before grabbing the kettle to fill it with water. When I switched it on to boil I returned to hover over the book for a closer inspection. It was A5 in size, perhaps a tad larger. The leather that covered it was rough-cut, which suggests that it had been made by hand. The yellowed stitching down the spine was unevenly crisscrossed with varying sized knots at the ends to hold them in place. There was an embossed picture of a raven soaring above a tree on the front. The back had two ravens that appeared to be conjoined, positioned above a skull. Slowly, I unhooked the leather belt, which was strapped around it. Opening the soft cover revealed a blank page. My fingers glided over the surface to feel the texture of the unusually thick paper. The writing began on the next page. I hadn't even started to read the first word before I subconsciously found myself closing it shut.

"Not yet." I whispered as I re-secured the belt around it.

While heading back up the stairs to my bedroom I could hear the boiling kettle switch off. Perching myself in the center of my bed I hugged a pillow, resting my chin on the end as I stared at the image of the glorious tree projected on the wall. The trunk had the subtle form of two human bodys intertwined. The mostly nude branches of the tree were outstretched across the width of the wall on either side. There were moments when it seemed to sparkle, attracting my eye toward its detail. The colors depicting the randomly set leaves held a deep saturation. I found it all soothing and somewhat hypnotic.

* * * * *

A sharp pain drew me to consciousness. I felt a twang as I tried to straighten my neck from the awkward position I found myself in. I'd fallen asleep hunched over the pillow with my legs bent at the knees. The circulation to my lower limbs had been compromised so I was rife with the sensation of pins and needles. Slowly, I rolled myself to the side to remove the pressure from my legs, lying as still as possible to give them a chance to settle down before I began wiggling my toes to encourage the blood flow.

As I lay there I thought about the book, which was still downstairs on the bench. My hesitation in regard to reading it encompassed the fact that it was likely Elon's wife's diary. I wasn't ready to embark on the journey of knowing what she had done to me. Especially given that he was driven to spend a decade of his life and a small fortune dedicated to the intricate design and development of this building as an apology. I secretly dreaded to think what had taken place. No doubt it would be the stuff of nightmares.

Bravely I stretched out my legs to release the last of the zing from the pins and needles. In unison, I rotated my ankles clockwise and then anti clockwise to ensure that I had regained full feeling. The pain in my neck had subsided but I could feel the pinch of the tightened muscle ever so slightly drawing my scapular up. A visit to my masseuse on the way back from my morning walk with Huckleberry would definitely be in order.

I didn't feel like having a shower this morning. I quickly freshened up before dressing, then headed out the door without giving the book another glance. Huckleberry seemed to have an added skip in his step almost pulling on the lead when we got closer to the dog park. The mornings were always busy. I could see as we approached that a few of his favorite four legged friends were already present. I left him to it while I walked across to settle down on the bench. I was keen to see what the vibe was now that a second full moon had come to pass. Eagerly I flipped through the media channels on my phone. It appeared that its presence was being played down. There was some acknowledgement by atronomers and escoteric groups that two full moons have occurred back to back, but the scientific communities offered no comment on how it could be possible. My team of hackers were continuing to work relentlessly to build the hype. It was obvious to me from what I was reading that we would need to somehow ensure that before this evening the word was spread far and wide on the possibilities of twin flame union. I looked across at where Mable had stood a few days prior and smiled.

"We meet again."

I turned my head. "Ouch." I said as I grabbed my neck to settle the throbbing pinch I felt.

"Sorry, I didn't mean to startle you."

I shook my head slightly, "You didn't. I accidently slept in a strange position and am feeling tension in my neck."

"Here may I?" He said holding out his hands.

"No, its okay. I'm planning to go to my masseuse straight after this."

"I'm an osteopath, I can relieve your pain right now if you would allow me to."

I looked at the expression on his face as I dropped my hand to allow him access to my neck. "Okay, thank you."

Grady positioned himself behind the bench and gently encouraged me to sit back.

"Close your eyes and relax."

I closed my eyes as I felt his cold hands clasp my neck. He began by rocking it from side to side while he used his arms as a bridge on my shoulders to engage the push and pull of a series of stretches. When he used his thumb to run down the tightened muscle I clenched.

"Relax," he whispered.

He persisted for well over twenty minutes. I felt myself fading in and out of being present to what he was doing. The warmth generated by the friction of his hands had my neck feeling flush.

"There you go." Grady released my neck and walked around to the front of the bench to take a seat beside me. "Does that feel better?"

I nodded my head, "It's made a big difference. Can I offer you some money?"

He smiled, "No, consider the first consultation free. I'll sting you triple on the second one."

I laughed, "Sounds like a plan."

"Actually, if you do feel like repaying me, perhaps you would say yes to joining me for a coffee sometime."

I looked into Grady's eyes as my smile slightly dissipated. "Are you asking me out on a date?"

He winked, "I am."

I turned to see what Huckleberry was up to. When I found him in the sea of wagging tails I felt relieved.

"Grady, I don't date. I appreciate the offer. Its very flattering but I have to decline."

I watched him readjust his seating. "Really? You don't date at all? How is that possible?"

Subconsciously I shrugged my shoulders, "I just don't see the point."

"The point is connection, intimacy, love. You can't be an island. We all need companionship."

I looked at my hands as I released a deep sigh.

"Who hurt you?"

I shrugged my shoulders again, "No-one."

"Something must have happened, unless what you mean by saying you don't date is that you don't hold interest in dating me."

I lifted my head to look at him, "No, it's an indiscriminate rule. I don't date and won't date until I feel I want to. Mostly, I don't want to. My life is complex enough without half-heartedly involving other people into the mix. I'm okay with being on my own. I get lonely sometimes but mostly I prefer the life I have chosen."

He looked at me for a moment before rising to his feet. "Well, if you ever change your mind, here's my card."

I reached out and grabbed the business card listing his practice details on it. "Thanks for fixing my neck."

"Not a problem at all. Try to keep that muscle warm, it will continue to release some more over the next couple of hours."

"I will." I said cupping the area with my hand.

"Well, I'm off to my practice to triple charge all my return offenders. Have a nice day."

I chuckled, "You too."

I watched him walk to the playground gate. He released a loud whistle that had most of the dogs freeze in their tracks. The St Bernard left the pack to join his owner. Together they walked down the path side by side, no lead attached. The strong bond between them was obvious.

It wasn't too long after that Huckleberry scaled the fence and came running to me. He had clearly had his fill of entertainment. I clasped his lead onto his harness and headed in the same direction that Grady had ventured. It was a nice day for a stroll.

* * * * *

There was a build up of anticipation in the air this evening. The third and final full moon would appear, solidifying the bridge of connection between lost souls universally. The clandestine team of underground hackers instilled a new approach on spreading the word to all the corners of the globe. They created a broadcast wave that interrupted all standard television and radio circuits to announce the need to take a chance on love during the third full moon this eve. It was pleasing to believe the notion that so many out there would be whispering and hearing the messages of love. I hoped my mom had kept her word to be among the ones who dare to call out to their twin flame.

To mark the occasion, I made myself a pancake stack with a generous serve of homemade raspberry compote poured between the layers, topped off with a scoop of ice cream and half a punnet of fresh blueberries. It was a rather indulgent treat. I served Huckleberry his mini stack minus the ice cream. Watching him waste no time with tucking in made me laugh. I cleared a space on the coffee table for my plate before sitting on the sofa. As I cut through the stack the juice from the compote oozed out. The first bite was heavenly. Often, I find that food can look better than it tastes but, in this instance, the flavors honored the presentation by being on par with the right balance of tart and sweetness. No sooner had I completed swallowing my first bite I found myself compelled to shovel in the next portion. I had no will to stop. The stack was consumed in less than five minutes, leaving me uncomfortably full. Not that this held me back from licking the plate clean.

Huckleberry joined me on the sofa just as I returned the plate back onto the coffee table. I patted his rotund little potbelly and smiled. He too, I suspect, had eaten too fast and was feeling the effects. I spontaneously grabbed the book my doppelgänger had gifted to me, the Conspirathorium Valedictorian. I placed a cushion on my lap to prop it up. Flipping through the pages I once again started to recognize some of the mathematical formulas. Slowly, I assessed each line to see if there was anything that might stand out. The later part of the book displayed chemical compounds and measures. To a scientifically skilled mind this information may be an instruction manual, but to me it still seemed like thought chaos randomly splattered on paper. Aside from the few macabre drawings of rat dissections, there was no hint as to what purpose the books contents served. My instincts still leaned toward this artefact being of great importance. After one final flutter through the pages I decided I would pack it away, for now. There was far too much going on around me to be concerned or caught up in trying to decipher the jargon. I couldn't even fathom allocating the time nor the energy that would be required for me to brush up my skills in biochemistry. I chose to place it in the hidden cavity below the floorboards, then I picked up Huckleberry and headed for bed.

Laying on the surface of the duvet I folded my arms beneath my head and stared up at the night sky. The luminescence from the moon was visible but it itself was yet to appear in my scape. Judging by the previous nights display I would expect there were a few hours still to pass before my eyes were greeted with its glory. Reaching into my dresser draw I pulled out the Cintāmani stone and placed it on my sternum. I closed my eyes to enjoy the subtle vibrations, while ruminating on all that had transpired since the time I had walked through the redwood forest. So much had come to pass.

* * * * *

A shock of electricity surged through my body as I reefed forward and gasped for breath feeling I had escaped from my dream just in time to evade certain death. In my nightmare, I had been trapped below the surface, a shallow burial ground with no coffin to house my rotting remains. The menacing muffled laughter above made my blood boil as I was tormented by my inability to scream. The roots were taking hold, invading my body to draw nutrients. I felt an excruciating torment wash over me while their slow extraction weakened my resolve to fight. I was dying, and every aspect of my being felt an oversaturation of pain.

The pulse beating in my hands commanded my attention. There was a burden of an unfamiliar weight encroaching as I tried to straighten out my fingers to reveal my palms. A purple stain of bruising created imagery of what looked akin to a network of veins. I switched on the bedside light and grabbed my cell to take some images. I stared at my hands. The purple stain had begun to rapidly fade. My surface pain was dissipating, leaving me with a new awareness that I was sitting in a layer of soil on top of my bed and had dirt embedded beneath my nails. The full moon was once more present in my skyline.

I jumped out of bed to search for Huckleberry, recognizing he wasn't with me. I felt a surge of strength in my body when I moved. Even my grip as I placed my hands on the balustrade to look down into the living area felt firm. Thanks to the position of the moon, the light emanating through the bedhead was once more projecting the image of a rather ornately adorned tree. It seemed to be even more beautiful than the night before. I immediately noticed that the secret door was open. I had a quick glance around the rest of the room below until I spied Huckleberry fast asleep nestled on a pile of cushions on the sofa. I returned my focus to clearing my bed of the soil. First, I shook the dirt off the duvet onto the bedding and then bundled the sheets in a pile. My next point of call was the bathroom to quickly wash the residual dirt and dust from my body. It took some rigour to remove the muck wedged underneath my nails. It was only when I came back into the bedroom that I realized that the Cintāmani stone was missing. I searched the floor and found it settled between the base of the bed and the side table. I placed it back in the top draw for safe keeping before setting out to remake my bed with new sheets. Once the bed was remade I headed downstairs to check on Huckleberry. He raised his head as I approached and begun wagging his tail. I leant in to kiss the top of his head then left him there to continue to rest.

Staring up from the base of the wall to where the secret door was ajar I no longer felt intimidated by the ascent. Without hesitation, I gripped onto the rough surface and started climbing up. In less than two minutes I was facing the opening and could see there was an envelope awaiting my collection. I arranged my position to free my right hand, so I could tuck it into my pants, shut the door and climbed back down. I knew by the time my feet reached the floor that something had altered within me. I felt no residual muscle pain from the previous climbs and was super agile this time around. There was definitely something happening that I was yet to understand but could appreciate that it seemed to be clearly linked to the vibrations generated from the Cintāmani stone.

Not wanting to disturb Huckleberry I decided I would open the envelope upstairs. I placed a towel on my pillows, as my hair was still wet from my impromptu shower. Once I found my sweet spot in the center of the bed I held the envelope out in front of me for inspection. It had the words '*To my beloved*' scribed with beautiful penmanship. I placed my finger in the section that was partially unsealed and used it to coax the rest apart. Inside there was a single parchment page. I unfolded it to reveal a hand written letter.

My Love,

The essence of you is the very same fabric that is contained within me. We are one. Your pain is my pain. Your joy is my joy. Not a moment has passed since the beginning of our time where I have not held faith that we will once more be in union. I love you with every beat of my heart and miss you in the spaces between. You are all of everything to me. Our turn draws near. It is time for you to feel this, know this and believe that it will come, for it shall.

The anguish endured across my lives has been served with junctures of pleasure in the all but fleeting treasured moments when our paths had crossed. Even in their greatest attempts they were unable to tear our mutual draw. It did not matter the shape, nor form for the vibration we have is set to the frequency of pure love. When you were presented to me as a child I loved you, as a woman, I loved you and as a man, I loved you. Fear not what the gauntlet holds for nothing can weaken the bond or our resolve to be together.

Your will chose the solitude of these remaining cycles, an entry not even they could predict. Still, you had left me behind in this realm. I felt torn. My countless efforts to cross over have fallen short of success only to later discover you had thwarted my ability to join you. My faith waned, for I thought you had abandoned me, us. It wasn't until I felt the presence of the guide that remained that I realized the extent of your sacrifice. It is a miracle that you survived and in the absence of such have thrived to the extent that you have gained the upper hand on all. Their ongoing fears have now been realized. You cannot be contained.

My love, the endless ache you bury deep is one I carry too. I miss you. Do not fear that I am lost to you, for I watch, and I patiently wait. I know now by the price paid there is traction gained assuring ours is the next true journey. This will be the final in the test of sins that has previously seen us torn from each other's arms prematurely, time and time again. Come what may, hold strength and do not yield for you have now made our union a certainty.

Eternally yours,
Beloved.

Tears streamed down my face as I felt a sense of relief in the words I had read. I placed the page against my chest then looked up toward the sky to the tri moon and whispered, "I love you. Always in all ways for always."

Duplicity

Leaping out of bed I walked the perimeter to ascertain how it was possible that my bed had returned to its original position, once again without detection. I shifted the edge of the rug and began tapping at the floorboards. There must be a false floor with a timed mechanism that allows for 360 rotations. I know the technology exists. I had seen it applied to the tops of narrow driveways to assist with repositioning the direction of vehicles. Even so, what mystified me is the fluidity of the undetectable movement and the fact that the floor appeared seamless. Just like the secret door and its hidden compartments, the craftsmanship is so superior that it tricks the human eye into believing that it is whole.

Huckleberry arrived with a wagging tail and sleepy eyes. He greeted me with kisses to my hands as I picked him up for a cuddle.

"Good morning," I whispered into his ear. The momentum of his tail increased. "Let's get you some breakfast."

I carried him downstairs and placed him on the kitchen counter where he sat patiently while watching me pull together a mini feast for his morning meal. He usually had a big appetite at the start of the day. I like to give him a small portion of raw egg, stirred through some lean fresh mince, which I sprinkle with a serve of quality dog kibbling. Huckleberry stepped forward as the last of the biscuits were released from my hand into his bowl. I placed them both on the ground, so he could begin feasting while I zipped back upstairs to get showered and dressed for the day.

Upon my return, I could see he was ready by the door waiting for our morning adventure. I smiled as he spun with excitement the moment he saw the harness appear in my hand. There was something blissful about the simplicity of his joy. A pat. A walk. A meal. He was easily pleased and consistently happy. I was grateful to be a contributor to this. I secured him into his harness and then we were on our way.

The dog park was a flurry of activity with people obviously taking advantage of the clear blue sky day. There was a crispness to the air that was vividly present while I stood in the shadows. The sense of it quickly faded when I stepped out to the welcoming warmth of the sun. Huckleberry happily scaled the fence the moment he felt the tension released from his harness. He ran as fast as he could and jumped straight into the thick of the canine activities that were taking place. I ventured across to the bench to rest. A couple taking turns to throw a Frisbee to their Golden Retriever caught my attention. The dog leapt into the air to catch it mid flight, often landing awkwardly before running back to deliver it to them to throw again. What I thought interesting is that they were standing apart and he seemed to consciously give them equal turns at throwing.

My thoughts drifted to the letter and how it made me feel. The sense of loneliness I have experienced throughout the course of this life felt abated, from the very instant that I read it. My faith was revitalized with a connection I had secretly always hoped existed but did not dare to seek for myself. In a sense, I had felt that I was burdened with a journey that demanded solitude. Based on the words contained within the letter I guess to some small measure I was right. I smiled, for I now felt the emotional resurgence of what it is to love and be loved.

"You seem deep in thought."

I squinted slightly as I looked up, "Hi Grady, take a seat."

"Thanks, how is your neck feeling today?"

"The stiffness is a distant memory. Honestly, since you worked on it yesterday I haven't really given it much thought."

"Hmm, so there's no chance of a triple charge then?"

I laughed, "Not a hope in hell."

He smiled as he leaned across to push a flyaway strand of my hair to the side of my face.

"You seem to be glowing today. Have you secretly received news about winning the lottery?"

"Glowing? Me? Really? No, I'm immersed in enjoying the glory of this beautiful morning. I love the atmosphere that's been created by the people and pets that come here. Look at that Golden Retriever and his slaves playing with the Frisbee."

"That's Marvin and his slaves are Ronald and Lucy," he said with a chuckle.

"Watch, Marvin consciously alternates between them. He gives them both equal turns at throwing to him."

Grady shifted his gaze to observe them at play.

"Well, I'll be damned, he does too."

"They never coax or call him, they wait, and he delivers the Frisbee. I think it's marvellous."

"I'm impressed that you even noticed. You must have a good eye for detail. What do you do for a living?"

I smiled, "I'm retired."

"Impressive, what did you do before you retired?"

"I was a behavioral scientist specializing in cognitive science assigned to the criminology department of the justice system."

Grady readjusted his posture, "Which explains the powers of observation. Wow, that seems like an intense gig for someone so young."

I laughed, "I'm no longer a spring chicken and yes the gig as you stated was somewhat intense."

"You seem to lead a rather fascinating life." He paused for a moment to release his breath. "I know you have a strict no dating policy, but would you accept my invitation to join me for a coffee in the spirit of forging a friendship? I would really like to get to know you better."

Subconsciously I began shaking my head. "I really dislike talking about myself and as I suggested yesterday my life is rather complex. I'm happy to exchange idle banter when we meet at the park, but my preference is to leave it at that. Once again, it's not personal to you, I would say this to anyone who at this stage of my life tried to connect with me. I have my purpose and cannot afford the maintenance or distraction that comes with social obligations."

"You make it sound like it's a burden to invest time in getting to know people."

"No, I'm brutally honest about the reality I see and the price I pay for getting to know people."

"What's the price? All I see are the positives, friendship, and support when you need it plus the bonus of someone to split the lunch bills with. How is that a bad thing?"

I closed my eyes and drew a breath. When I opened them, I checked on Huckleberry before engaging Grady's eyes. "You are interested in me. If you were remotely honest with yourself, you would acknowledge that your current request to engage in a plutonic sense is a hopeful bridging element into creating an opportunity to segue back to the original intent of pursuit of intimacy. I see no point in allowing this. It will bring you pain and me a sense of loss because you were not able to keep to the suggested friendship. Hence, to me there is no point in taking a course that leads to a state that I want to avoid. We cannot be friends because you are not capable of being my friend. You like me and will always wish for more than what I want to offer. It is a cruel dynamic that would consume your thoughts and distract you from searching for a more suitable companion. You deserve better than that."

"I'm starting to think you have tickets on yourself and are too caught up in feeling that you know it all that you aren't able to extend beyond it to accept the simple gesture of friendship."

I nodded my head doing my best not to smirk at his tell-tale reaction.

"I feel sorry for you. I really do," he said in a harsh tone.

Huckleberry came running up to me and in a single leap was on my lap standing on his hind quarters fixated on kissing me on my face and neck. I smiled as I contained his wriggling long enough to attach the leash before I stood up with him settled within my arms.

"Have a nice day, Grady."

He gave no reply.

I walked down the path continuing to hold Huckleberry until we were a few hundred meters away. Just before placing him down I gave him a big squeeze, "Thanks for the save buddy." He released a bark and had a skip in his step as we meandered through the park.

We stopped at the ice-cream truck to purchase a cone to share. I watched as the man serving, scooped a generous amount of the ricotta and lemon myrtle sorbet into the cone. The last time I had one of his flavor inventions it was the extraordinary combination of olive oil and tangerine. His interesting blends have been written up in several of the culinary magazines as the treat to eat, which is how I first heard about him. Huckleberry knew that he was going to be given the bottom portion when I neared the end of the cone. On the way back to the apartment I broke off small bite sizes for him to consume and then stopped just outside the building to give him the rest of it before we ventured indoors. I wasn't big on diversifying his palette with human food, but the odd indulgence was acceptable.

Once inside Huckleberry helped himself to some water while I grabbed the diary from the kitchen bench and brought it with me to the sofa. I no longer felt hesitant about reading its contents. I had faith that whatever resided within these pages were set to be revealed to me at the right time and for the right reasons.

I opened it up and went to the second page where the writing began.

I've never been afraid of the dark even though they wanted me to be. Sometimes I would pretend to react to the things they did to try and scare me just because I could see that it seemed to please them. Then in my moments of rebellion I wouldn't provide any measurable response, which I guess was one of the reasons they decided to segregate me from the others. I held the potential to be a bad influence; and on occasion I could hear their whispers suggesting I may be tainted.

During the early years, I thought my life was normal, holding no reason to believe otherwise. My brothers, sisters and I went to school every day, played in the evenings, and were lovingly tucked into bed by our mom and dad each night. It was the perfect little bubble that was set to burst for each of us when we turned eleven years of age. I remember celebrating mine and my sibling's birthday, eating lots of cake and falling asleep with a smile on my face. It was the last time I recall that I had ever felt truly happy.

The keeper at some point had taken me during the night to a place that was to become my home for the remainder of my adolescent years. My quarters had no window. Only a tiny crack in the broken mortar invited a slither of natural light to invade my tomb. The furnishings were rudimentary with a mattress and some bedding strewn on the floor. The poorly plumbed toilet and small basin both were situated in the far corner of the narrow room. To me, the worst discovery was that I had shackles on both my ankles that were connected to thick linked chains protruding from the wall. I was at their mercy and time would soon reveal that they possessed none.

There was no light provided when my meals were delivered. The couriers were always dressed in black and had their face covered only revealing a narrow window for their eyes to guide them. No amount of pleading to set me free drew a response or if it did I couldn't tell. The meals were small in portion but delicious to consume. With the boredom of entrapment encroaching on my state of mind the sound of footsteps delivering my food became the only thing I had to look forward to. Then it started....

I closed the book shut as I felt my stomach wrench at the words 'then it started.' This wasn't at all what I was expecting. I just know that there is a high probability that nothing about what this person has to say from hereon is going to be pleasant. The only grace my mind can allocate is that they recorded their account of their life, which means that at some point she or he must have escaped from their persecutors.

I went to the kitchen and switched on the kettle. Huckleberry was fast asleep in his bed. I watched the rise and fall of his body as he took each breath. He looked so peaceful. While waiting for the kettle to boil I went and stood in front of the stonewall in the dining area. Across the tri moon phase, I was presented with three items, a letter from Elon, this diary and the letter from my beloved. All of them must somehow be interconnected. I can surmise that it is probable that his wife had something to do with the fate of this person writing the diary, but how did Elon manage to acquire the letter written by my beloved and more so know to give it to me?

I returned to the kitchen, made my cup of tea and decided to go back and continue reading.

At first it was presented as flashes of images and words projected on the wall. My eyes took some adjusting to the introduction of the bright light. Initially, I wasn't sure what I was looking at and hadn't understood the meaning of the words being presented. It was all happening too fast for me to make any sense of it. If I covered my eyes with my hands to try block it out, a male voice would immediately yell, "WATCH." It scared me enough to make me do as commanded.

It happened in random spurts throughout the days and nights too. While sleeping I would be woken by a sound that indicated more images were ready to be projected. If I didn't stir, the chains were pulled through the wall drawing my legs toward the air. Once I began to pay attention to the images the tension in them were almost immediately released. I stared and tried to think about other things, but it was no use. Their technique of exhaustion and repetitive exposure to the images and words had become so familiar to me that I could see them playing on the wall even when no projection was taking place.

Usually, once every couple of days, I was escorted out of the room to the shower where I was stripped naked and scrubbed from head to toe, then dried, dressed in clean clothes and returned to my confined space. I recall the first time they stormed in, removed my chains and dragged me to the bathroom as I fought, kicking and screaming. There were five of them. One secured to each of my limbs, carrying my unwilling body while a person walked behind holding a cattle prod. He never used it on me but the threat of it was always present. As time passed and I became more compliant to the routine, they reduced down to a total of three. Two walked at pace on either side while the third remained lagging slightly behind with his cattle prod in hand. I was gradually afforded the opportunity to shower and wash myself unaided. They would be present in the bathroom with their backs turned to give me a modicum of privacy. Except the cattle prod man. He, however, was always silently watching.

During my absence from the room they took the opportunity to clean it. I could smell the bleach that was used on the facilities and fresh bedding was provided. On the odd occasion, I would discover I had been left an after dinner mint hidden out of sight near the edge of the pillow close to the underside of the top outer most sheet. I would savor the taste of the treat and wonder who among them felt pity on me enough to risk providing such a gift. To ensure it was never discovered I would wrap the packaging in toilet paper and flush it down when I used the facilities.

Once upon a time I believed that there was a single defining moment that a person can pin point in their life that held such significance that it could be used to trace back almost every stimulus that drove their justification for their on going behaviors and decisions. Mine was when on this one occasion they returned me from my routine shower with the absence of clothes. I felt exposed and vulnerable without fabric to shield my skin. They fastened my ankles to the clamps and left. A short while later the signal went off to indicate that the images would start projecting, except this time the chains were drawn reefing my ankles in the air. My back was flush against the wall as I felt my legs being slowly drawn apart. The images and words began to flash upon the screen when a commanding voice stated abruptly, "MASTURBATE."

Initially I was twisting and turning, trying to find leverage to attempt to pull against the chain. Each time the voice yelled the same singular word. If I didn't comply the chains would separate my legs further. Inch by inch I was pried apart until the muscle pain became too much for me to handle. I recall how it felt placing my hand on my clitoris for the first time. The moment my finger touched the velvet of its surface, the tension was released from the chains as a reward for my compliance. I did as I had been taught by the flashes of imagery and played with myself. It was only when my body released into a brief state of climax that the chains would be fully released, and they would leave me alone for a while.

Months would pass with the same routine repeated at a frequency that fluctuated from multiple times a day then nothing for a few. I became obsessed with conditioning my legs to stretch, ensuring that eventually they could no longer hold the threat of prying me apart beyond my threshold. I would remain in position for hours to train my muscles to become elongated and supple. The angle from which the chains were mounted, and the width of the room meant they could no longer gain the leverage to extend me beyond my capacity to spread my legs. This pleased me, and I suspect infuriated them.

I am unable to ascertain the precise time when I switched from being driven by them bellowing a command to me versus me feeling a compulsion to execute the act of my own volition. All I understood was that I no longer felt uncomfortable being naked, rather it was somewhat empowering. I knew they were watching. I wanted them to watch.

The next phase of what I had come to know as my education involved taking me into a room that was decorated with a bedroom suite that had purple velour material draped from the posts and along the length of the beam. I was placed in an old Edwardian wing back chair with my wrists shackled to a loose length of chain. The person with the cattle prod was the only one who remained present in the room with me as the other two escorts exited. When orchestral music begun to play a male and female entered the room. The crushed velvet cloaks they wore matched the color *of the purple décor in the room. Ignoring my presence, they faced each other, and both synchronized the lowering of their hoods. She had a vibrant deep red lipstick that emphasized the plump pout she displayed. Her mid length wavy auburn hair was partially trapped within the robe. He ran his hand on the underside, gliding his fingers across her neck to release it. Both wore masks to cover the upper portion of their faces. I wasn't sure what my mask looked like but could only assume it was similar in style to hers.*

He untied the bow that secured her cape in position to remove it from her body. As it fell to the floor it revealed her pale curvaceous flesh in all its glory. The man stepped forward running his hand down the length of her arm, gravitating to her waist before raising her leg to pull it toward him. The other hand was used to encourage an arch in her back as he bent his head to greet the rise of her mound with his mouth. I watched her lips part to release a gasp when he bit her protruding nipple. His tongue left a shimmering trail of moisture as he licked and sucked her bosoms raw.

There was a point at which I noticed her hands had moved from bracing his shoulders for balance to pushing him down to his knees. He released her leg and raised the other dropping it over his shoulder before burying his face between her thighs. I had seen all this done before through the pictures projected on my wall. What held my attention were the noises being generated from his deed and her response to it. Intermittently he would raise his saturated face from her privates to look at her. To which she promptly either thrust forward or used her hand to place his head back into position. I noticed as she was close to her climax she wriggled and thrust at his face until her body released a quiver of pleasure that made her coo.

The man stood up and began pleasuring himself while she took her position on her knees. I could see that his cock was hard. She glanced for the first time across at me to smile before opening her mouth and taking him in. She used one hand to stroke him slowly while she licked and sucked the end of his penis. There were lipstick marks on different parts of the circumference of his cock that were left there when she paused in places. He groaned at the times she took him completely in and then slowly drew him out.

"I want you to stain me." I said.

She turned to look at me and then up at the man she was sucking. He stepped back from her and turned to come toward me.

"No, not you. I want her lipstick to stain me." I perched me legs on the chairs left and right arms then ran my hand slowly down my belly and stopped to hover above my clitoris, then drifted lower to insert my finger into myself.

The woman rose and came over to me. She looked at the man with the cattle prod as she bent down onto her knees. My body felt a pulse of electrtcity when her hands glided from my knees in toward my thighs. She took my hand and brought it to her mouth. I watched as she first inhaled my scent and then tasted it. She sucked my finger hard and then pulled it out slowly. I touched the side of her face before dropping my fingers down to explore her warm breast. She licked her lips when I squeezed her nipple.

"Stain me with your lips." I said.

She dropped her face between my legs and began licking my clitoris. I looked at the man who was staring at us and commanded, "MASTURBATE." He dropped his hand down to grasp his ridged penis and began to pull with slow steady strokes. I lifted the girls face so I could see her covered in my moisture. This pleased me.

"Play with my tits as you stain me."

Thrusting my hips forward I pushed her head down to grind her tongue hard up against my nether region. She lifted her arms and began squeezing my breasts. I gyrated when I felt the tingling build from her licking working me into a quivering frenzy.

"PULL HARDER," I yelled at the man who immediately complied with my command.

I closed my eyes as I released a groan of pleasure cumming on her face with an intensity I had not felt before. My hands pushed down on the back of her head to deepen the contact as I continued to climax.

Unexpectedly the man stepped forward pushing the woman to one side. I screamed "NO," as I lifted my hands to protect myself. Out of the corner of my eye I caught a glimpse of his body jolt across the room when he received the sting of the cattle prod to his cock and balls. He convulsed on the floor as the music stopped and the two men who usually escorted me back to my room came in to remove the man by dragging him out the door. The woman quietly followed suit.

I stood up and looked at the person with the cattle prod. "Thank you."

He nodded his head slightly, knelt down to release me from my wrist shackles, removed my mask and then gestured with his hands that we should leave. He walked me back to the room, allowing me to enter first. I heard the click of the door shut. He had left without placing me back on the ankle shackles.

I reached for my cup of tea to take a sip while I contemplated what I had just read. This girl was abducted when she was only eleven, and from what I can ascertain has been placed in some elaborate program to condition her into being a sexual slave or perhaps a mistress. I'm not too sure which one it is but am leaning toward believing that they are grooming her to be a complete deviant. If the intent were to have a slave I would expect that her perpetrators would have been more invasive and physically penetrated her by now. They have exercised a huge amount of restraint not to have done so given everything seems to evolve around sex. It's odd that they have spent countless months placing energy into making her watch pornographic material, taught her to masturbate and then introduce her to a room where she is set to observe a couple engaging in coitus. She mentioned having breasts, so she must have graduated into a pubescent state, which suggests she is around thirteen or fourteen by now. They clearly want her to feel comfortable with sexually explicit scenarios. Was she being groomed in preparation to be sold off as a sex slave? Perhaps she has been involuntarily recruited for grooming to later be assigned to spy on high profile people for collection of Intel?

It made me wonder who this person was and why she was selected. There had to be some significance behind the choosing of this child. To have her taken from her family means that she is missed, and people must be looking for her. That would have been a far higher risk scenario than grabbing an adolescent crack head or child prostitute from the streets whose absence wouldn't be noticed. She seems rather extraordinary to be developing in strength whereas most people would understandably become wrecked. Instead her recount of the experience suggests that she developed a sense of empowerment and was trying to find her own rhythm within the fate that had been dealt. Taking her tender age into account, I admired her for that.

The next evening, I was taken to a room escorted only by the man with the cattle prod. A bath had been set with milky water; where a combination of deep red and light pink rose, petals were freely floating on the surface. There was music softly playing in the background with a few candles lit. The aroma in the air was sweet. Initially, I stood there staring at my surrounds. The mirror held a distinct fascination for I realized upon engaging my reflection how much I missed my siblings. I turned to look at my escort who gestured for me to enter the bath.

I watched my toes on my right foot disappear into the clouded water. The heat was initially searing. I shifted my gaze to see that he was now sitting on a chair with the cattle prod resting across his lap. He never speaks a word and given they all wore the same head to toe covered black outfit I wasn't ever sure it was the same person each time. All I could see were his eyes and they rarely gave much away. Once I was completely settled, I closed my eyes to remove the visual presence of him.

Time seemed to pass slowly. I only considered exiting when the bath water began to cool. I enjoyed the wrinkled feel of my hands as I grasped the edge of the bath to prop myself up to a standing position. He rose to his feet at the same time and reached for the towel. Instead of passing it to me he placed the cattle prod on the chair, so he could hold the length of the towel up. When I got out of the bath he gently wrapped it around me. As I clasped onto it he released and stepped back.

"Thank you," I said with a slight smile.

He turned, picked up his cattle prod and gestured for me to exit the room.

Still wrapped in the towel I walked forward as he followed slightly behind. When we neared the door of my room I slowed down. He ventured past signalling for me to follow his lead. I hesitantly continued in the direction that he went feeling some apprehension about the sense of freedom I was suddenly being afforded. When he stopped outside a red door I froze in place. He twisted the handle to release the latch then pushed it open before stepping back to allow me to enter. I slowly walked to the opening peered in and immediately turned to look at him. He ever so slightly nodded his head. Stepping over the threshold, I entered into a beautifully decorated bedroom. The turquoise baroque styled wallpaper accentuated the shimmering dark grey duvet cover with matching pillows on the double bed. There was a single nightstand with a lamp switched on. In the far right corner a small library of books were neatly lining the shelves. My excitement rose as I placed my hand on the thick black velvet fabric curtain. I drew it back expecting a window but instead found that it was covering the entrance to an ensuite. I opened the cabinet and saw it had fresh towels with an ample stock of toiletry supplies. When I re-entered the bedroom, the red door was shut. It felt strange to be standing in such a large space on my own. It took me a little while to realize that the wardrobe contained clothes. My abductors had forced me to remain nude for such a great length of time that I no longer felt any compulsion to wear anything. Deciding not to suffocate my skin with fabrics I used the towel I had wrapped around me to dry off my hair then placed it in the wash basket.

Hours seemed to pass as I explored every inch of the room. The books on the shelves were authored by the likes of the father of sadism himself the Marquis de Sade, with titles such as Justine, The 120 Days of Sodom, Juliette and so forth. There wasn't a single title within my library allocation that was not related to some level of perverse erotic suggestion. I of course never knew this at the time and blindly launched into pouring over the literature as a way of escaping from the boredom of entrapment.

By the time I reached the age of consent I had already been privy to ten lifetimes worth of sexual exposure and still my virtue remained in tact. It appeared that my clandestine abductors were men of patience. Over the years, they introduced me into controlled situations whereby I was permitted to unleash my developing interest of exploration without the allowance of others to reciprocate. If I commanded I would receive cunnilingus but only ever from a woman. The men were forbidden to touch me, and I was not allowed to touch them. Hence my curiosity and hunger grew insatiable.

The sound of my cell ringing broke my concentration. I fumbled about to find it and then swiped to accept the call.

"Hello"

"Hi, can speak with Harper Perelle please?"

"Yes."

"Hi Harper, its Officer Bradlyn here. How are you?"

"I'm good thanks. What can I do for you?"

"I am just giving you a courtesy call to let you know that no charges will be pressed by Houghton House, so you are in the clear. I have finalized my report and the matter will be deemed as closed."

"Me, charges? What grounds would they have had to press any charges?"

"They initially called me in to investigate the trespassing of a secure facility, and to get endorsement for a psych evaluation order given the behavior demonstrated in the footage."

"But I thought we had established on the day that the footage was tampered with and that I was actually in the studio located behind the facility."

"Yes, correct which is why the charges cannot be executed and the case is being dropped."

I scratched my head, "Okay, so you called me to let me know that there were intentions to have a case built against me, but now in light of the evidence I am no longer under investigation. Is that correct?"

"Yes. We are satisfied that you were not trespassing, and the tampering of the footage provides the explanation for the otherwise rather odd behavior."

"Hmm. Okay. Are you investigating anything further into this fake studio and why the footage was altered to look like I had been trespassing, or the fact that some-one out there went to some pretty elaborate measures to have me depicted as a lunatic?"

"No Ma'am. I've been told that the matter is addressed, and the report can be closed with no further investigation required."

"Who told you that?"

"My superiors Ma'am."

"Okay." I paused for a moment. "Well thank you for your assistance and for the call. I appreciate everything you have done and tried to do for me."

"Thank you. Take extra special care of yourself."

"You too. Bye."

"Bye."

I placed the phone down and took a sip of my now luke warm tea. Officer Bradlyn was tipping me off that he was being pressured to stop sniffing around. I could tell by the tone in his voice that he was conscious of his environment. When he suggested I take 'extra' special care of myself I knew that he was aware that something isn't right. What he doesn't realize of course is that I am not naïve to the dangers that lurk all around me. In actuality, I'm safer than he is, so I'm glad that he is stopping the investigation, although my instincts tell me that he may be less inclined to cease under the circumstances. Officially he might appear to have closed the case but unofficially I think he will continue snooping. I can only hope he gets bored or finds enough to satisfy his curiosity and then leaves it be. If there is one thing I have learnt so far is that I can't protect anyone who tries to protect me. We each have a role to play and choices to make on this arduous journey. I hope he makes the right ones for him.

I tapped my finger on the page I was up to and re-read the very last sentence. It would seem that this little one has developed into a minx with a veracious appetite for sexual interludes. She has come of age and managed to still have her virginity intact. How is it possible that she hasn't been deflowered under the circumstances? I'm not sure what that's about. I've heard of so many horror stories regarding sexual predators that I find this whole scenario rather out of the ordinary. It brings me back to the same conclusion that she must be a person of significance to them. Who is she?

Her reference to missing her siblings when she saw her reflection in the mirror was a curious tell. You would think after not seeing yourself in the mirror, the first thing you would do is inspect how much you had changed. It was odd to have her siblings overshadow any other thoughts at that precise moment. I wonder if she has a twin? The literature on her book shelf that she referenced is centuries old. I'm struggling to pin point what era she lived in given there are so few markers to go by. Her tone and use of vocabulary denotes education but the language used isn't distinctly aligned to any particular timeline. I think the challenge here is that if her vocab was likely influenced by the restrictive nature of the literature that she read. There isn't an easy way to precisely pinpoint the era. In saying this, she also mentioned some-one sneaking her an occaisional after dinner mint. That suggests that she is from this current century. I thought that the fate of this person may have been connected to Elon's wife, but now I'm not so sure. The connections between the three items delivered to me during the tri moon phase are making less and less sense to me. How is any of this inter-related?

At the early stages of my exposure to them I was almost always presented with people in pairs. Masks adorned, cloaks worn and nudity a must. The backgrounds supplied would vary as were the furnished settings too. Painted scenes on floating walls in the room with a bed or at times a marble top alter. My favorite was the bi-directional rack. I discovered that I had a penchant for ensuring I had complete access to their front and back. Watching them be constrained in a taught spread of limbs made me moist. Blindfolded they knew it was time for the receipt of pleasure, while the absence of one meant the deliverance of pain.

If there were a man mounted on the rack I would instruct the other person present on what he or she is to do. It removed the element of surprise in the racked man's experience but heightened his anticipation of what was to come. During the moments, I could see a man was building to a brink, I would slink forward to whisper in his ear the filth I wanted to say to contribute to the intensity of the orgasm.

"Thrust into my mouth deeper. I need to feel the swell of your cock in my throat as you cum." The reference to me being the receiver seemed to send them into frenzy even though they knew otherwise. Their desperate need to have me, and the fantasy pertaining to the suggestion that they have, become a necessary part of the play. I was the unattainable object of their desire.

The occurrences of the interludes were usually three times within a week and on the occasion as many as five. I knew by the chime that an event was nearing. It usually allowed me a window of two hours before a man with a cattle prod would arrive to escort me to the room. When I entered, the patrons acknowledged me with a bow. I would assess the scene while they awaited my instruction. The first time I had an orgy to command I found challenge in how to address and draw the attention of the people who I wished to issue demands to. It didn't please me as much as I had imagined it might given the tales I had consumed in my younger days. This is what drove my imagination to start to invent new ways to enhance group sex.

When the silken room was launched, I wasn't certain that it would be a success. It was born of my enjoyment of the fabric on my skin and the sensation I felt when touching myself through it. Yards of the textile had been draped from the ceiling in long drapes and some were loops. People had to walk around and through the forest of material. The lack of visibility of the consortium meant that hands could reach and explore the bodies of each other using only the tactile sensation of touch to glide along the surface of the fabric against another's skin. Some looped silks were designed for men to wedge between their legs. A single window was present for their penis to protrude and another for ease of access to their ass. Other silks were raised to hold a woman with her nether regions on display at a height that signaled the invitation of penetration. At a twist of the fabric they were flipped with ease to be invaded from behind. Similarly, the ties along the sides of the silk could be pulled to raise them to the height of one's mouth to indulge in the delights of cunnilingus. This erotic venture removed the vanilla of command and held emphasis on developing the individual's pursuit of fantasy of either being the giver or receiver of a stranger's ecstasy. None were to speak, and none were to refuse. Once entry was made into the forest of silk no one could be denied. The music selected was hauntingly beautiful and adjusted to sit just above the groans and screams emitting from within. The lights in the room were faded only to occasionally pulse, so glimpses were provided of the debauchery. I sat on the outskirts and savored my creation. There was no entry allowed for me, yet I yearned to commit the sins.

Huckleberry jumped up on the sofa and placed his head on my lap as he settled in between two cushions beside me. I gave him a little pat then looked up at the sky. The sunny morning had passed to a gloomy setting. I was torn between continuing to read or finding something else to do to distract me from having to read. I wanted to understand who she is and why she was raised to be that way but without having to participate in her account of all that had taken place across her life. I wasn't a prude but reading this made me feel intrusively voyeuristic. This was after all her very intimate details captured with I suspect no expectation of it being seen by an outsider.

I released a big sigh as I acknowledged to myself that I needed to continue.

On my twenty first birthday, I was summoned to the room after I had been given a decadent meal for dinner and a small cake in celebration. There was no warning that I would be called upon so my entry into the chambers held me unprepared. Inside the décor was sparse with the exception of a nicely dressed rather handsome man sitting on a stool directly in front of my wing backed chair. I wondered why he was not masked, and nor was I. They had always gone to great lengths to ensure no visitor could see my face.

The door closed behind leaving me unescorted.

"Come, sit with me."

I jumped at the sound of his voice.

"Please, join me. I don't bite." A wry smile appeared on his face, "Unless you ask nicely that is."

"Who are you?"

"I'm just a man who has a weakness for the finer things that this life has to offer."

I looked around the empty room and then at him, "Then why are you here?"

"For you my lovely Libertine. You are renowned to be the finest."

"Libertine?"

"Yes, that is what they call you."

I fumbled to say, "They gave me a name?"

He smiled as he leaned forward and patted my chair, "I insist you come and sit with me awhile."

I walked over to the chair and sat down as he had asked. "What is wrong with your eyes? I have never seen such a pale blue in all my days."

"I am blind."

"My sincerest apologies, I did not know."

"It doesn't matter. I was born like this, so I have known no other way. It is fine for me."

I waved my hand about to see if he would jitter. "I don't understand why you are here without a woman on hand to please you at my command."

He laughed, "I may be blind, but I can still sense the flow of air you cause by the wave of your hand."

I tucked my hand under my thigh and bit my bottom lip as I continued to stare into his beautiful eyes.

He leaned forward and whispered, "I don't want the aid of another woman. I only wish to experience the reaction your tone delivers and perhaps if you wish you may please me in other ways of your choosing."

"I am forbidden to touch, and you are not allowed to attempt transgression with me." I said looking at the closed door and wandering why the guard was not present.

"My wager is far too high for me to consider executing such a deed."

"What wager are you referring to?"

"If you in the absence of aid and my absence of sight can still make me cum, then I must pay triple the price for this night. The sumtotal is otherwise paid to me if I leave unencumbered by such a deed.

"What are you suggesting?"

"I'm suggesting that the great Libertine will fail at pleasing me, and as such I walk away a wealthier man for it."

"Are you reducing me to comparison of a lowly whore for hire?"

The expression on his face changed, "I can tell by the change in your tone that you are annoyed. You didn't know there was a fee charged to be in your presence, did you?"

I folded my arms and shook my head, then realized he couldn't see. "No, I was never advised."

"My, my we do find ourselves in a predicament. I thought you were well aware of the demand your services fetch. It is nothing short of a king's ransom."

"How much would that be?"

"A couple are charged five thousand a piece to enter this chamber. There are additional costs associated to the scene created for their evening of frivolity with you. It can be upwards of twenty thousand for the experience. It is why the influential and the elite are the only ones who can afford to visit. To all others, you are an unobtainable dream."

"What of the nights that are set in mass?"

He smiled, "It is as I understand it a variable sum of anything from fifty thousand to as much as two hundred and fifty thousand per head. Your reputation for creating unique orgasmic events is held in the highest of regards."

"Have you attended any?"

"Me, no I couldn't afford it even if I wanted to."

"If you are not rich enough to afford that sum then how are you able to afford this evening?"

"They pay me if you fail remember?"

"So, you were so sure that you wouldn't ejaculate that you entered into a wager and they accepted. There must be more to this that you haven't divulged."

"Let's just say that they owed me and I in turn opted to sate my growing curiosity about the famous Libertine. I traded the favor for a visit and then for interest threw in the wager as an added incentive to the mix."

I looked around the empty room and then back at him. "Then let us begin."

I reached across and placed my hand on his trousers and ran it slowly up his leg to rest on top of his penis.

"I thought you were forbidden to touch," he said surprised.

"I am." I whispered. "I want you to pull it out of your pants for me. It's not fair that I am the only one naked." I sat back in my chair to watch him remove his clothes as I spread my legs and began to lightly touch myself.

"You don't play fair." He said with a cheeky smile.

"I don't like to fail." I said while running my wet finger across the surface of his lips. "I know you smell me and thought you might like a taste of what you cannot touch or see."

He slowly licked his upper lip and then sucked on his bottom lip as his pale eyes stared in my direction.

"Play with yourself. I want to see you ridged."

He lowered his hand and gripped his penis tight. I watched him squeeze it and release a few times before he began to graduate to lengthened strokes.

"I'm squeezing my erect nipple with my left hand. It feels so nice. Can you hear the sounds I'm making with my fingers?"

"Yes." He whispered.

"I'm inserting them in and out of my vagina for you."

"I know. I can smell your sweet nectar of arousal."

"Would you like to touch me?"

He reached across and glided his fingers over his own nipple as he licked his lips, "Oh God, yes."

I smiled, "It's a pity it's against the rules. Savor the taste on your lips for it is all you will ever have of me. Inhale my scent deep within your lungs and imagine the caress of my tongue pushing up against the length of your shaft as I suck your cock."

I stared at him wanking as I masturbated.

"I'm saturated just thinking about it. Can you hear the dulcet sounds of my aching wet pussy?" My back arched when I released a groan from the intensity of being in close proximity to what I had craved.

"I want you inside me, penetrating deep. Pushing so hard that I whimper as you force me to ride the full length of your enormous cock."

I stood and turned my body to bend forward so the smell of my sex could rise to his nose. I reached under and inserted a finger into my sphincter, while I used the other hand to continue stimulating my clitoris, plunging my finger in and out, in and out, over and over.

"Don't you just want to fuck me hard and cum all over my ass?"

He shut his eyes as he began to pull harder. "Yes."

I closed mine to imagine being penetrated by him as I squirmed in delight.

"Oh, God that feels so good, taste me while I cum on your face."

My lower body gyrated as I entered into a state of bliss quickly building up to my peak of release. Beads of sweat trickled from my brow. I could hear him groan as he continued to jerk off. The sound of my stimulation was making a sloshing noise when I penetrated my own oversaturated pussy.

"I'm going to cum," I said panting as the all too familiar delicious tingling sensation took over my body. I shifted to straddle my arm rubbing my clitoris hard against it to maintain the stimulus.

"*Fuck me now,*" I growled then reefed my head up, arching my back to increase and savor the explosion of my senses into orgasm.

When I was able to compose myself, I turned to see whether he had managed to achieve the same. Much to my dismay I noted I was in the presence of a flaccid penis with no evidence of discharge to be seen.

"*I don't understand, how is it possible that you didn't achieve climax?*"

He shrugged his shoulders and smiled, "*Lord knows I tried to play along but you simply don't do it for me. I guess we will have to remain friends.*"

I could see that it was red from being handled. I glanced around the room to check if there was anywhere he could have hidden his ejaculate.

"*Is there something diminishing your capabilities?*" I asked peering a little closer.

He smiled and gave me a partial wink as he placed his finger to his lips, "*Shh, that has to remain our little secret.*"

Initially, I stared at him while I pondered the situation before releasing a hearty laugh. "*Good, let them pay you what they owe and perhaps if you have the gall you might offer them double or nothing in that case.*"

"*You're not angry then?*"

"*Not in the slightest. I may not ever see a dime for my efforts but to have them lose some to the likes of you is a joy to consider. Besides, I rather enjoyed the chance to hold a conversation with such a handsome stranger.*"

He began to place his clothes on and paused, "*Do you mean to tell me that you don't have anyone talk to?*"

"*No. The last time I recollect anyone conversing with me at length, I was eleven.*"

I could see by the expression on his face that news brought him sadness.

"It was a pleasure to be enlightened by you, my clever blind man. Enjoy your richly sum of good tidings."

He reached out and secured my hand, confidently bringing it to his lips. He hovered for a moment and then kissed it. "I assure you the pleasure was all mine, Libertine."

As he released my hand I let it casually fall to my side then left him in the room to finish dressing. My escort was waiting in the hall. I walked ahead, went into my room and shut the door without providing him a second glance. I placed my back against the door before lifting my hand to my lips on the area he had kissed. He was so cautiously gentle with his touch.

I placed the book down and went for a quick pit stop to the toilet before making myself a fresh cup of tea. They called her Libertine, which means a person who is morally or sexually unrestrained. Judging by her writing she was aptly named. The scientist in me can't help but wonder whether she is a product of her environment or whether her environment nurtured an aspect that was already a part of who she innately was. Even the way she manages herself when confronted with information that affects her, like the fact that they charge a fee for people to be in her presence. The composure she maintains is irregular. Most people would be pushed over the edge, but she just shrugs it off. I wonder why she hasn't got any fight in her to try and escape. She's very compliant, which makes me want to understand what drives that behavior. It is possible that she has a form of Stockholm syndrome where by her feelings have developed for the people who have held her captive for the last ten years. It's a phenomenal length of time to be subjected to solitary confinement. The strongest of minds would struggle to retain their sanity under such circumstances. Yet, the way she writes suggests to me that she has managed to thrive. Her only engaging human contact evolves around sexually driven events. Understanding that she was abducted at the age of eleven means she doesn't know any different, so within the confines of what she does know she is managing to find her own level of happiness.

When I was in university there were cases that we studied covering scenarios of a similar ilk. One that stuck with me was a twenty-year old hitchhiker accepting a ride with a family because the husband and wife had an infant in the car. Visually they presented as a wholesome family and so it was easy for her to make the assumption that she would be in safe hands. In actuality, the couple were on the prowl for a victim because the husband who had very violent sexual tendencies had made an agreement with his wife that if she allowed him to have a slave then she would no longer be subjected to his darker more brutal fantasies. The wife agreed and the poor girl who had the misfortune of crossing their path was subjected to decades of horrendous violation both mentally and physically. The power of fear and manipulation is demonstrated perfectly in this case because the hitchhiker was eventually allowed to baby-sit her abductors children, go for jogs around the neighborhood and even visit her own family. She never sought help because she believed all his threats regarding the consequences of trying to leave. In order to protect her parents and siblings from the threat of punishment, she remained silent and continued to be subjected to the abuse, eventually even providing her abductor with a brood of children of their own.

As an outsider peering into these snippets of another person's experiences it's hard to fathom how survivors manage to retain their sanity, let alone rebuild their lives afterwards. Libertine is strong, and I sense very adaptable to her surrounds. There must be a significant portion of what took place that she is choosing not to write about. Looking past the façade I sense deep down that she is lonely and truly very sad.

Family

Entering my parent's home I quietly snuck down the hall and peered from the side into the open space of the kitchen and dining area. The smell of the food was tantalizing, it wasn't surpising, given that mom would have spent the entire day preparing all our favorite dishes. Huckleberry started squirming in my arms signalling he wanted to be placed down. A quick scout indicated they were either in the living room area or out in the backyard. I put my wriggling worm down and watched as he ran straight out the back door.

Placing my bag on the kitchen bench I found the bottle opener to uncork the wine. Just as I managed to pour myself a glass I heard the voices greeting Huckleberry and felt my heart skip a beat when I saw my brother come running inside to greet me.

He squealed, "Beanie Bear," with his arms spread open. "Oh, my God, look at you." He wrapped his arms around me and swung me in the air as I laughed.

I gave him a hug and kissed him on the cheek as my feet returned to the ground. "How are you Baby Bro? It's been too long."

"You look amazing. I've missed you so much." He gave me another hug then grabbed my hand. "Come I want to introduce you to some-one."

I followed his lead as we ventured into the back yard.

"Kichiro, this is my sister Harper. Harp's this is Kichiro."

"Hello, I see you have met Huckleberry." I said smiling while pointing to him nestled happily in Kichiro's arms.

"Hai Huckleberry et to, berry kawaii."

I looked at Dylan.

"Kawaii means cute."

I nodded my head, "What's 'et to' mean?"

"That's equivalent to a pause. It's kind of like us saying Umm."

I turned to Kichiro, "Hai, Huckleberry is kawaii." I then repeated it for him, "kawaii, cute, kawaii, cute."

Kichiro nodded his head, "Berry cuto," he then nuzzled into Huckleberry in the most adorable way.

"Hi guys." I leaned in and gave my mom and dad each a kiss on the cheek. "How are you?"

Mom was beaming with smiles. "I'm so happy to have both my children home."

Dylan and I looked at each other and laughed.

"I'm super Harps. How is everything with you?"

I looked at my dad with a quizzical expression. "That was rather formal sounding. What's up?"

He shifted his body slightly, fighting off the urge to fold his arms. "Nothing, I'm happy to have Dylan here and his friend too."

"That's not just his friend, that's his boyfriend." I said poking my dad in the ribs.

Dad stepped back slightly, "I know, I know. I'm just feeling a little awkward. I don't know what to say."

Dylan stepped in to give him a cuddle. "Relax. You're doing great dad." They hugged each other tightly.

"Okay break it up you two. The smell of this food is too hard to resist, let's eat."

We all went inside taking our positions at the table while mom did some final fussing in the kitchen. Kichiro still had Huckleberry with him. He was now nestled on his lap resting as Kichiro slowly stroked his curled up body. I could tell that Huckleberry was giving him a sense of comfort.

I threw a piece of crust from my bread roll at my brother, "How did you manage to score such a hottie?"

Dylan picked up the crust and popped it in his mouth. "Just lucky I guess."

I turned to look at mom in the kitchen, "Have you already heard the back story, or should we wait for you?"

"No, wait, I've heard it, but I want to hear it again. I'm almost done."

"Okay, well dad that leaves you in the spot light. How's work going? Are you enjoying being back in the swing of things. Mom mentioned your working late to catch up. Are things settling down or are you still behind?"

"Urgh, work is a nightmare. We have a request for audit on our books, so it looks like we are under investigation again. This will be the third time in less than two years. I don't know why they are being so persistent in trying to find something untoward. It's like we have a spot light shining on us and they are waiting for an excuse to pounce. It's been really stressful."

"I'm sorry to hear that. Is there anything that I can do to help?" asked Dylan.

"No, I've got nothing to hide so I'm letting them look at all the records. They can knock themselves out. They won't find anything."

I repositioned myself in my seat to sit up straighter and cleared my throat. I noticed mom picked up on my discomfort. "Dad, you need to get someone to shadow these auditors and ideally have their activities video recorded. You don't want to be in a position where the company somehow gets set up for a fall. Especially given that they keep returning to sniff around. Something about that is not right. You should approach their behavior with more caution. What if someone affiliated with the company is doing something that is triggering this interest to Dynamically Global?"

He released a sigh, "It's a small team of people. I'd know if there was an issue. I'm across every aspect of the company's operations, nothing gets past me."

"That's such a naïve and dangerous statement to make. I hope you didn't say that to them."

"I most certainly did. I've got nothing to hide. They've done this twice before and found zilch and it will be the same this time."

I rolled my eyes, "Not necessarily. This is where your complacency might bring you undone. Yes, the team is relatively small, but you leverage off a large network of contracting groups so any of those could easily be the tainted link leading to the business. Did you consider that?"

"Yes." He said folding arms.

"Right, judging by the response, that's a resounding no. Having the IRS sniffing around is not a game and pleading ignorance won't be an excuse they will accept no matter how valid it may be. You need to get onto this and treat it as seriously as they are to ensure that you uncover what they are looking for and severe the ties with any contracting group that doesn't come up to par."

Mom mouthed the words thank you as she made her way back from the kitchen. She had obviously had the same discussion with him. I nodded and then turned to Dylan. "I'm not sure how much English Kichiro understands so let us know how to best include him given the language barrier. I don't want him feeling excluded."

Dylan leaned across the table to give me a kiss on the cheek, "No matter how many years have passed you never seem to change. He understands English reasonably well but is still building his confidence to speak the language. He's sneaky like that."

I looked at Kichiro, "Hontō?"

"Hai, hontō des."

The three of us laughed.

"Let us in on the joke. What does hon toe mean?"

"It means honest or honestly. I was asking him in Japanese if what Dylan said was true and he replied yes it's true."

Kichiro had a spark in his eye as he smiled at me, "Anata wa nihongo o hanasemasu ka?"

I considered carefully before I responded, "Hai watshi wa dekiru"

Kichiro bowed his head slightly in acknowledgement.

Dylan looked at me puzzled, "When did you learn to speak so well?"

"Mom told me that you were coming home for a visit and that Kichiro was trying to brush up on his English skills, so I thought it would be nice for me to do the same with my Japanese. I was surprised with how easy it was to pick up from where I left it in college. Looks like the old grey matter is still firing on some levels." I said with a chuckle.

Dylan leaned across the table to plant another kiss on my cheek, "Thank you."

I nodded, "Watashitachi no kazoku e yōkoso."

Kichiro bowed his head again and whispered, "Anata wa anata no kotoba de watashi o uyamau. Dōmo arigatōgozaimas."

Mom had now laid out all the food and was settled in her seat. "Okay fill me in on what I've missed out on."

Dad piped up, "Well from what I can gather Kichiro can actually understand most of what we are saying but is still finding his confidence with speaking the language. Meanwhile, Beanie Bear has been secretly brushing up on her skills to be able to speak with Kichiro. It seems that they have become fast friends."

An image of Liam popped into my mind as dad said the word fast friends.

"That's really wonderful. What did you say to Kichiro?" asked mom.

"He asked me if I understood the language and I replied yes. Then I said, welcome to the family, to which he replied that I honor him with my words and that he thanks me."

"Oh, how lovely. I want to say that too."

"Okay. Repeat this, Watashitachi no kazoku e yōkoso."

"Wa tash chi kazoo yok so Kichiro" said mom enthusiastically. "Pleeease eat," her hand moved over the food in a slow motion robotic wave.

Dylan and I burst out laughing while Kichiro politely said thank you in English.

"Mom we've established that he comprehends the language, so you don't need to exaggerate your words. He gets it. Watch." I looked at Kichiro, "Can you please pass me the bowl of bean salad."

"Hai." He picked up the container and passed it across the table to me.

"Dōmo." I said as I took it from him.

Dylan waved his hands to draw our attention, "Let's eat. Mom you have outdone yourself, this is an unbelievable spread. Marinated eggplant, stuffed roasted peppers, dill and cucumber yogurt salad, bean salad, stuffed cabbage rolls and cannelloni with ricotta and spinach. Are you expecting another ten guests to arrive?"

She looked at all the food, "I have gone a bit overboard."

"Nonsense, we'll consume this in no time at all," said dad licking his lips as he began piling a little of everything onto his plate.

"It was very considerate of you to brush up on your skills of the language," said mom as she tucked a piece of my fringe behind my ear.

"Well to be honest I was more driven by the entertaining idea of sneakily eaves dropping on what they were going to be saying to each other under the false premise that no one could understand. I never planned to immediately let on that I'd been relearning the language. It was going to be more of a surprise."

"That explains why you started out asking me what kawaii meant when we were outside. You were going to feign ignorance," said Dylan throwing a dressing soaked French bean at me. "Cheeky monkey."

I poked my tongue out at him. "Yep, that was the plan. I wasn't expecting Kichiro to ask me whether

I knew the language. When he did I got the guilts and decided to come clean. I'm too honest for my own good, damn it."

We all laughed.

Just before taking my first bite of my stuffed pepper I decided to set the scene for the next topic of conversation, "While we're tucking into our feast why don't you tell us the story of how you two met?" I shoved a mouthful in and cheekily smiled at my brother. I'd never seen him look so positively radiant.

Dylan maintained his composure while he finished pouring the wine for everyone. Just as he sat down again he raised his glass signalling for us to do the same.

"Here's to family."

We all looked at one another thoughtfully as we took a sip.

"Enough stalling, give me the long drawn out version."

Dylan glanced at Dad.

"Don't look at me. I've already been grilled. It's your turn kiddo. Quite frankly I'm enjoying having you here to share the heat with me again."

Dylan smirked. "Alright. The long version it is." He took a bite of his cannelloni, making sure to chew slowly as he stared at me. When he swallowed it down he indulged in sip of wine and then cleared his throat to begin.

"Just before Launa and I agreed to part ways I was feeling pretty disillusioned in the relationship. I mostly put on a façade, pretending to be happy for the sake of everyone else. We were great at being friends but anything more than that fell short of what I wanted. It's not her fault or mine, I guess we were learning and didn't know until we were well into the thick of the relationship, living together and trying to make a go of it. I felt obligated to make it work. I didn't want the stigma of being associated to yet another failed relationship."

Dylan was focused on me the whole time he spoke. I blinked slowly and nodded my head to acknowledge his words. I wasn't expecting him to go that far back but respected his choice to do so. Everyone was quietly eating their meal while listening. Dylan took another bite from his plate then glanced to smile at Kichiro before continuing.

"In the end we agreed that we were better off as friends. Well to be honest it was more driven by me saying the relationship wasn't what I wanted. Launa would have stayed if I let her but I knew we weren't right for each other. The problem partly stemmed from me not knowing what I wanted. I only held a level of certainty that what I had going on with her, wasn't it. You know?"

"It makes it challenging if you don't know what you want. Lots of people go through it. The difference is that you knew enough to recognize at the very least what you had with Launa was not what you desired. It takes a lot for people to be honest with themselves and leave the comfort of what they know for the trade off, of being alone. It's a brave move to opt to be in solitude while trying to figure things out. There are so many people stuck in unhappy relationships for that very reason." I said.

"Exactly. All I had to go by at the time was that I didn't want what I had. Receiving my orders from the air force about the two-year relocation opportunity was the perfect distraction at the time because I was completely lost and could feel myself sinking into a depressive state. I really felt like a failure."

Mom reached across and placed her hand on Dylans, "Why didn't you tell us? We could have helped you through it."

"No, I don't believe you could have. I needed to figure things out for myself. You would have just spent the whole time worrying and the rest of the time trying to set me up with your friend's eligible daughters. It has disaster written all over it."

I laughed as I lifted my wine glass to take a sip, "I'll cheers to that."

Mom gave me a light slap on my back in protest but didn't saying anything else knowing that Dylan was indeed spot on with his statement.

"Are we getting any closer to the juicy bit?" I said, giving Dylan a wink.

Kichiro shyly smiled.

"I arrived in Tokyo a few days early to assimilate before I was required to report to base. The ryokan that I stayed at was very traditional and rather low key. It had a segregated bath house for men. The room I booked contained a small decorative table and a tatami mat for sleeping. The mat was in a rolled state during the day and then set up in the middle of the room on the floor before lights out. I was spending the days sight-seeing while the evenings were mostly consumed by the use of the hot baths and then sleeping. Just before I went to bed I would flick through the images on my camera to look at the pictures. This one night a couple of days into my trip I noticed this person in the frame. I enlarged it on the screen to see who it was. There was something about this stranger that made me want to stare at him. I felt drawn to the image and would find myself subconsciously thinking about it. There's no other way to describe it other than I thought he was beautiful."

Dylan reached for Kichiro's hand brought it to his lips, gave him a light kiss on his ring finger and then placed it back down. They then intertwined their fingers to hold hands.

"The most amazing thing happened after that simple epiphany occurred. I realized that I was smiling again. Each time the thought of him popped into my mind I was happy. I didn't know who he was, I just knew that there was something about him that made my soul shine. It was liberating to feel that way."

"If he was a stranger how did you meet?" I asked.

"Unmei," said Kichiro as he squeezed Dylan's hand.

"Destiny. How beautiful." I said.

"Mom are you crying?" quizzed Dylan.

"No, I just have something in the corner of my eye."

"It's called a tear." I said teasingly.

Dad picked up his napkin and passed it to her to use.

"Back to the story then." I said reaching to take another sip of my wine.

"One day I met a fellow traveller who told me that there was this noodle house that was located only a couple of blocks from where I was staying and that it was renowned for its cuisine. He kept insisting that I go there before I leave Tokyo. On my fifth and final night, I went. This guy Travis I think that was his name, had told me to order the ginger and sesame dressed noodles and a beer. So that's what I planned to do. When the waiter arrived at my table I pointed to the dish on the menu and asked for a single serve. As I looked up I realized that the person leaning down to read what I was pointing to was the very same person in my image that I had been admiring."

My mind was immersed in the imagery of the experience Dylan was describing. "You could make a movie out of this story."

"It gets better. Here I am completely speechless staring up at him like a complete fool. Meanwhile, he politely smiled and walked off to process my order. I honestly couldn't stop my heart from fluttering. I kept glancing across to see where in the restaurant he was standing and if he was looking at me. It was the most ridiculous feeling and at the same time so exhilarating."

I chuckled, "You sound like a school girl. You were totally crushing on him."

Dylan bounced in response to my words, "I know, right? I really was. It was unbelievable. I had never had anyone evoke that response in me. It wasn't until I returned to the inn and was laying in my bed that it dawned on me that I was into a guy."

"Wait, what? You had already been thinking about him previously because of the photo you took. You knew his gender. Why did you have such a delayed reaction?"

"Yes, but that was an image. He might as well have been a model in a magazine I was flipping through. He didn't become real until he was standing right there. The reaction I had was unexpected and so intoxicating that once the euphoria of the experience dissipated I was left with the rude awakening that I was deeply attracted to a man."

"Okay, he's sitting right beside you, so I know it has a fairy tale ending. Keep going."

"I left for Osaka in the morning and decided on the flight there that it was for the best that I was leaving.

I tried to put the idea of him out of my head but was sad that I wouldn't get a chance to sate my curiosity and learn more about him. In my typical style, I threw myself into my job and did my best to stay busy. Of course, no matter how much I tried, I found myself looking at the photo."

I raised my hand to get him to pause. "I'm calling a brief intermission for the purposes of a wine refill and, also because I need you to pull out your wallet. I have to see it."

Dad jumped up from the table, "I'll go get us another bottle."

Kichiro looked at Dylan, "Anata wa imōto wa dō yatte shitte imasu ka?"

Dylan pulled out his wallet and passed it across to me. "She knows because she has this uncanny ability to profile people and mostly gets it right."

I jokingly snatched the wallet from his hand, "What do you mean mostly?"

Mom leaned in to have a look as well. Kichiro was positioned to the left of the frame in the background. The foreground had an ornamental tree with the prominent feature being a couple of woman dressed in traditional kimonos.

"If you had waited twenty seconds more before you took the shot he would have been out of view. Goes to show that timing is everything." I passed it back to him. The image provided me with an appreciation of the genuine draw Dylan had to Kichiro. There were so many interesting elements in the foreground of that image, yet he only had eyes for him.

Dad returned with the wine.

"Carry on." I said unashamedly sliding my glass across to be refilled.

"My plans to erase him from my mind were futile and I was quickly getting bored with doing nothing more than sleeping and working long hours. I decided that I would use my accrued time to take a trip to Kyoto for a few days to watch the up coming Gion festival. I'd heard so many good things about the place, so I was super keen to get out and explore. Once again I booked a ryokan to stay in."

Dylan paused to indulge in a big gulp of his wine.

"The first day I decided to explore a district on the outskirts of Kyoto called Arashiyama. Anyway, without going into too many details I spent the day wandering around visiting one breathtaking garden after the next. The temples were incredible too. I thoroughly enjoyed it and realized that it was precisely what I needed to get my mind focussed on something else. When I returned to the inn I headed down to the bathhouse to indulge in a soak before bed. This particular inn was built on a natural underground hot spring, so the bath had steam rising up from the water and it was reasonably hot in comparison to the one in Tokyo. There were already two Japanese men in the water. I quietly entered, found a position where I could lean against the rock and closed my eyes to relax. I'd say approx. twenty minutes had passed before they left. Finally, on my own I figured I had another ten or so minutes before I was cooked and ready to call it a night. I was just about to close my eyes again when I heard the door swing open. I looked and there he was, confidently walking toward me naked as the day he was born. It took me a moment to divert my eyes. In all honesty, I didn't know what to do. I became nervous when I heard him entering the water. Thankfully my face was already flushed from the heat, which I might add, had suddenly become sweltering hot. All I knew was that I felt awkward as fuck and was sporting a raging boner in a bath filled with crystal clear natural spring water. My only hope was that the steam rising would be a saving grace in assisting in masking my um… condition."

"Oh, too much detail," said dad as he placed his hands over his ears.

"Mom get that husband of yours under control. Hey dad, penis, penis, penis, erection, blue balls…. smegma." I said laughing.

"No, no what on earth are you doing?" he protested.

"I'm trying to desensitize the fuddy duddy part of your psych." I replied completely amused. I leaned forward looking straight at Dylan. "Ignore him. Keep going with the story. You were hot and horny, then what?"

"I waited until Kichiro was settled and then casually twisted my torso away, so it was less obvious. I closed my eyes and pretended to be relaxing but inside my heart was racing so fast I thought I was going to have a heart attack or something. I keep taking quick glances to see what he was up to. Seriously, I must have looked like a total pervert."

I could see a slight smile appear on Kichiro's face as Dylan was recounting this portion of the events.

"When he finally closed his eyes, I took the opportunity to casually head out of the water. He did open his eyes slightly as I went past but closed them rather quickly again. I used the shower to rinse, wrapped my dressing gown on and got out of there. When I arrived in my room I was still feeling a bit flustered. I flopped into bed, placing my hand on my heart to feel it pounding, while recreating the scene in my head. The overwhelming sense of how stupid I must have looked to him, made me cringe but at the same time I burst out laughing."

I glanced across at dad who was munching on some salad. Mom was staring at her wine glass with a smile on her face. She seemed to be consumed by her own thoughts. Kichiro was listening, but his focal point was fixated on their clasped hands.

"Anyhow, the next day I got up extra early to head to this temple that was positioned on a mountain top. I really wanted to beat the tourist congestion, so I grabbed my pack and set off on this hike. When I reached the peak, the sun was still on its way to rising, which meant it didn't quiet have the bite of the looming summer heat that usually brought humid cloud condensation along with it. The view of the skyline was super clear and truly spectacular. It felt magical to stand there in silence thinking about him and how wonderful it now felt to be alive. I heard a noise, turned my gaze in the direction where I thought it was coming from and watched as Kichiro walked up the path toward me. We looked into each other's eyes and without a word exchanged I knew, this was it for me. He was the one I had been restless for."

I raised my glass to them both. "It's the perfect beginning."

Dylan and Kichiro looked at each other and smiled. "Yeah, I guess it kinda was." Dylan gave Kichiro a light peck on the lips. I was tempted to look at dad to see what the expression was on his face but chose not to. I could see from my peripheral vision that mom was still off with the fairies. Personally, I felt stoked that my brother was so happy.

"I think dad's experiencing the first stages of food coma and mom's mind has clearly been abducted by aliens."

Dylan smirked. "In her defence, she has heard this story before."

"Oh, sorry I was just thinking about something ..."

"Don't keep it to yourself," said Dylan playfully.

Mom looked at me and then at Dylan and shook her head slightly as her face flushed. She then glanced at dad before returning her attention back to us.

"I'm surprised you haven't prepared any dessert." I said clearly changing the subject.

Mom placed her hand under the table and squeezed my knee, "I was going to but thought that it would be nice to go for a walk and head down to the ice-cream parlor for a fresh sorbet."

"That sounds like a plan but I'm going to propose a new one. Why don't you and I stay here and clear the table and get that kitchen back in some order while these three take Huckleberry for a walk in the park, and then on their way back they can pick up some sorbet. This should cater to everyone's needs just nicely."

Mom hestitated for a moment. "Ah, yes okay. Are you happy with that Dylan?"

"Sure, it looks like Dad and Huckleberry could do with a little exercise. You've developed a bit of a gut. I might have to teach you a few of the good old fashioned exercise drills that we do on the base every morning."

Dad patted his stomach, "You leave Bertha out of this. We are getting along just fine."

I stood up to begin clearing the table, "Oh lordy lord he's named it. There's a sign of acceptance with no intention to change."

Dad rose from the table, "I'll go put on my sneakers and meet you out the front."

"Okay dad. Hey Harps, do you have a leash for Huckleberry?"

"Ah, yes that would be useful. It's in the car, one minute, I'll get it for you."

"Sure, I'll come with you," said Dylan following suit.

When we got to the car Dylan did a quick head check to make sure no-one was in ear shot, while I rummaged around in Huckleberry's doggy travel pack to look for his harness and lead.

"What's up with mom and dad?"

My lips pursed as I shook my head, "I'm not certain but there is stuff going on for them. They've been growing apart awhile now. I don't know where they are at, but we just need to give them the space to figure it out for themselves. All we can do is be supportive of them."

Dylan had an expression of concern, "Yeah, sure. Its just hard to watch without saying anything. Isn't there anything we can do to help?"

"Yes, don't behave like mom. Do you remember what it felt like when she kept trying to help you after your split with Launa? These things are never pleasant." I placed my hand on his shoulder and gave it a squeeze. "Sometimes, its best to let people figure things out for themselves. Try not to interfere."

Dylan smiled.

"On a brighter note Kichiro is a dish and I can see that you are smitten with each other. I'm so happy for you."

His face lit up, "I'm completely in love with him. He's just so, perfect."

"ARE YOU READY?" yelled dad.

Dylan planted a kiss on my cheek while he simultaneously grabbed the harness and leash from my hand before running over to join them. I waved as they walked down the path then returned to the kitchen to spend some time with mom.

"What would you like me to do?" I said rolling up my sleeves.

"Nothing, just keep me company. I'm happy to potter."

"Okay," I said as I refilled my glass with wine and then perched myself up on the bench.

"What's new?" I asked.

"Nothing much."

I sipped on my wine while I watched her flit about in the kitchen. It took her close to fifteen minutes before she cracked from the silence.

"I'm sad Harper."

"I can see that. Do you want to tell me why?"

"Watching them together and listening to Dylan tell the story while it makes me happy to know my son is so happy, I was feeling a little envious that I can't be allowed to express the same."

She paused to look at me. I took another sip of my wine.

"You don't know what its like to have to pretend, to feel the need to conform so that no-one is hurt or disappointed. I live a lie everyday just to protect you from the truth."

"Don't project onto me. If you're compelled to express what's going on for you than be brave enough to say it as it is, but don't include me as your reason or your comparison."

She released a sigh and took a large swig from her own glass of wine. "I've told your father I want a divorce. He knows about Devon. All he said was that he wanted to wait until after we had received a chance to be acquainted with Kichiro before anything was said. He didn't want to detract from Dylan's visit."

"That seems fair."

Mom nodded, "It is, yes, of course it is but today when Dylan was exuding so much joy while recounting their steps toward union, I found myself thinking about Devon and our story. I realized that I would never be welcomed to share my new found joy with the very people who are the most important to me."

I tapped my fingers on the bench and pondered on her words for a moment.

Mom leaned forward to still my hands, "Say something."

"You've obviously made some big decisions and put the steps in motion to have things geared toward a certain outcome. Yeah, you're right in a sense. Dylan and I won't want to hear all the details for it's a story that led to the separation of two people that we love. It would have been different if you both divorced and established separate lives prior to meeting new partners. As I see it, Devon is the catalyst that contributed to you looking outside of your marital communion for companionship and love. If you're truly happy with this guy, then I'm happy for you. I just can't help but wonder why you had to wait to meet someone else before you made the move to separate. If you weren't happy and couldn't find how to fix what you felt was broken, why did you stay?"

"I thought I owed it to your father."

"I call bullshit on that statement. That's just a convient story that you can sell as a palatable image of sacrificial nobility. Try again, and this time be honest, at the very least with yourself."

She looked at me for a moment and then down at her glass of wine. I watched as she ran her finger around the rim of the glass.

"I was scared to leave because I didn't feel like I had anything to offer anyone else. When you kids grew up and started living your own lives I realized I had somehow lost my identity as a person. All those years had gone by where I blissfully immersed myself into being a mother, and a good wife. When one role was largely completed, I started to recognize that the other remaining role didn't satisfy the void I felt."

"What did you try to do about it?"

"I feel like I genuinely tried to make it work. Eventually, I became complacent and just accepted my lot."

I shrugged my shoulders, "So what changed?"

"I met Devon. We hit it off and new possibilities grew from there."

"What's the difference aside from the ignition of stimuli? You are still just trading one dependency role for another, aren't you? What happens when the spark dulls or at the very least tempers? Won't you still be left with the same feeling of void?"

Mom leaned forward again to place her hand on mine, "No it's different with Devon. He wants to do things, travel to places and explore. We have so much in common it's uncanny. Your father only wants to continue the charity work we started together at Dynamically Global and at the end of a day come home to tinker in his garden."

"I feel you're missing the point mom. You need to find your happiness and sense of fulfilment independent of others. When you discover it, acknowledge it, and embrace whatever happiness is for you, then it is the very component that allows you to participate within a relationship and share, instead of your current position of expectation and dependence to simply fill a void."

"I get it, I do. It's just that with Devon I feel I can be myself and he likes who I am."

"Well, all I'll say is that I want the very best for you just as you want that for me. Make your decisions, live the life you want and try to have no regrets in the process. That's the best any of us can do."

Mom patted my hand, "I know. I can't wait for you to meet him. I know when you spend some time getting to know him, you'll understand why I needed to leave your father."

I shook my head, "Sorry mom. The stunt you both pulled at the restaurant sealed the deal for me. You both screwed the pooch on that one."

She stood upright and looked away, "I know. I'm still so ashamed. I don't know what I was thinking." I watched as her eyes returned to greet mine. "It wasn't his fault Harper. He didn't know that I was going to be there."

"STOP. Even if that was true it doesn't make a difference. He chose to wait on our table instead of getting someone else to stand in. He openly flirted with you and made it clear that he didn't care that dad and I were there. I'm sorry, I've told you before, that is nothing short of shit in my books and no amount of excuses will quantify the behaviour into another light. That singular event represents Devon's choices as much as they did yours, and I want no part of it."

"You're upset."

"No mom, not in the slightest. Well, that's not entirely true. I am feeling a little irritated by the way you are trying to protect Devon as though he didn't equally contribute. Ultimately, I'm trying to convey that we all have choices to make. You have chosen Devon. I want to be supportive and am doing so by stepping back to allow you the space to do anything you feel will make you happy." I reached across and squeezed her hand, "I sincerely hope it all works out. Just don't expect that I'm going to be an active part of it. He's not welcome in my life and I'm not going to pretend to like a person just because my mother has taken him in as a lover."

Mom pulled her hand out from underneath mine and folded her arms, "So I was right."

"Not totally. You are welcome to tell me anything, the highs, the lows and the in-betweens. I will always be there for you mom. Just don't ask me to be there for him. I hold no obligation or interest in doing so. Don't go beating yourself up about the incident either. What's done is done. If it weren't that something else would have cropped up which led me to the same conclusion and therefore the same result. He is who he is, and I am who I am."

She stared blankly out into the yard only nodding her head slightly to acknowledge my words.

Decree

Dylan and Kichiro were spending some quality time doing a combination of flights and road tripping around different states to see the main sights. He was sending me text messages every couple of days to let me know where they were at and what they were planning to do next. He wanted me to join them, which in theory sounded like it would be fun, but I had a suspicion they would enjoy it more on their own. I agreed that I would meet them in Joshua Tree if they gave me enough notice closer to the time. Right now, they were living it up in Viva Las Vegas. It turns out that Kichiro is quite the Elvis fan and loved the karaoke scene out there. I had a hard time imaging him up on stage burling out a Presley classic to a room full of foreigners. It seemed to be a far cry from the person I met a little over a week ago who was conscious of his pronunciation of the language. Then again, it is something that Dylan would be up for, so perhaps they are closely matched in this regard. I'm just glad they are having a blast.

I'd purposely not called mom or dad to see how they were going. I knew Dylan would be regularly keeping in touch, giving them the low down of his and Kichiro's adventures. I'm sure they appreciated the upbeat energy he was providing in what was possibly one of the most challenging times in their lives. I wasn't certain whether mom had told dad that I knew about their impending divorce. My instinct told me to give them space. They knew how to reach me, if and when they needed me.

It was time to venture back into Libertine's world. I placed the cell on the coffee table exchanging it for the diary. I was left feeling rather intrigued about her dynamic with the blind man. There was something he wasn't telling her, that I knew for sure. The story he told her about the trading of a favour to meet her and the wager possibly had an element of truth, but there was more to this guy than what he presented. I don't get why she seems so smitten.

My desire for attendance to the room quickly began to wane post acquiring the knowledge that my acts were reduced to the services of a whore, albeit the sums allegedly commanded were impressive. I saw none of this. Indeed, I was denied any sense of freedom. My thoughts were evolving to a new suite of relization. I now recognized that I craved companionship. Too much of my time had been traded for the benefit of others. There was a growing need for me to take a stand.

During my sessions, I began to intermittently deny the patrons my instruction. There were times I feigned illness and other times I would not leave my quarters to participate at all. My rebellion grew as I sensed their tolerance for my fragmented behavior was wearing thin. I knew it was affecting their business. This was evident to me in the decreasing frequency of engagement. It was reduced down to one a week and sometimes as far between as one a fortnight.

When I felt my point was clearly demonstrated, I alerted them to my requirement for a companion, together with my need to gain access to a greater portion of the housing than just my room. I wanted to feel the grass between my toes while the wind danced on my skin. I explained I knew they had profited more than a tidy sum from my services and that I would agree to continue once more, if they only conceded to provide me with these few things. I left it at that, feeling any conversation relating to a bargain for my freedom may have had them not listen to me at all.

In truth, I missed the stimulation of the erotic play and was mostly left to my own devices to manage the entertainment of my time alone in my room while, I assume, they deliberated. I'm uncertain of how many months had passed but knew there were more than a few that had gone by. I recall with precise clarity the day that I received a knock at my door. I could barley muster my voice to make the sounds required to have the visitor know they could come in. When the door was opened, there before me was the blind man with the extraordinary pale blue eyes.

"Hello," I said peering past him to see where the guard was. I noted the hallway was empty.

The blind man turned his head slightly to be closer to the proximity of my neck as he inhaled deeply. "Ah, my Libertine. You smell just as delicious as the first time we met."

I stepped back, "Thank you. Can I ask what you are doing here?"

He bowed slightly, "I'm at your service as a companion if you shall have me as such."

I looked at him and smiled. "They engaged you to be my companion?"

"Engaged, no, it was rather a rigorous process that all applicants had to endure to be considered for the honor of being your companion. May I come in?"

"Sorry, of course you may. Here, take my hand, I shall lead you to my bed where you may have a seat." I led him to the bed and then returned to shut the door. I spun around once it was closed and smiled, "How is it possible that you passed? What were the criteria for entry? How long did this all take? Were you in competition with many others?"

"Whoa, please take a seat with me so I may begin from the top."

Eager to know more I settled beside him, "Go on then."

"There was a notice placed in the social section of the paper announcing that a companion was sought for you. As I understand it, the powers that be were supplied with an overwhelming number of expressions of interest. After much deliberation only a handful of people were selected to go through the arduous process of submission."

"Submission? I'm not sure what that suggests. What did you have to submit?"

"Complete loyalty to the brethren and their code. We all were expected to unveil our secrets and render ourselves vulnerable so that should something unsavory be attempted when acting within the role of companion they could utilize all that was known against us."

"Blackmail?"

"Worse, they made it clear that they would kill any that contained my bloodline and described the merciless ways in which it would be done."

"Why didn't this deter you? No one is worthy of such a high price. Surely many would have hesitated to persist beyond this."

The blind man shook his head, "The names I had given were none who were related but all would vouch that they were, in exchange for money and secrets of trade. My family is in essence untouchable and their lineage will continue unscathed for many generations to come."

"So, you progressed through this with a web woven in lies and then what occurred? How did they make their final selection?"

"They wanted to ensure that the companion was unable to perform any sexual favors that would allow for penetration to deflower your virginity. This was of paramount importance to them. They insisted that you must remain in tact and any attempt to taint your good standing would result in the aforementioned death of all the bloodline. I'm not sure who you are set to be reserved for, but it was clear that you are reserved."

I sat upright, "It doesn't make sense. Why would a person wish to wait so long to take what they no doubt paid handsomely to claim?"

The blind man shook his head, "I'm unsure, but suggest that it may be linked to something astrological. It appears that these people are very driven by the signs associated to the alignment of the stars and numerology. All the masked balls that have been arranged were done so by the charts. There must be something of ultra significance that they are waiting for. I see no other reason."

"How odd. I know little about astrology and haven't seen the light of day for many years. The only darkness I have been afforded exists by the containment within this room. I've all but forgotten what if felt like to lift my gaze to admire the heavens."

"Well perhaps with time we can do something to correct this together." He said sweetly.

"How?"

"I feel that it is only a matter of trust that is required and then the maintenance of the trust. If we can demonstrate together that we are worthy of a chance, then perhaps I will be permitted to take you into the courtyard of an evening for a stroll in the moonlight."

"This all feels like a dream of wonderment that is set on a course for another."

He placed his hand on my knee, "No-one is more deserving than you."

My heart fluttered. "Thank you."

"Now on with the story I still have much to tell."

"Oh, yes, please do tell. I am intrigued to know more."

"Each of us had to explain how we could provide certainty that we would not attempt anything beyond the permitted act of cunnilingus. The women who were selected were assured to progress beyond this phase of assessment, as they didn't have the appendage to cause any notable threat. The men on the other hand needed to convince them. One by one they failed to pass the stimulation test with the exception of myself. In turn one woman gave us all hand jobs while another woman who held a striking resemblance to you danced provocatively for them. I was the only man who didn't become erect and thus did not ejaculate. They added further rigour to my exposure by having her stimulate my cock with her mouth. Once again, I didn't respond. The others were offered the choice of amputation as the only way to progress any further."

"What does amputation mean?"

"They would have to agree to have their penis severed so it would be guaranteed to be dysfunctional. They had already established mine doesn't work so I passed with no concern or need for further tampering."

"Did any of the other men progress past this point?"

He shook his head, "No. None opted for the amputation."

"I'm glad. What else did they make you do?"

"The final step was an evaluation of the mind. They wanted to understand what drove the reasoning behind wanting to be your companion. I'm unsure of what the others had said but mine was simply put. I am a blind man with little opportunity to become a scholar or person of any importance. What I have are confined to simple joys and none give me more pleasure than the scent of an incredible woman. I not only feel that I am the right person to enact the role of companion for Libertine. I believe I was born for it."

I clapped my hands to applaud his speech, "That was truly beautiful."

"They must have thought so too for here I am, officially assigned to be your companion."

"It's curious why they would entertain going to such lengths to meet my demands instead of using brute force to try and make me concede to their will. They obviously hold the capacity for violence and yet they never seem to direct it at me. Why are they being so accommodating?"

"I am unsure. Perhaps you have enchanted them as you have all others. Can you take me for a tour of this room, so I can become acclimatized to my surrounds? If we are to spend time here I would like to at least formulate an idea of how things are structured. Assuming you are happy for me to stay on occasion."

"They permit you to remain here with me?"

"Yes, I may not be available to be here all the time, but when I am, I wish to be present to address your every whim. We can listen to music. I could show you how to dance. Perhaps you could read to me. I can teach you the few things I know of the sciences. If it also pleases you I will share your bed, and have you sleep within my arms."

I reached across and clasped his hand, "I like the sound of all of that. Come, let me first be your guide so you may gain your bearings."

This has completely thrown me. Why would they entertain her request for a companion? It goes back to my original question of who the hell is she and why on earth is she so important to her abductors? I'm glad for her in the sense that she isn't being subjected to extreme abuse like so many people have in similar situations. This guy must be lying to her. There is no way that he could be an outsider suddenly accepted into a sacred inner circle and hold the priveliage of being placed in the presence of what seems to be their prized possession. That prime role would have to be enacted by their most trusted resource. His story of how he got appointed is in my opinion, poorly fabricated. I detect a rat.

The elation I felt having someone to share my time with made me feel a sense of perpetual euphoria. The way he held me at night, skin close whispering stories until I drifted to sleep was nourishing my soul. It didn't take long before I could feel my heart yearned for him during his times of absence. He would always return with a gift of perfume, clothing or flowers. He conveyed the torture he felt when apart with expression so poetic it made me swoon.

On the anniversary of our first month together he had made arrangements for privileges to be given to enter the courtyard post the hour of the sun setting across the horizon. I was blindfolded and guided to the open space to sit on a bench in the center of the garden. When the blindfold was removed, I looked up and was greeted by a thousand stars in the dark night sky twinkling back at me. The cool of the night breeze on my skin gave me goose bumps as I stared in awe at the wonderment of the universe. It was my first recollection of the enormity of my surrounds, which only set to amplify the stark contrast to my life of confinement. He patiently sat in silence as I soaked in the beauty.

It was that evening that I unknowingly entered the precipice of change. When we returned to our room I prepared for bed with a quick bath while he waited. When I re-entered the room, it was lit with candles. I'd been forbidden to have such luxuries before, so to behold the space awash in dancing light, I felt completely romanced. I leapt into the bed and kissed him passionately. He returned my intensity then positioned my body underneath, so his chest was heavily set on mine. Instinctually I parted my legs to wrap around his waist as I felt my body command with ache to hold him close.

He raised his lips to hover over my lips as he whispered, "Brace yourself."

I felt his hand glide down toward my nether regions. My body tingled in anticipation. It took a moment to realize he had released his ridged cock from his underwear. He smiled as he placed it at the entry point of my throbbing vagina. I gasped when he partially entered and then swiftly pulled out. My eyes widened staring into his as he continued to do this several times until I could no longer bear the tease of *his shaft and chose to thrust forward to greedily consume his length. Initially, I felt a slight sting that quickly dissipated as he pulsed rhythmically in and out of my soaking wet pussy. His penis plunging deep into me was satisfying my senses. He placed his hand gently over my mouth as I began to release groans of pleasure. My expression perfectly depicted the bliss felt in being fulfilled in such a manner.*

Lifting my head from the pillow I removed his hand as I pressed my lips on the lobe of his ear to bite, "Roll over so I may taste the flavors of our love."

He did as I requested.

I relished in the delight of playing with his manhood. My hand grasped firmly as I glided up and down his cock. When I felt the rise of his arousal I squeezed tight to prevent him for cumming then released to begin again while I savored the taste of the droplets that managed to surface. My tongue celebrated in the exploration of the velvet of his swollen knob. I found pleasure in watching the intensity on his face grow while I worked his dick into a state of purple before mounting him to allow the magic of his release to geyser inside me. I rode him hard until I felt his body quivering, and then soften.

We lay there for a while panting. I wondered how I could have previously endured all the past sexual escapades with such crave to be penetrated and have never known this intensity of delight.

"What miracle took place for it to work?" I asked still laying upon his chest.

He shifted from underneath me so that we were side by side before kissing me gently on the mouth.

His hand pulled back the hair from my face. "Allow me to tell you a story."

"Okay," I whispered.

"I was born in a small village to a very poor family. My brothers, sisters and father were struck by a sickness that swept through the town and killed many. I was only five when it occurred so most of my recollection and memories of these times had been formed by my mother's recount. The loss held devastation for all and my mom as a widower could not bear to remain there. She took all she was able to carry and set off with me to find a new place to call home. There was little favorable work available for women, so she had to become extremely resourceful in obtaining the money she needed to support us. As time passed she developed her ability to fool the locals into believing far fetched tales that she had spun. She was mastering the art of manipulation and quickly managed to place herself in an advantageous position. Not satisfied with the comforts she had begun to acquire, she concocted more elaborate ruses."

He fumbled below the blankets to find my hand. He placed it in his, then lifted it to kiss my palm. "The greatest of which was her idea to teach me how to convincingly feign blindness."

I sat up, "You aren't blind?"

"Lay with me. Allow me to explain."

As I dropped back down onto my side to stare into his eyes, he returned my gaze and continued.

"You see, people feel a comfort in being themselves when they believe that no one is watching. That is why the presence of a blind person or in my case back then a blind child, held no threat. My mother sold the benefits of engaging my services to the circle of people who held shady dealings. Once I was proven to indeed be of use the word was out and I quickly became the runner to execute tasks that involved things such as the delivery of secret messages between lovers, while other times I carried packages that contained

money or illegal subtances. The point person would be unmasked because they believed they didn't need to disguise their person. This is largely how I gathered the Intel that my mom would then use to gain exchange for power and money."

"Blackmail?"

"In a sense, yes. She preferred to call it trade."

"Can you see me?"

He adjusted his position to free his other hand so that he could stroke the side of my face, "You are the most beautiful creature I have ever been blessed to lay eyes upon."

I leaned in and kissed both his eyelids. "Tell me more."

"By the time my mom had remarried I was well on my way to being a confidant for the leading front men of the major crime syndicates around the country. None ever suspected that I was anything other than a blind man. The few times I was intercepted by the local authorities I was able to state that I was unaware of what was contained within the packages and comparatively could not stand witness as to who provided it to me for I was unable to see. Given that I was deemed to be legally blind they found it hard to prove otherwise. It was a win, win situation."

"Is that why you leave me from time to time? Do you go and execute such jobs still?"

"A man must eat and therefore must earn a living. I do still execute such errands but only to the elite and only when a high price opportunity arises. In short, yes."

"What happened to your mother?"

"She lives well with her husband and three children."

I let my eyes wander the length of his torso, "How is it that you were able to become erect? I thought it was damaged beyond repair."

He chuckled, "There is a combination of herbs when prepared in a certain way that will cause a man to become temporarily flaccid. My mother created the concoction to use on men who would insist upon engaging her services as a prostitute."

"Your mother was a whore?"

"Well had she not been ingenious about managing her predicament perhaps that would have been her fate. Instead, she would provide them with expensive booze that they would greedily consume. She laced the alcohol with the herbal concoction. They were none the wiser for the taste as it was masked brilliantly. She drank as well so no suspicion would be drawn to the beverage. It took less than ten minutes for it to begin its effect. The men being embarrassed by the realization that they were not able to become erect would insist on delaying by consuming more of the alcohol. Inevitably they would find themselves inebriated and used that as their reason for not being able to engage in sex. Given their embarrassment they would always pay their dues and often provide a handsome tip in exchange for her discretion on the matter. To which she always obliged, that is until she needed to call on a favor."

"You drank the herbs to pretend you had a limp dick?"

"Yes. Initially I wanted to meet you and saw an opportunity to make some money at the same time through the wager I had arranged. I drank the herbs but remained flaccid for weeks post our meeting. It appeared that the strength of the concoction had a lasting effect in my system whereas most other men would recover by mid-morning the following day. When I came across the opportunity to become your companion, I simply knew I needed to be the one selected and did all that I could to make it so."

"It would seem that your whole life is built on lies."

"Yes, it has been a monumental castle constructed of fabricated stories." He shifted to nuzzle into my neck. "I have wanted to tell you from the moment my eyes saw you how captivating you are. Alas, I knew the release of such a truth would have me condemned. I needed to ensure that there was trust built between us. My life from hereon is within your hands."

"Then you are safe for I will never betray you."

He leant in and kissed me. We spent the rest of that evening in silence, using only our senses to explore each other while we made love.

Lies, lies, lies, that is all she seems to be getting spun. He has totally sucked her into believing that he's a good guy, a regular knight in shining armor. I'm certain he must be one of her captors. It's the only thing that makes sense. She's been in lock down with minimal contact from the time they tore her away from her family. Why would they allow anyone from the outside to be near her unsupervised? They wouldn't. He is one of them for sure.

My blood was boiling at the thought of her naivety. It almost felt personal. I simply hated that they were taking advantage of her trust. She was so lonely and desperate to be loved that he immediately became her world. There was a part of me that wanted to cry for her and another wanted to punch a wall. Libertine was being used. It seemed such an elaborate game that it didn't feel too dissimilar to my own. Sure, I wasn't kidnapped and subjected to sexual depravity, but I did feel I was trapped and being toyed with. My life is no longer my own. I am confined by the knowledge that there is a very real struggle between the universal balance of good and evil, and that somehow, I had become the pivot point for both to gain advantage.

There was something compelling about Libertine and her story. I'm still unsure of what era she was born in. I know that Marquis de Sade lived within the seventeen and eighteen hundreds. She was given a copy of his works in her library, but this literature was originally written in French. The translation of the books were only starting to be executed around the nineteen thirties, so unless she was multilingual she must have been born sometime within that century and this current one. Her use of proper English throws me off and he seems to match his language to hers. That might be because I am reading her recount of the story and she only has her voice to capture the memories, hence there is synergy in the expression. I suspect there is a very real possibility that she is still alive. I wonder….

Feeling a little stir crazy, I decided some fresh air would do me some good. I placed Huckleberry in his harness and headed out the door with the book in my bag. The streets on the way to the dog park seemed eerily abandoned. There were hardly any cars on the road and I had not encountered a single pedestrian. It was an oddity for this time of day. Mid-afternoon was usually a slow build onto the looming peak time traffic that kicked off from three.

Huckleberry went into his playpen to mingle with his friends while I sat on the bench. I could see across the way that Grady was also on a bench. He looked like he was transfixed reading his paper. A part of me wanted to go across to say hello but I thought better of it. His true colors shone through in our last meeting. There was no point in trying to appease the situation. It would only be set to be worse.

A butterfly flew into my direct field of view, hovered for a moment then continued its journey. I realized I hadn't seen a butterfly in quite some time. I wonder why they were named butter flies. I was about to pull out my cell to look up the answer when the sound of footsteps heading toward me distracted my random train of thought.

"Hello again."

"Hi Grady, how are you?"

"I'm good thanks. Would you mind if I sat next to you?"

I shuffled across slightly, "Not at all. I saw you over there and contemplated going across to say hello but thought it might not be well received."

"I figured as much. That's why I decided to come over here. I behaved like a total jerk the other day. I'm sorry. It was part pride and the fact that what you were saying reflected the truth. I reverted to being defensive and projected insults toward you to mask my vulnerability. I'm really sorry if I hurt you with my words."

"It's okay. I didn't give it a second thought. No harm done. I appreciate the honesty and am truly glad that you are feeling better."

"Well I wouldn't say that I'm feeling better. I spent the first week carrying around a bunch of flowers to the park every day in the hopes of making a formal apology, but you never returned. The thought of you not coming here because of me made me feel like a complete heel."

"Hmm. I decided that I would take Huckleberry on a morning exploration of other areas for a short while instead. It was a chance to give him the stimulus of new sights and smells and I guess I felt you needed the break from seeing me. I left you in a rather annoyed state so in my opinion there was a need to provide us with some distance to allow things to settle." I looked into his eyes, "I only come here because Huckleberry loves to interact and play with the other dogs. I don't want to deny him his simple pleasures. That's the only reason why I returned."

He shook his head slightly, "Your honesty is refreshing but it sure does make me feel like shit."

"I can't help how you choose to feel. It's not my intent to make you feel bad. In fact, I'd prefer that you didn't." I turned to focus on the dogs playing.

"What's the book you are reading?"

I looked down and saw that the journal was partly jutting out the side of my bag. "Oh, it's from an unknown author. I had it given to me as a gift."

"May I?" Grady put out his hand.

"Sure." I said passing it to him. A hot flush rose to my cheeks as I realized I hadn't thought this through. The text was going to be invisible to him. My mind searched for what spin I could put on explaining why the book was content free.

Grady stared at the cover. "It's beautiful." He opened and began to flip through some pages and then paused to stare at a particular section. I watched as his lips moved silently mouthing the words. "Whoa, this is some raunchy stuff." He looked up at me with a glint in his eye. "It appears to be a hand written diary. It's got some flavors of Lolita jumping out at me."

I could see by the way he adjusted his seating position, that the words within the book weren't all that was jumping out at him. I casually reached for the diary to glance at the page he was on. "Ah yes, the stain me jaunt." I flipped a couple of pages over and then closed the book, returning it to my bag.

"I'm surprised I wouldn't have pegged you as the type of person to read smut."

I smiled, "Like I said, it was given to me as a gift. I started reading it and now I'm curious to know how it ends."

Politely I returned my gaze to watching the dogs in the park as I could see Grady needed to readjust himself. On cue, he shifted the position of his erection, so it wasn't as obvious and then placed his suit jacket over the top.

"I'd best be going. It was nice to see you again."

"Thanks Grady. Have a lovely afternoon."

"I will." He headed to the gate, whistled to call his St Bernard over and then together they trundled down the path.

When they were out of view I pulled out the diary to look at it. If he could read the text that meant that it wasn't one of the four books that I was destined to find. This was something else altogether, which meant I still had two more books to locate. I had read the story of York and then the tales of Patience. Libertine I would have thought is a fit and yet her thoughts are clearly not reserved for my eyes only. Who is she and why did Elon have her journal presented to me during the tri moon phase?

"Hand it over."

I jumped at the sound of a familiar voice speaking to me. Confused I looked to the side and saw her standing there with her hand reached out. I returned the book to my bag.

"Why, what does this book have to do with you?"

She flinched slightly. "How did you get it? Who gave it to you?"

I looked her up and down. It was remarkable. "I know you've been following me. I've seen you every day since the time you dropped off the package at my doorstep." I lightened the tone of my voice. "What's your name? I know you already know mine."

I watched her eyes jut down to briefly look at the spine of the book and then back at me.

I felt a hot flush rise as it dawned on me, "The note in the scientific journal you left on my doorstep was signed Lib. Are you Libertine?"

She stepped forward, "GIVE. IT. TO. ME."

I rose from my seat holding my bag tight against my chest. "I will give it to you, but first can you tell me why you gave me the conspirathorium valedictorian to read?"

Her disposition softened when she heard me state that I would return the book to her. She smirked, "They say you're a genius. Figure it out for yourself."

I dropped my head as I considered her words, "I thought it might have just been sent to bait my online transactions with a tracer tag that would reveal my network. The word conspirathorium valedictorian turned out to be hot."

She shrugged her shoulders seemingly unimpressed.

I took pause to stare at her.

"I'm thirty seven, judging by the way you look I would guess that you are no more than a year or two younger than me."

Libertine shifted her weight to her left leg.

"I'll take that as a yes. You mentioned 'they' say that I'm a genius. I'm assuming that you are referring to the Interferon's."

I noted her pupils dilated.

"Why did you fuck that guy Ross and say it was me? I saw the footage of you sucking his cock. You intentionally had him come to the restaurant that night to approach me. What were you expecting me to do? Freak out? What was the point of it all?"

She went to shake her head and then froze momentarily before making a face to mask her emotions. "I was just having a little fun."

"Intercepting my calls to know my every move and then banging some guy while pretending to be me. I don't buy it as just a little fun. The Interferon's obviously wanted you to execute the act and you did it. Why?"

She went to look over her shoulder then stopped herself by awkwardly pretending she had an itchy chin. She rubbed it against her shoulder before returning her head to face me again. "I just felt like fucking someone. I don't answer to you."

While watching her I realized it was quite possible that she had no idea that he was sent to me after her interlude. Judging by her demeanor there was an air of naivety about her. Whether she was blindly instructed or in cahoots I knew for certain she was not acting alone. I stepped forward to change tact. "I'm sorry for what they did to you. I'm sorry for what they did to your siblings too."

She folded her arms, "What would you know? You get to live free and be revered like a God, while we were reduced to nothing more than lab rats. Experimented on for some ludicrous cause."

"How many of you were created?"

"I had seven brothers and six sisters."

"You were all the same age, weren't you? In the diary, you say that you and your siblings were celebrating your eleventh birthday."

She nodded her head.

"Fourteen children…. That's why when you looked in the mirror you missed them. Were all of you created to look the same?"

"What do you think?"

I paused for a moment pondering whether I should ask.

"Did any of them survive?"

She looked down toward the ground, "No, just me. I didn't realize. It was too late to save them. By the time I understood the truth, they were long gone."

I pursed my lips as I bowed my head, "The seven sins enacted. Seven aligned to the boys and seven to the girls. A gauntlet run and lost."

"Yes. How do you know that?" She asked gritting her teeth.

"Libertine lived the life of lust. Your story, it makes sense now. You weren't abducted. The person you thought was your mom was a scientist who I believe bore the last name Braymer. She would have been the geneticist or the person working closely with the geneticist who developed and perfected the formula which created you all from my parents and possibly my own genetic material."

Libertine stood there glaring at me.

"You, your brothers and sisters were under the false premise that you were being raised in a normal environment when all the while you were likely living in a simulation of my childhood, which had no doubt been under close observation. I'd hazard a guess that the numerological significance of separating you at the age of eleven is possibly due to the connection of twin flame energies to that number." I shook my head. "This was all an experiment to see how my perceived male and female replicas would behave under the various rulings. They were using you to understand how I might behave so that they could try and pre-emptively prepare." I paused for a moment to stare into her eyes. "I'm so sorry. I honestly had no idea."

A single tear rolled down her cheek. "Give me the book."

I reached in and pulled out the journal. "Libertine, please wait I want to..."

She snatched it out of my hands and immediately ran away.

I stood there watching the mirror image of myself disappear into the distance with a single thought on my mind. I have a sister.

Dominion

Staring up at the millions of stars in the sky I couldn't help but drift into thoughts of the moment that Libertine described about her first time being allowed in the courtyard with the blind man. The intense beauty of the vast universe before me had me mesmerized on this perfect night. I tried to imagine how captivating it must have felt for Libertine to witness the twinkle of the stars in the sky. After the length of time she had been confined, simply inhaling the cool freshness of the night air surely would have tasted like freedom. Two weeks had passed from the time she appeared before me at the park. I hadn't seen her lurking about since. At a guess, I think she was rattled by the fact that her diary was in my possession. It was a vulnerable position to be in, especially with the likes of me.

"Here you go Harps." Dylan wrapped a blanket around me while Kichiro passed us a beer each.

"Thank you."

Dylan opened his bottle and took a sip then placed his free arm around me before leaning his head on my shoulder. "I'm so glad you decided to come. It makes this trip all the more special."

"The last time we were at Joshua Tree was in our early teens. Do you remember when mom tried to get you to climb the Great Burrito with her? Dad and I were belaying. Part way through the ascent mom looked down and caught you licking the rock."

Dylan burst out laughing, "Oh my God yes. I had been visiting the hippy camp and got intoxicated by the barrage of smoke from their pot. By the time we went on the hike I was tripping my balls off with the biggest craving for munchies. Mom wouldn't stop calling it a burrito and went to check on me just as I tried to sneak a bite."

"Yep, 'inadvertently inhaled.' You're still sticking to that story, really?"

He lifted his head to look at me, "Okay fine, a cute hippy chick sat on my lap then handed me the pipe. I took few puffs. It was obvious to everyone that I had no idea what I was doing. Once I started coughing and spluttering they all laughed and encouraged me to have some more. In the end, the tent was spinning and the smell of the incense they were burning to mask the scent of the weed was making me feel awfully nauseous. I wanted to sneak into our tent to try sleep it off but then ran into you guys set for the hike."

I laughed. "Yes, and hike we did. I'm not sure what you were doing but it made for some hilarious moments and brilliant memories."

"Yes. You were merciless and I'm pretty sure mom and dad were trying to teach me a lesson."

I smiled then kissed him on the cheek. "They aren't stupid. It was pretty obvious you were high as a kite."

I pinched his cheek, "You're welcome for the relentless teasing."

Dylan shifted his head out of reach of my pincers and laughed.

Kichiro seemed content listening to our conversation while remaining fixated on staring at the stars.

"When are you planning to tell me?" I whispered.

Dylan scrunched up his face as he tapped on the end of my nose, "Tell you what Beanie Bear?"

"About secretly getting hitched."

He reshuffled his position, so he could face me. "I don't get how you figure stuff out. What could have possibly given it away?"

"Mom happened to mention that you said you were making a special stop in Canada first before coming across. I didn't really think much of it until I noticed that day at lunch Kichiro was rolling his finger over the position of where a wedding ring would be placed. I couldn't see any tan lines to delineate if one had been worn so I assumed that if it did happen then it was recent. I suspected that you noticed me watching him, which is why you grabbed his hand to hold it. What you may not have realized is that when you kissed his hand you placed your lips on the area where his wedding ring should have been. A silent reassurance of the secret vows that were exchanged perhaps?"

"It blows my mind how you do that? We did get married. I wanted to exchange our vows before … actually no, you tell me smarty pants."

"Before you started a family. You're planning on adopting a child or two."

He playfully pushed me, "Get the fuck out of here. There is no way that you could possibly know that. You're spooky."

I laughed as I let the momentum of his push place me onto my side, "I'm no shaman I can assure you. It's just a matter of applying logic. You always said that when you were ready to have kids you would get married." I sat up and tapped Kichiro on the shoulder, "Congratulations. You can start wearing your ring again."

He smiled at Dylan and I as he pulled the chain from around his neck up from behind his T-Shirt. He removed the ring and placed it on his finger.

"Show me." I reached for his hand. The ring was simple in design with a picture of a wave etched into the surface. "It's lovely."

"Thank you." He said beaming.

Dylan shuffled to one side to retrieve his ring from his wallet.

"When are you planning to start the adoption process?"

"Actually, we have already begun the meetings and are in the middle of reviewing the piles of paperwork. Its trickier than I thought it would be."

"Why? Is it because of the same sex thing?"

"No, that's sort of manageable. It's more that neither of us are residents of each other's country. I'm trying to figure out whether I can get Kichiro to qualify for residency here. We all know what a ball buster it is for foreigners to get a green card and our marriage isn't recognized, so it leaves me with either working in Japan permanently or the two of us migrating somewhere else that accepts us both."

I turned to look at Dylan, "Tricky. The world is so closed off and filled with ridgid rules. It's a rude shock to grow up believing we're free and then see that really at the end of the day we're not. All of us are restricted by lineage and birthplace. To change our residency, we are made to jump through hoops, being scrutinized to validate that we meet the stringent criteria some bunch of pen pushers concocted as a faux necessity for maintenance of the country's security. However, if you have enough collateral to financially 'invest' you are easily able to buy your invitation. It's elitist, selective and entrapment at its finest."

"Exactly. Before we can make our official submission to adopt I have to find a solution to this for us. It's crazy," said Dylan shaking his head.

"Mom is going to be livid that she has missed out on attending your wedding. I can't imagine how she is going to accept you having a family and not being nearby for her to fuss over them."

"I know. She will never let me hear the end of it. Leaving Launa and heading over to Japan nearly broke her. When I told her about Kichiro she became silent. It was an awful feeling to experience the possibility of being rejected for my life choices."

I placed my arm around Dylan and pulled him in, "Try not to take it personally. She's always looked forward to the idea of being surrounded by grand kids. She'd given up on me years ago and pegged all her hopes on you and Launa delivering the goods. When you fell in love with Kichiro, she knew that dream might never be realized biologically."

"Actually, we have been exploring the idea of a surrogate. Ideally, we want two kids, one from each of us from the same egg donor if possible. It's rather expensive but doable, maybe, eventually. Even that route has its own suite of complications and challenges to face."

"How much is it?"

"It varies but can be anywhere from twenty five thousand upwards plus expenses."

"At the very least you have some options. Adopting a child in need is also a beautiful gift to offer." I kissed my brothers hand. "Things will fall into place for you both. First try and get your residency situation sorted. Then focus on the brood. Does Kichiro have any relatives already here? I know that family can become sponsors for their relatives. It might not be a permanent solution but it's a start towards the possibility."

"He does but they aren't very close and from what he told me they are unlikely to assist."

"That's a shame. Oh well, you are obviously not destined to be afforded the easy route. Get some professional advice and find a way to make it happen or be prepared to receive never ending grief from mom." I said chuckling.

"I've been struggling to think of how to tell her and when. I'm having such a good time I don't want to invoke any unnecessary drama."

I leaned back so I could get a better view of the sky. "Then don't tell her. Just trust you will know when the time is right."

"For once I'm going to take your advice."

We all sat there in silence enjoying the incredible view.

My brother wanted to avoid the drama and I couldn't help but think about the drama. Our mom's having an affair, her and dad are getting divorced, and we have a sister who is being controlled by evil forces that are doing everything in their power to penetrate my psych in order to obliterate my free will. It was simply madness at every turn.

"I'm going to head to bed. I'd like to get a decent night's sleep so I'm feeling fresh for the hike we have planned." I kissed Dylan on the cheek and then gave one to Kichiro. "Goodnight."

"Night sis."

"Good Nighto," said Kichiro as he waved.

I headed off to my cabin to try and get some rest.

Snuggled under the covers I recognized how much I missed Huckleberry. I left him with my parents primarily because I was worried about him being taken by coyotes out here. This was the first time I had been separated from him since he entered my life. There was a sense of emptiness that I felt in his absence. I missed feeling the joy of hearing the pitter-patter of his little feet. In hindsight, I should have been more persistent in finding a way to bring him with me. I know for certain he would have loved it out here. I'd tried to get him an on board seat allocated but the airline was already at their maximum so my only option was having him caged and checked into the cargo area. The thought of having him reduced to being confined in a box and shoved into a dark, noisy compartment where I had no way of checking on him to ensure that he was safe, felt wrong. I decided that would be a selfish ask by me, which added to my reasoning to leave him with mom and dad. Flashes of what happened when he was a puppy crossed my mind several times, but I knew my fears were linked directly to the horrendous experience we had with Vernon. He was banished so I trusted that my sweet Huckleberry was in safe hands.

Folding my arms behind my head I stared at the ceiling while I tried to untangle a mottle of thoughts that were tirelessly running through my mind. Bahrain and Zivah were two of five entities that Zivah mentioned I had selected to be present to provide me insight when I required it. I wondered when the others would manifest and through whom. They both arrived in quick succession with no one else appearing since. Was that the reason why Vernon murdered Liam? Did the end of Liam's life close off the channel? There seemed to be an extraordinary amount of premeditation to my whole life experience. The Interferon's as I recently discovered have been actively designing elaborate schemes to control me since before I was even born. They knew that I was going to be present in this lifetime and they also somehow discovered who my parents were destined to be. I know this because they set up the ruse to collect my family's DNA to manufacture my replicas. The curious thing is that I too appear to have pre-planned my entry because I selected spirits to guide me, along with the way they would be allowed to enter and were given specific instructions on what to divulge. It's the same with the books that were created specifically for me to find. I'm the only person, who can read the stories, which I'm sure contained countless secret messages I am yet to unravel. I get now that the birthday cards delivered each year on a specific date were likely related to my fourteen doppelganger's date of birth. What throws me is who orchestrated the delivery of the cards each year and why they were motivated to hand over those enchanted relics. It doesn't make sense to have priceless artefacts delivered to a child as a gift. My mom had no capacity to protect them from falling into the wrong hands and yet it all somehow worked. The precious items remained in our attic undetected. They would have cost someone a fortune to obtain, most are considered to be objects of legend rather than real. Maybe that's it. Perhaps no one was looking for them because most people believed they were items born of fiction. Even then, I'm not sure how it was possible to find and acquire all of them without drawing any attention. I know at some point I need to work to understand each of the objects and what they could be used for. I'm just not ready to dedicate the time to do it yet. The three items that I have explored thus far all have contained a force I am unable to fully understand or remotely command. The incident with the crystal ball was truly amazing but the energy exchanged left me feeling depleted for days. The thought of Maat having the ability to so easily gain entry to possess my body when I grabbed the Ostrich feather still freaks me out. I know I took hold of the feather to invoke her assistance but had no idea how fluid her entry would be. Then there is the vibration of the Cintāmani stone that feels soothing and yet, in unexpected moments through the sequencing of dreams as a channel it catapults me into heinous scenarios that have me facing death. I'm sure when the time is right I will be drawn to explore the other relics out of necessity. In truth, I am not looking forward to it.

Each time I try to take an aerial view of what I know I continue to draw the same conclusion. Simplistically this could all be a game associated to a high stakes wager. What if after all this I eventually discover that I was the pawn who accepted the role to run the gauntlet of the seven sins. The spirits mentioned that no one was able to execute it under seven cycles and most took hundreds of attempts, even thousands. Bahrain said that my next life would be my final entry, which if I am to trust what he and Zivah had told me would make that five in total. He also said that Vernon would be an aspect of my past, present and future. Post this Vernon did return as a spirit before Maat banished him. Does that mean I am now free from binds with him? The letters he wrote to me are still locked in a cabinet in my apartment. There seemed to be so many loose ends that need to be tidied up before I can pass this life and re-enter for my final jaunt. I wish there were ten of me to…. I stopped mid thought when I realized what I was thinking. There had been thirteen who had already suffered and passed. The seven sins enacted, gluttony, greed, sloth, wrath, envy, pride and lust. Just knowing a little of what Libertine had been through I didn't want to entertain thoughts of the experiments the others were subjected to by the Interferon's.

Reshuffling my position to lie on my side I closed my eyes and tried to focus on images of Huckleberry. My stomach wrenched at the thought of the thirteen. I wanted to drift off to sleep thinking about little Huckleberry. He is the joy of my life.

* * * * *

"Hurry up Dylan," I said as I paused at the foot of the rock.

Kichiro was unpacking the gear from his pack while the climbing instructor set up our base. Once Dylan finished taking some photos he proceeded toward us. As he reached me he took my pack from my back and began prepping my harness before doing his own. None of us were experts but we had ventured on hundreds of hikes and some mountaineering with our parents when we were young. Since then sporadically both Dylan and I had done a few trips where we abseiled, and rock climbed together in our early twenties. That's why we selected the easiest route on the Great Burrito called the Quesadilla and paid for a climbing guide to assist.

I knew within a few minutes of the accent that this moderate climb was going to get our hearts pumping. Kichiro seemed to be a natural at finding solid grips in the cracks to leverage from. We were together and yet there was a sense of solitude in the journey. My mind was emptied of thoughts, all I focussed on was the sound of my heart beating and where I was strategically going to place my limbs next. The silence this vigorous activity invoked made me appreciate the draw some people have to doing this regularly. Living for the climb.

The day passed quickly with the climb achieved and then the descent back to where we planned to make camp. We had prepared some salads and of course the beer was on ice. All we needed to do was set up our tents in the designated area before we ventured off again, this time for a late afternoon hike to help shake out the lactic acid build up in our lethargic muscles. This first day established the pace for our next five. We had organized to set off each morning to be guided on a new climb while fresh supplies were delivered to our campsite daily. Dylan and I agreed up front that this was going to be a no cook adventure.

The funniest moment of the whole trip was hearing the screams come from Kichiro and Dylan when they turned to see a coyote was marking his scent on their tent. Each evening the coyotes brazenly lurked about waiting to see what scraps were available from our meals. They were not as shy as I expected them to be. It was a testimony to the parkland visitors either being lax with putting away their food or outright feeding them, rather than leaving the coyotes to fend for themselves as nature intended. One ventured an arm's length away from us. It was unbelievable. We sat and watched them skulk about but made sure to never interfere.

The remaining five days had flown by with a myriad of challenging routes tackled and conquered. They may have been small feats in comparison to what is out there to climb but it was pretty well done for us rookies. We were proud of our achievement.

Sitting out enjoying our final night together, Dylan and I were the last to remain awake. We had a blanket wrapped around us to counter the slight chill in the air. Feeling muscle sore and tired I was tempted to head off to sleep but felt equally content where I was.

Dylan leaned into me to whisper, "I don't want you to go."

I knew he was referring to my decision to leave in the morning. "It's been an amazing trip and I've really enjoyed getting to know Kichiro. He's lovely. I think you chose well."

"Thanks sis. He is pretty special."

"I would hope so given that you married him."

I could see out of my peripheral vision that Dylan was smiling. It was super nice to see him so happy.

"Do you think you will ever settle down?"

"Sure, next life." I said feeling rather upbeat about the fact that there was truth to my statement.

Dylan released a laugh, "Really? Aren't you lonely?"

I released a sigh and turned my head up to stare at the stars. "Sometimes," I said in a whisper.

"Even Kichiro was quizzing me the other night about why you are single. Honestly Beanie Bear you should try and find someone to share your life with. I worry about you."

I poked him in the ribs, "You sound like mom."

"Even if I do, she has a point. You're amazing and you deserve to be happy."

"I'm as happy as I can be. Let's drop it. I don't want our last evening to be tainted by unnecessary concerns. If it's meant to be it will happen. Look at what you and Kichiro have. Would you want me to settle for anything less? Do you remember how unhappy you were with Launa and how long you stayed in that unhappy relationship? To my mind, it's better to be alone than to be with the wrong person. That's why I am genuine when I say I'm as happy as I can be. Sure, I would dearly love to be in a relationship, but only with the one who is designed by the same fabric as my soul. I won't compromise on this for anyone."

"You're right. I was miserable for years in that relationship and made a million excuses not to do anything about it when in reality the moment we parted I felt this enormous weight lift. I was completely free. I don't understand why people subject themselves to it when it's clear that it's not working. Look at how happy mom and dad are. I mean I had the perfect role models and still fucked up."

I shook my head slightly, "Given you lived the dream yourself you should be able to appreciate that there isn't a singular reason for the behavior. It is completely subjective. Honestly, it could be environment, culture, upbringing, religion, self-worth, fear, pick one, select them all. At the end of the day it's about the person's experiences and more importantly their interpretation of those experiences. What you and mom need to recognize in order to stop the unnecessary worrying is that I'm not that kind of person. I couldn't stand being in a relationship that was anything short of fulfilling. Until the love of my lifetimes comes along, I'm far happier on my own."

"I always thought Peppy might be the one. I'm so sorry about what happened to him and Sam. That guy Liam, mom told me was in your apartment when he…"

I placed my hand up to signal for him to stop. "Don't go there. I don't want to talk about it. I'm still trying to make my peace with what transpired. Peppy and I were always the best of friends and I will forever love him and Sam dearly. What happened was an awful shame. Liam too. It's all a tragic waste of life. Please Dylan, drop it."

Dylan released a sigh. "I just want to say that I love you and have had the best time this week. I'm really glad you came. I'm going to feel devastated when you head home tomorrow."

I looked across at him and smiled. "I love you too. You didn't fuck up with Launa. You obviously needed to be in that relationship and perhaps it was that experience that prepared you for Kichiro to enter your life. Don't dis the value of what you two shared. It held purpose for both of you." I shifted my position, so I could lie down to stare up at the sky. Dylan followed suit.

"Dylan"

"Yes."

"Mom and dad aren't perfect role models and they aren't happy."

"I know Beanie Bear. I know."

The next day as I was boarding the plane I felt a deep sadness about our trip coming to an end. Earlier in the morning before I left them at Joshua Tree Dylan continued toying with the idea of staying longer in the hopes that I might extend too. I kept a poker face the whole time, knowing there was a part of me that wasn't ready to leave. I thoroughly enjoyed having a chance to spend time getting to know Kichiro a little better, and its always great to catch up with my brother, but there was so much unfinished work for me to do. I couldn't eradicate thoughts of Libertine from my mind. I needed to find a way to track her down.

* * * * *

Entering the hallway of my parents house I felt my heart skip beats as Huckleberry came running toward me. I dropped to my knees, so he could reach my face as he propped himself up on his hindquarters to lick me all over. He released little sounds of whimpering while wagging his tail in a frantic swish back and forth.

I heard a scrape of a chair against the floor. "Come into the kitchen Harper. I want to hear all about the trip," called out mom.

"Okay, I'll be there in a moment." I picked up Huckleberry and headed down the hall.

"Hi Mom." I said leaning in to give her a kiss. "Thanks for looking after him. He's chubby." I flipped Huckleberry upside down. "Feel that little protruding pudding belly. What on earth have you been feeding him?"

Her eye's flittered, "You can blame your father for that. He's been sneaking him off to the ice cream parlor every chance he can get."

I laughed, gave Huckleberry a squeeze before placing him on the ground. "Where is dad?"

Mom glanced at me with an odd expression and then down at her hands.

"What is it?"

"I promised not to say anything. He's still furious at me for telling you about us getting a divorce. He would be beside himself if I betrayed him again."

"Then don't tell me."

She looked at me while fidgeting with a dishcloth, "As simple as that? You won't try to pry it out of me?"

"You know it's precisely what I'm going to do but without compromising your promise to him. I'm only doing this because I can tell by the furrows across your brow that you are seriously worried. Whatever it is seems to be causing you to be really anxious. Look into my eyes."

Mom straightened her posture and began staring into my eyes.

"Breathe and relax Mom," I said while stepping closer. "Place your palms on top of mine to hover not touch."

She did as I had instructed.

"That's it. Stay like that and keep watching me." I changed the tone of my voice by dropping it down an octave, "I don't want you to speak. Just think of the answer."

I paused for a moment.

"I'm going to start now, so listen carefully. Does it have to do with the divorce?"

I waited a moment.

"Okay that's a no. Does it have to do with his health?"

Once again, I paused.

"That's also a no. Hmm, does it have to do with the affair?"

Mom presented a slight reaction.

"Maybe. Does it have to do with his work?"

This time mom's signal was far stronger.

"Yes. It is realted to Dad's work."

Mom stepped back, "How did you do that?"

"Pupil dilation is a signal that often gets read but it can be misleading. What I was looking for was confirmation queues, which your hands were set up to provide. You had them hovering over my hands and were told not to touch mine. When I asked questions around items that were sensitive to you, which of course were all the questions, your pupils naturally dilated. When your hands could maintain position, that was a definite no. Your hands only dropped slightly at the affair question but were heaviest when I mentioned dad's job. You dropped them onto mine and then bounced back up."

"Incredible. Did they teach you that at college or on the job?"

"Neither it's my own technique I developed while working with criminal cases where the assessment involved children. Some of them were so proficient in lying that it was hard to discern when the truth was being told. I wasn't allowed to utilize hypnotherapy, so I developed this as a way of bypassing their cognitive engagement. Our bodies have never been trained to lie so it's an easy barometer to use as a guide for honesty queues. It's not something I could use officially but it helped me better understand what I was dealing with. Psychopaths are master chameleons."

"Amazing, simply amazing," she said nervously clasping her hands together.

"Through practice I realized not only can I use any part of the body as a gauge, I discovered it was more accurate when I got the person to remain silent. Its seems that the comfort of not having to say anything out loud made them more inclined to think the truth and that makes it even harder for them to resist presenting the queues."

"You should write a book or get a research grant for further studies of the technique. There is definite merit in getting this methodology formally acknowledged. You're so clever Harper."

I smiled, "You're relieved that I now know it's about dad's job but you're also very nervous. That's why you're trying to steer the conversation in a new direction. You're trying to distract me from something." I paused for a moment. "It's okay mom, I'm not going to ask you anything else. I have all I need to know, the rest I've figured out on my own."

"You have?"

"Yep. If it's associated to work, then I'm leaning toward dad finding out the hard way that he is being targeted and that there is something company related that he might become the fall guy for. I'm assuming he has had to lawyer up again. The last time it was an accusation of a biosecurity breach in Africa, which he managed to successfully defend. Whatever it is that they believe they have on him this time no doubt also holds significant threat to the company and might lead jail time. It must be reasonably serious because they kept returning to assess the company books. They are looking for something or have something and are looking to pin it on someone."

"I'm truly worried that he won't withstand the pressure. He was already struggling with the idea of the divorce and now this."

"Do you think he will be home within the next hour?" I asked looking at the clock on the kitchen wall.

She shook her head, "No, he's being staying at the office late and then checking into a hotel. He doesn't want to see me at the moment."

I nodded my head then wondered, if that were the case when would dad have been home to take Huckleberry to the ice cream parlor. I was only gone a week.

"I don't know what to do Harper. I've made such a mess of things of late."

"How often has he been home in the last week?"

"Only once to pick up some clothes. He was in and out in less than an hour and hardly spoke a word to me. He's really upset."

I looked around the kitchen and then the dining room behind me. I noticed a cigarette lighter on the table.

"Go see a therapist to help you talk things through. You obviously have some changes happening that are driving this desire for different. I'm not going to lie to you. To me it feels like you are struggling with facing yourself and are grasping on to Devon as a crutch to make you feel better. It will work for a while but it's not sustainable. You need to make yourself happy, it's no one else's responsibility. It starts and ends with you. If you can master this, then you won't be so easily led astray."

"You don't think I should have left your father."

"It's not for me to say whether you should or shouldn't. Mom, I don't know how to say it any clearer so that you can hear the message I am trying to convey. You need to find what makes you happy outside of anything or anyone else."

"Devon makes me happy," she said pleadingly.

"I can see by the fact that he has been here that you obviously aren't respecting dad's feelings or boundaries for that matter. Is it any wonder that he has resorted to staying at a hotel? Honestly mom what has gotten into you? It's completely selfish."

"How did you…"

"The lighter on the table." I pointed directly to it. "He left his lighter here." I watched her disposition alter causing me to feel an instant flush of anger. "Oh no, are you fucking kidding me? He didn't leave it here. He's still here, isn't he? You know how I feel about it and knew I was on my way to pick up Huckleberry. What the fuck?"

Mom covered her face as she burst into tears.

"Jesus, I'm out of here." I picked up Huckleberry and stormed down the hallway and out the door. Taking off without a second glance at the house, I held an image of Devon rushing to her side to console her. It made me feel annoyed to think that she was being intentionally insensitive. I wanted to defend her and say that it was out of character but her continual inconsiderate actions told me it was a part of who she is. The restaurant was one poor choice but bringing him into the family home while in the midst of divorce is something else altogether. I was going to have to accept that I currently held no respect for her shit behavior. Part of my anger was associated to my annoyance that I picked up on her feeling nervous and assumed it was related to what was happening to dad, but instead it was really due to Devon hiding somewhere in the house. The whole experience to me was nothing short of pathetic and I found it outrageous that she had succumbed to becoming this person.

* * * * *

I was relieved when Huckleberry and I finally entered my apartment. I'd already dropped off my dirty clothes at the local laundry service, so now I wanted to have a quick shower before settling on the sofa to call dad. The fact that they might have found something else to use against him worried me.

The mineral mask I plastered into my hair was alleviating the itch I developed while hiking through Joshua Tree. The fine dust seemed to irritate my eyes and clogged my pores. I decided to pull out the salt scrub to give my body a complete once over, then pulled out the razor to shave my legs. As I sat on the base of the shower I enjoyed the sensation of the soft falling water cascading down my body. When I finished shaving I lazily swivelled around to place my head centrally under the water and began to massage my scalp. The new conditioner I have been using of late combined with this mineral mask has transformed my hair to feel like silk.

It was hard to drag myself out from the shower but the call of my jim jams and a hot cup of tea was equally as enticing. Once I dried off and finished applying moisturiser, I slid into a fresh pair of pyjamas before venturing downstairs to switch on the kettle. As it started to boil I prepped my cup before dialling dad's number.

"Hi, you've successfully reached Max at Dynamically Global please leave a message and I'll get right back to you. Thanks, a zillion."

"Hi dad, it's Harper. I've picked up Huckleberry. Thanks for looking after him. I'm sorry we missed each other. Call me back when you get this message. Bye."

It was unusual for dad's phone to go straight to his voicemail. I considered redialling but thought better of it. He would call me back when he was ready.

I grabbed my laptop and scrambler from my office in the back room and brought them both into the living area. Huckleberry was already on the sofa waiting for me to join him. As I sat down he positioned his head on my lap. I switched on the computer, so I could connect to my web service. Prior to doing anything else I verified that the scrambler was activated, then proceeded to sign in to my email account to check my mail.

The first email that initially caught my eye was a message from my hacker friends.

Sorry for the delay, their network wasn't a quick one to crack without being detected. ZeonMark sold 2500 limited edition Flight Flo spy drones of which 300 reside within New York area. The full list of purchaser's details is attached.

We have tagged your cell as requested. Awaiting your next instruction.

I was hoping that they would be able to narrow down the purchaser's list further than by region. Still, I opened the file and began to scan for anything that might help me identify who owned the drone that was taking images of my apartment. After a quick run-down the page one name stood out:

Purchased by: Braymer Architect Inc

Delivery Address: Elon Braymer, 13 Warra Wrinkle Way Drive, New York.

I issued a reply to my covert hackers:

Thanks Team. Please quietly draw down on Dynamically Global. Set markers to trace hack lines both in and out. Cast the net wide, personnel view covering both professional and private. Something stinks in Bangkok.

<u>Warning</u>: Hyper encryption with multilayer tracer required. If you can't ensure you aren't followed in and out of the rabbit warren, don't go. Set up a dummy first with false leads to test. If toxic, abort this request.

Also, now that you have hacked my cell, please provide instructions of how to hack proof my cell. Let me know what malware is hidden, what it is exposing and to whom it goes to. Then shut it down.

Forever Grateful,
H

The next email I chose to open was one I had been avoiding for a while.

Dear Ms Perelle,

The property you wished me to purchase on your behalf in San Francisco has settled. The funds held in escrow were used to clear the title with the balance returned to your account less my agreed fees. The breakdown of the total costs and my invoice are attached.

The title has been sent to your solicitor as instructed. Please advise if you would like me to make arrangements to have the property cleared and cleaned in preparation to rent.

Regards,
Josh Pelgrin
Pelgrin Realty

I'd asked the local realtor Josh, to keep an eye out, as I suspected that the landlord would try to sell the property after what happened to Peppy and Sam. It didn't feel right to have anyone else stay there. I still needed to come to terms with their deaths, and I wanted to find a way to provide closure for their spirits. Josh was keen to make a sale, so he proactively approached the landlord to make an offer. It was a low ball proposal that neither of us expected would be entertained. The strategy was set to use this as a starting point to begin a conversation. However, much to our surprise he accepted. Part of the terms were written to ensure the property with its contents remained as is. This seemed to suit him. Post the forensic cleaners entry, no one else had been in the house or removed any of the furniture. Sam and Peppies respective families made claim to their personel items, but largely the rest remained. I knew I would have to get across there at some point to do whatever it was that I felt I needed to do, but now was not the time.

I sent a reply to Josh.

My apologies for not being available to respond sooner. Thanks for assisting with the purchase. Please send me the keys via a secure courier. I currently hold no intentions of letting out the property. I'll reach out to you, if I change my mind.

Take Care,
Harper.

I sifted through the rest of my emails amazed that with all of the ingenious technology today, we still haven't won the war on spam messaging. The amount of erectile dysfunction and penis enlargement emails that managed to bypass my spam filter was staggering. The pictures were even more so. My favorite is a before and after shot of a penis that has been subjected to the use of a cock pump that looks akin to a modern day torture device. The only enlargement it was sure to produce was swelling. The authenticity of the images were compelling. I had no doubt it was a best seller.

Once I completed my bill payments, I closed down all the windows, cleared my cache and began to surf the web to see what the latest news was on Anathema. Millions of articles were returned with my first hit. There was still a large swag of believers driving the cause via a variety of different activists and underground networks. This was only set to continue to gain momentum. My next phase of the plan may have been interrupted by the Interferon's games of distraction, but I was by no means finished. Timing was everything.

I looked across at my cell and wondered why my father hadn't returned my call. Even Dylan seemed to be silent. I shut down the computer and decided it was time to get some sleep. Tomorrow's plans were now revised to include an unannounced visit to Elon Braymer. The last I had heard he was retired and living overseas. I wondered what he was doing back in town and more importantly why he would be spying on me.

* * * * *

Thirteen Warra Wrinkle Way Drive was nineteen blocks east of my apartment building in an industrial estate. Initially, I thought I might take Huckleberry for a long stroll, but then decided it would be reckless of me to do so. I could tell by the expression on his face that he was none too pleased about it as I headed out the door. It's not as though he had missed out on his routine walk. I'd taken him for an early morning stroll and stopped by the park, so he could have some play time with his furry friends, but this didn't appease his need to stick to me like velcro. It seems he missed me as much as I had missed him during my trip away.

Meandering down the network of streets I allowed my mind to drift. Dad still hadn't return my call, I haven't concocted a way to locate Libertine and I held an awful negative feeling about this Devon fellow mom was besotted with. Kichiro on the other hand seems lovely. Dylan and he are quite the match. I really like their energy. I wondered what events would not have occurred had I not found the first book in the woods? The story of Illuminarium woke me up from a dream state into reality. If this didn't happen then I wouldn't know the Interferon's exist, I therefore wouldn't have spent the time I did with Liam, which means he never would have met my friends. Was it inevitable or was Peppy, Sam's and Liam's deaths a biproduct of a series of events that were determined by the axis of my direction? I'll never know the answer. I guess it doesn't matter. Knowing in hindsight won't change the fact that it has happened. A flush of heat soared to my face making sweat beads formulate on my brow. I recognized my bodies signal for me to stop thinking about it.

A quick glance at the GPS indicated that the destination was only a few blocks away. I began to pay conscious attention to my environment. It was not an area I was familiar with and for some reason it felt eerily void of any signs of life. There were no cars on the road, none could be seen parked on the streets either. Not a single bird was visible in the tree's or flying across the cloudless sky. This whole industrial sector appeared to be abandoned, yet smoke was coming out of a few of the buildings chimney stacks.

Warra winkle drive was easy to find. I surveyed the area as I walked towards number thirteen. Standing outside the building it seemed rather nondescript. I would have expected an architect's residence to be a showpiece of unique features. Stepping forward to press the doorbell I realized that the door to the main entrance was already ajar. I did a quick head check left and right to establish that everything was clear before giving it a nudge to widen the entry point.

"Elon, it's Harper Perelle are you in here?"

I couldn't hear anything.

"Elon are you home?"

I had no desire to press on. If I didn't get a response, then I was going to leave it for another day. Stepping slightly over the threshold I reached in to clasp the handle, so I could close the door shut. Just as I started to hear the lock click over the floor beneath me gave way and I found myself falling down an enclosed metal shaft. I grappled at the sides to find something to grip but the momentum gained was too quick to allow me to build any leverage. In a matter of moments, I landed onto a pile of cushions. Catching my breath, I tried to get my bearings as I jumped to my feet. I swivelled around to gauge my position within the dimly lit room. Three sides bricked in and one caged like a prison cell.

"Why have you come here?"

I leapt back losing my balance causing me to fall onto the cushions. I squinted my eyes to see if I could get a better view of the person while my eyes were adjusting. All I could ascertain was that there was someone sitting in a chair.

I rose to my feet and stepped forward, "Elon? Is that you?"

"Why have you come?"

"I found out that you owned the drone that was hovering over my apartment. I wanted to know why you were taking surveillance imagery?"

He raised himself off the chair and stepped forward, tilting his head slightly to the left. "How did you acquire this information?"

I recognized the expression on his face was emanating signals of mistrust.

"I received the letter you wrote to me. It was revealed during the tri moon phase. That was one of three items the apartment disclosed across the three days. I know about my genetic replicas and have met the only surviving one they call Libertine."

His head jerked further to the left when I said her name.

"How many times have we met?" He asked.

"Once."

"Who orchestrated the meeting?"

"My realtor."

"What were my parting words to you?"

"I wish my wife was here to have met you."

His eye's widened, "Harper, I'm so sorry, let me get you out of here. One moment."

I watched him scurry away and then return with a rather large key. He used both his hands to guide it into the lock and then twisted it counter clockwise until the mechanism released. He opened the door and stepped in giving me a hug.

"Are you okay? Was the landing soft enough?"

"Yes thanks, what would have happened if I had stepped into the house?"

Elon twisted his torso and pointed, "You would have landed over there."

"Oh, so either way I was set up to fall."

"On cushions," he said nodding his head.

I don't know why I found his reassurance of the cushions as amusing, but I did. I muffled my laugh. "We need to talk. I think there is some information that you might be able to provide that could help me."

"Sure, follow me and don't step there, or there." He turned to look at me, "Just watch me and follow my lead."

"Okay." I did as he asked.

The length of the building was deceptive from the outside. The twists and turns of the narrow corridors had me feeling we were venturing in circles. "Have we entered into a maze?"

Elon turned and smiled, "Why yes, it's precisely what it is. Only one correct way in or out, the rest if walked through trigger a trap door to be sprung so the person is locked into a sector until I release them." He turned and continued to walk.

"It's a pretty neat set up you have here."

"Precautions had to be made." He said walking forward at a quickened pace. "Ah, here we are."

We arrived at a spiral stair case that was the same design as the ones that are in my apartment. When Elon reached the top, he pushed up to pry open a trap door that instantly flooded us with natural light from above. He momentarily disappeared and then his hand reappeared, held out to offer assistance. When I was clear from the port hole he released the cover to the hatch that automatically sprang shut. I looked down and couldn't see the seam.

"How is it possible that I can no longer see the door or even have an indicator of its outline?"

Elon seemed to beam with pride, "It's my signature trademark."

"It's impressive. The rotating floor, the tree of life projected on the wall, it's incredible. I secretly think you might be a wizard."

"Oh, I'm so pleased. Yes, yes the rotating floor." He said scratching his head. "Would you like me to make you a cup of tea?"

"No thanks," I said looking around the vast room we had entered. "I'm surprised that there are only two levels to this place. The basement and this open expanse?"

"Yes, two levels but the open expanse is only how you see it today. Visually it would appear this way but technically that is not always the case."

"What do you mean?"

"The walls of the maze below are designed to rise to create dividers for rooms within here too. It's a brilliantly orchestrated evolving design."

"Incredible."

His expression changed as he grabbed my hand and patted it. "How are you holding up?"

I looked at the liver spots on his weathered craftsman hands, "I'm just trying to take things day by day. I won't lie, it's been a struggle. There is a lot to absorb and even more to absolve."

He bowed his head, "Yes and my dear late wife Candice is definitly a contributor to this."

"Was she a geneticist?"

"She held an engineering degree, was an inventor and foremost a passionate scientist. Solution driven she wound up specializing in genetics and reproductive cloning. Harper, you have to understand that she was the leader in her field that had developed techniques that were ground breaking. Candice made the impossible, possible."

"Did she create my replica's?"

He placed his hands on his lap. "Yes, but it is not what you would think. She was hyper intelligent in the field of mechanics and science but not equally so when it came to applying logic to human nature and people's capacity for evil. Candice was born without a uterus or the reproductive elements typically associated to reproduction. She was so desperate to have children that it caused her to be manically driven to find a cure."

"Adoption sounds like it would have been a simpler solution."

"Indeed, but we are all born with a cause and she felt that this was her way to contribute. Candice worked tirelessly at it. In those days, we weren't financially established, so she applied for grant after grant. The idea of cloning in those days was seen as far too controversial and considered to be a pipe dream born of too much exposure to science fiction novels. She was disheartened by the continual rejection but wasn't deterred from her plight. She attended science fairs, spoke at conventions and wrote a book on the subject. One day a man who said he represented a pharmaceutical company by the name of Dynamic Life approached her to present an offer that included her own fully kitted laboratory with state of the art equipment and an annual salary of two hundred and fifty thousand dollars. He assured her that the full rights of anything she discovered or created would be hers to patent and retain. He referred to his client as enablers. In exchange, they wanted to have her focus solely on cloning. Who would say no to such an offer?"

"What was the catch?"

"At the time Candice was too swept up in the deal to consider this, we both were. The money she brought in allowed me to complete my studies in architecture and have the business established. Prior to this I was struggling to attend part time while I worked onsite construction as a carpenter's apprentice. We went from rags to riches practically overnight."

"It sounds like an alternate version of a fairy tale."

"Well how true that is, for every fairy tale I have come to know has a sinister undertone and ours was no exception. The company kept to its word and gave Candice the space to execute her work without any interference. She kept a journal, which was written in a code that only she had the capability to decipher. Although she was naïve in many ways, she was aware that what she was venturing into could be applied and misused. In that regard, she was very cautious to ensure that no staff member was privy to the entire procedure. Mostly she operated on her own and only requested assistance when she felt she couldn't complete something in solitude. It took her well over a decade to develop a definitive solution that was intermittently successful but yielded flaws in the clones that caused premature death. Proving it was possible only fuelled her determination."

"How did the cloning of my replica's come about?"

"I don't know the full details but as I understand it she was given a surplus of genetic material from a variety of human donors to use as part of her development of the technique. This was provided to signify her graduation from mastering the art of cloning healthy mammals successfully. They led her to believe that it was a top-secret government sanctioned research program. She was relocated to a new facility and received an increase in wages of a whopping two hundred and fifty thousand dollars. There were significant incentive bonuses offered for her to create an equivalent healthy human clone within a three year period. They would pay her millions for her contribution to science. Candice could see the application of such a feat as a solution for those couples with infertility issues. The success of this would mean that we would be able to create a perfect image of ourselves from virtually any cell that held our DNA without the need of a human body as a host during the incubation period of a typical pregnancy."

"She was obviously successful. Why hasn't anything been published about it?"

"It was a completely clandestine operation. The facility was located in a high security precinct that allowed absolutely no-one entry in or out of the premises without being heavily sedated and blindfolded. Even the vehicles were equipped with white noise to distract the mind from hearing any other sounds that could be used as a landmark. Candice sometimes wouldn't be home for weeks at a time. She was tirelessly working on the project and felt that she was close enough to developing a repeatable technique. At least that is what she had me believe." He paused for a moment to release a sigh. "Candice returned to me one day a shadow of herself. She was riddled with cancer and was coming home to die. That was when she told me the truth."

Elon's posture drooped as he sat down on the stool behind him.

"Take your time. I know this must be hard for you."

His lips pursed, "When you watch the person you love dearest lay there unwell and crying about the regrets they have, its hard. Knowing that there is nothing that can be done to console her pain. She was at the end of her life and found herself feeling devastated that she had chosen the path she had, albeit initially unaware."

I released a sigh. "Tell me."

Elon placed his hands on his face, rubbing his eyes, and then returned them to his lap clasped.

"Candice had never worked on mammals. Nor was she taken to a new location, it was the same one just a different sector of this vast complex. I was just repeating the lies she told me so that you can appreciate what I knew at the time. From the outset, she was supplied human samples to experiment with and would implant them into mammals. They had already advanced somewhat in this area and were looking to leverage off Candice's brilliant mind to progress further than they found themselves able to achieve. The struggle was finding animals that had the capacity to carry and allow the human babies to survive the birthing process. In the end, it appeared that horses were the best incubators with the benefit of having room to support multiple human foetuses concurrently. Post birthing these babies would be taken from Candice to another location in the facility. Although a horse's uterus functioned well she wasn't satisfied with the use of any beast given it held its own biology and could therefore inadvertently pass on its own genetic markers, possibly causing an interspecies mutation. She had seen enough to know that evolution and the need to survive were perpetuated at a cellular level. Things could and did happen that she would not speak of. Eventually using her engineering background, she created a prototype called the utero incubator. She cloned the amniotic fluid from her donors and grew the sac in petri dishes. This was all placed into the incubator, which was connected to a tube that had the inner layer meshed with the genetic material of the umbilical cord. At full term the sac would be sliced open and the child retrieved. It was this method that yielded the uncompromising results she had dearly hoped to achieve. After a few trials of the prototype produced further success she was instructed to build fourteen and have them carrying the same clone. On the day she was ready to begin the process she entered the lab and found all her genetic material had been removed and the laboratory was scrubbed clean. The only donor sample provided was in the temperature-controlled fridge with a note saying: *Clone this, seven of each.*

"Seven of each?" I knew what it meant but wanted to see if he did too.

"Seven Boys and seven girls. Seven of each."

"Elon, you were married to the female counterpart of Josef Mengele. Where did all the children go that she created?"

His hands gripped together tightly at the receipt of my words.

"I'm never going to apologize for something I didn't know or unconsciously contributed to, although I feel sickened by what my wife had devoted her life to doing under the guise of making it possible for us to have a child. On her deathbed, she called them sacrifices that needed to be made. The repulsion I felt for the words I was hearing from her mouth had me torn."

"What do you mean by unconsciously contributed to?"

"There were nights where we sat at the table discussing this machine she was trying to construct. I was misled to believe it was an advanced incubator that would eventually be utilized in hospital paternity wards to aid premature babies. The motion sensor and rotation axle were my idea. Candice was looking for what might be missing from her rudimentary design. The obvious thought I had was the emulation of movement and positioning. It wasn't natural for a mother who is carrying a child to be in one position all the time, so it didn't make sense to have the child remain stationary. I helped her design the mechanism that allowed the structure of the cribbing system to move in any direction. This was connected to a twentyfour hour counter that would split the percentage of angles into mimicking the crib in a standing and walking motion, then switch to alternate to a sitting position. Of an evening the rotation of lay down positions from how the host would be on their back, then left and right were also mimicked. She reached out to specialists in biomechanics to understand the movement babies would experience in utero when the mom was walking, running and so on. That's where the motion sensor played a role." Elon paused for a moment, then shook his head, "I was so damn proud of her and felt pride in myself for helping. I don't know if the design made a skerrick of difference, none the less, I unwittingly contributed."

A part of me wanted to console him but I felt to do so at this point would come across as disingenuous given I had just called his wife a monster. "Perhaps a legacy can be left by actually designing an incubator that could be utilized in paternity wards to aid premature babies. From what I understand about limited mobility the human body does not bode well with adapting to stillness. I'm sure there is value in creating a psuedo environment that nurtures the same stimulus their mother would have otherwise provided."

He looked at me with moistness in his eyes, "I'd do anything to make things right."

I placed my hand on Elon's shoulder and gave it a squeeze, "Nothing will alter what is done but to live within a future of new possibilities you must first release the harrowing burdens of the past. I think what you said you had designed is a solid idea. I can even see valour in applying the same concept to people with short term restricted mobility or more serious conditions such as paraplegia."

Elon's posture altered from slouching to more upright, "I could do that." He stood up while clasping his bottom lip with his right hand, "Yes, yes that is definitely possible. I need to write this down." He rushed off to the table in the far section of the open room. I stood up and followed.

He was leaning over busily writing something on the blank A3 sheet of paper. My eyes scanned over the mass of blue prints, and the piles of cut out clippings of the articles that discussed Anathema, the tri moon phenomena and the swat team take down of the Telco operator service division called Point to Point. There were also blown up surveillance images he had captured with the drone and others I never realized had been taken of me. A few were while I was in the park with Huckleberry and other public places.

"Elon, what's all this?"

"It's just a precaution. We have them follow you to make sure you're safe. We need to know that you are protected when you aren't within the security of the apartment."

I could feel myself getting angry. "Listen to me very carefully. I need you to stop the surveillance. You have no way of knowing who you are hiring and might well be enabling the very people you think you are protecting me from. It needs to stop immediately."

He stood up to look into my eyes, "No, I can't. I've joined the order. We are devoted to ensuring that you remain safe."

I took a step back, "We? What are you talking about?"

"The holy war, of course. We are on the precipice of succeeding in getting the gates of Equanon opened and you are believed to be the sole key to this occurring. We cannot allow for anything bad to happen to you. It's why so many people work tirelessly to protect you." His hand waved over the pile of articles. "This agitation you insist on creating only aggravates the purveyors of evil. It is placing everything that has been worked towards in jeopardy."

I noticed a muscle twitch below his right eye.

"What is the name of the order?" I asked, as I shifted my bodies position to face him.

"Mahdi."

I stared at him to ensure he knew I was reading his body language.

"We protect the guided one, which is you from the Masih ad-Dajjal who is the false Messiah. There will be a holy war if you don't cease your toying with them."

I readjusted my position to fold my arms as a false read for him to think I am in a space of feeling defensive. "I'm not sure I follow. Who is the false Messiah?"

He dropped his head, "The one they call Libertine. You met her in the park. They wish to replace you with her. No one would detect the switch. Look at the photos if you don't believe me. She had been following your every move trying to establish patterns to ensure a smooth transition. They know they cannot kill you, but they have the means to replace you no thanks to the work of my wife."

As he lifted his hands from the table I noted the sweat patches that remained. His hands were very dry when he previously touched my hands.

"How did you come to know of the Mahdi's existence?" I asked.

"Candice told me on her deathbed. They approached her to convince her to join to help protect you. It was too late given her illness took hold, so she begged me to do what I could to assist. I've been with them ever since."

"That explains the apartment. You built it under their instruction then?"

"Yes. The apartment, the surveillance it's all there to protect you."

I glanced over at the table, "That reminds me, do you have a spare copy of the blueprint of the building?"

"Unfortunately, I was looking for it recently myself and I can't seem to find where I put it. I'll have a copy delivered to you as soon as I remember where I hid it."

I stepped in and gave him a hug. "I can't thank you and the order of the Mahdi enough for sacrificing your time to protect me. It is a relief to know I'm not weighted with this burden alone."

"You're welcome, it is the least I can do under the circumstances." He licked his lips and then repositioned his body to face the table, "Do you know how to open the doors to Equanon?"

I shook my head, "No, not yet."

He swivelled to grab my arms just above the elbows giving me a gentle shake, "Time is of the essence Harper. You must figure out what you need and then let the order enable you to do this. Promise me."

I looked directly into his eyes, "I promise Elon."

"Good, good," he said releasing his grasp.

I glanced across at what he had written down on the piece of paper. He misspelt the word incubator and had written the word crypt instead of crib. I smiled and grabbed his hands gently in mine to feel his temperature while I lightly rubbed my thumb on the surface of his hands, "You mentioned your wife kept a journal, which was written in a code that only she had the capability to decipher. Do you have this in your possession? I'd like to take a look at it if you don't mind. It sounds complex and likely way too difficult for me to even try to decipher, but I would still appreciate the opportunity to see it for myself."

Elon's eyes darted to the table as he shook his head, "I'm sorry my wife took it upon herself to burn the journal. It no longer exists."

I nodded my head, "No need to apologize. It's no doubt for the best. Hopefully they can't reproduce her work without it."

His jaw clenched then released. "Hopefully."

I released a deep sigh, "Thanks for explaining everything to me. The context gives me peace of mind. It's probably best that we don't see each other again unless we have to. I'll be in touch as soon as I know anything with regard to opening the door to Equanon."

I began walking toward the door, and then swivelled to face Elon once more. "Oh, and I should warn you that I accidently mentioned your wife's name to Libertine when we met in the park the other day."

"That's okay, she went by her maiden name for all her work and she's long passed now. No harm done."

"I wasn't aware of your wife's maiden name. I mentioned the surname Braymer." His eyes widened at hearing this. It was hard not to break out into a smile. "Please take extra care, the one you suspect is the Anti-Christ is possibly preparing to seek retribution for the ruthless torture and tragic death of her siblings."

"Of course, yes, not to worry. I will most certainly let the order know. Thank you, Harper."

"No Elon, thank you, for everything. I'll be in touch." With this I leapt over the front door foothold landing directly onto the footpath.

Elon gave me a wave then quickly shut the door.

When I was clear of the street I stretched my arms out to glance at the underside of my thumbs while I continued to walk. They were coated in streaks of brown makeup. Liver spots my ass. He initially had me fooled with the caution he took in establishing who I was. The dramatic entry and his line of questioning threw me into a defensive state, where I was so busy trying to authenticate who I was, that it deterred me from executing the same. It was a clever approach but clearly, he didn't have enough information to sustain the ruse. Faux Elon stuffed up when he became inconsistent with his responses and clearly demonstrated that he didn't know what the real Elon had written in his letter to me, with regard to his wife's wishes.

There were three things I now knew for certain:

a) That wasn't Elon Braymer.
b) The Interferon's are desperate to discourage me from persisting in my plight to have them exposed.
c) Libertine trusted me enough to give me Candice's journal.

If I play my cards right, my sister may inadvertently become their undoing. I saw how petrified faux Elon was when he heard that Libertine now knew his family name. Game on.

Sibling Rivalry

Dad had not responded to my request to return my calls. It was obvious that he was clearly avoiding any interaction, at the very least with me. Meanwhile, Dylan was still happily travelling the country with Kichiro. The last message he sent had a photo attached of their cattle wrangling adventure in New Mexico. The expression on his face was priceless. It wouldn't be too long before they returned to New York to say goodbye on their way back to Japan. As much as I was going to feel sad about having him leave, I would be relieved that he's not here to be subjected to what was happening between our parents. Dylan idolized them. I wanted to protect him from having to experience the realities of who they had become to one another.

Mom seemed to also be intentionally keeping a low profile. This was completely understandable given my reaction to discovering that her lover was in the house. Now that I've had some time to assimilate my thoughts I have concluded that it didn't matter how I was feeling about it all. The reality is that she is still my mom and despite not appreciating her approach to things, it was her life and her choice to manage what was happening, in any way she saw fit. I'm no longer going to advise or impose my perspective on her no matter how much she baits me. It's the only way under the circumstances that I see that we can move forward amicably. I must try to create a genuine space where I offer her total acceptance of who she is with no expectations.

Each morning as I ventured out with Huckleberry for his walk I now tried to peg who were the surveillance crew on duty. A few of them had gotten sloppy by utilizing the same vehicles in the same parking spots. They were the easiest to mark. What I was missing was how the photo's I saw at Elon's house were taken at such close proximity without my detection. There had to be more crew roaming about that I was not able to see. I wondered if they had invested in remote control portable spy cameras. It would make sense to have them set up and camouflaged within areas that I frequented such as the dog park. I put my theory to the test by paying a local crew of kids who I had often seen use the adjacent skateboarding park. I gave them some pictures of what I thought they might be looking for and had them run about from tree to tree searching for spy cams. They found nine situated in the dog park and another twelve at the other routes I commonly used. The best part was that being skaters they recorded their hunt and made a video compilation of the pictures that were taken of locals within the area. This triggered the start of an investigation, as the residants in the district were none too pleased about being watched. I knew that it wouldn't lead anywhere. I just liked the idea that I had found another way to piss the Interferon's off.

I'd stepped through what had happened at Elon's house over and over. There were so many alternate scenarios that I had to consider. The Interferon's had planned many threads across decades, so I couldn't exclude the possibility that this whole apartment may have been a place that they designed for me to reside in. It would, after all, become the perfect control point. The constant reference to it being safe with the encouragement to stay within its walls I'm sure was a ploy to make me suspicious. The counter to this is that the Elon I met the other day didn't seem to react to my mention of the letter, nor did he flinch when I spoke about the tree of life. He only seemed to get visibly aggitated when I said Libertine's name. My suspicion was that the Interferon's had been waiting for me to visit Elon for a while. The traceable drone was possibly their concocted ruse to get me to find the connection and therefore be motivated to visit. Just like they did with Digby. Everything was perfectly orchestrated to try to have me believe that I was interacting with Elon. When he led me to the table that revealed all the images of me being monitored it was designed to make me feel panic. This provided the space for him to sooth me with his reassurance that it was to protect me. They want me to be less resistant to their presence.

It didn't make sense that Elon would have clippings of the Telco Point to Point's take down. The articles about Anathema and the Tri Moon phase fit, but I can't see any way he would have an ability to link me to what happened with Point to Point. The fact that he specifically looked at the Point to Point article when I asked about Candice's journal tells me they are still under the impression it exists and that it may be residing somewhere within that company. Yet, he told me that Candice burnt it.

When the faux Elon went into the explanation of the order I suspected by the confidence in his delivery that he was giving me some partial truths, but I didn't believe a scrap about the references to Libertine being the Anti-Christ. Overall, I had to say that the faux Elon's performance was impressive. He had the initial compassion and sorrow portions executed to perfection. I only began to wane confidence in what he was presenting from the time he tried to make me fearful of being replaced. When he suggested that he was part of an order that supported me in my plight, I knew he was lying. How stupid do these people think I am? I find their whole approach quite ludicrous. It mystifies me as to why the almighty Interferon's who have demonstrated in many aspects that they hold the capacity to be heartless, immoral and heinous in their actions are hesitant to be cruel to me directly. Instead, they target people around me to try to influence my behavior. It's a weak hand to play. I need to figure out what it is about me that they are afraid of.

There were only a few hours left before it would become dark. I went upstairs to have a shower and prepare for an evening out on the town. It appeared that Libertine was no longer going to seek me out. Hence, I decided that I had to venture into venues where I suspected she may frequent. I wasn't entirely sure of her playground, so I was working on a hunch and planned to muster up the energy to attend every BDSM club I could find to see if she was about. I was working on the assumption that even if we didn't cross paths tonight, I may get reactions from the patrons who think I am her. That would at the very least let me know which of them she attends, if any. There were twelve known clubs of which only five were publicized. I immediately scratched them off my list. If they were mainstream, then it was unlikely to be of interest to her. It was tricky to identify the unpublicized clubs. I had to resort to joining a few online BDSM forums to build up rapport with people before I could get any insight into the more exclusive venues. I'd created the scene name 'Dom De Plume' and spent a considerable amount of effort to establish a rather impressive backstory on all the social networking profiles so my alter ego 'Dom De Plume' was adopted as a known entity in international BDSM circles. I told my newly acquired BDSM crew on the local chat forums that I was moving into the area and was looking to see what the happening clubs were in New York. I knew if I presented as a rookie they would be unlikely to provide me any details. Even now I wasn't certain they had revealed all the clubs to me, but there were enough to get me started. Some of them had such vanilla names that I wondered if they were authentic. Spank, I mean really? It hardly sounds enticing. The place called Club 120 caught my attention as a possibility. I found out by a regular on the forum that it was by invitation only and there was a graduation process required from its sister clubs Marquis and Juliette. My instinct told me just by the name of the clubs alone that if Libertine were hovering about, this would be where she may venture. The owners were likely admirers of Marquis de Sade's literary works as it seemed the establishment names were a signatory insight into his influence. That alone may have drawn on Libertine's curiosity to explore them.

My biggest concern leading up to this night was what I should wear. I had laid out three outfits on my bed, each one raunchier than the next. I didn't mind bearing my skin but wearing three inch high heals all night was going to be a killer. My hair for this evening's event was slicked back and tucked into a tight low placed ponytail. The wax in my hair gave off a shimmer and held every follicle in perfect order. It took me three attempts before I got the smokey eye shadow effect to appear semi respectable. The application of my makeup on the first two attempts left me looking like I was sporting black eyes from a bar brawl. I finished my application of makeup by using a pencil to darken my eyebrows with the final touch focussed on the perfect placement of my porn star red lipstick to accentuate my lips. It felt stifling to have all these layers of primer, foundation, skin glow and blush plastered on my face.

Huckleberry was curled up on the main pillow that I use to sleep. He knew I was heading out and seemed to have the sulks. He mostly kept his eyes closed pretending to be asleep. On the odd occasion, he took a quick peek to see what I was doing. Believe me, there was nothing more I would have preferred to do then to jump into my pyjamas and join him in a snuggle, but I had to press on and do this. I needed to establish Libertine's position on whether she held any interest in helping. I believe that she may be my one degree of separation to the Interferons. My sole objective is to get an introduction.

There was a growing hesitance in me about going out. The more I stood there fussing and checking my appearance in the mirror, the less inclined I was to leave. Finally, I decided I just needed to stop procrastinating and go. Switching off the bathroom light I re-entered my bedroom to give Huckleberry a kiss. I paused for a moment to watch him continue to pretend he was sleeping. Releasing a deep breath, I walked down stairs, tucked my credit cards into the left cup of my bra, some cash into my right, grabbed my apartment keys and headed out the door.

I decided to begin with attempting to gain entry into a club called Juliette. I was super glad by the time I reached the non-descript metal door down the back of an alley, that I had chosen to switch out my stilettos and wore knee high lace up black suede paisley boots instead. They weren't completely comfortable, but the height of the heel was far more manageable at an inch. The venue was located down a cobblestone laneway, which was not the easiest path to walk on. There was so little light available that I felt partially blind as my feet became a beacon for wedging the point of my heel into every crevice. Just in that short distance I thought I was going to sprain my ankle or worse, do a humiliating face plant. Thankfully for me even if I did, there wasn't a soul about to witness it.

The outfit I chose was the least ostentatious of the three I had prepared. I opted to maintain an air of simplicity, which led me to select the black slim fit dress. It had a loose section in the upper quadrant at the front that draped nicely giving the illusion that my breasts were bigger than they are. I finished it off by wearing a turquoise blue wide band chocker. I didn't own a strapless bra to counter the plunging open neck, so I accented my lingerie to match the necklace. The straps didn't seem out of place and a hint of the peacock blue scallop lacing on the main part of my bra was occaisionally exposed when I moved. I felt sexy.

I released a breath while mentally composing myself as I pulled the metal door open to enter. The room was lit by a black light with only a small space that would accommodate no more than five people at best. The sign on the elevator door said 'Fuck the shaft. Use the stairs.'

Carefully traipsing down the steep stairs, I used my hands to brace against the walls on either side. I felt it was odd that I couldn't hear any music or patrons talking. When I reached the bottom, I turned toward the bright light on my left. A huge well-built black man with a shaved head wearing skimpy pleather hot pants that made tracing the placement of his bulge impossible to miss, stepped forward.

"Pleasure or pain?"

His stare felt intimidating, but his deep voice was ominous.

I glanced down at his cock, intentionally holding my gaze for a lengthy couple of seconds prior to slowly graduating up the length of his torso, and finally reconnecting with his unflinching stare. "Both."

He smiled to reveal a panel of gold plated front teeth.

"As you wish." He passed across two tickets. His rather large hand then pointed to the booth situated behind me.

I walked over, gave the coupons to the woman whose hair was so wispy and frazzled that it looked like it had been exposed to static electricity. Her otherwise gothic styling reminded me of something out of the rocky horror picture show, although when she looked up I realized she bore a striking resemblance to the character Uncle Fester from the Adams Family. She blew a puff of her cinnamon scented cigarette in my face as a silent protest to my stare.

"Left arm pleasure. Right arm pain."

I looked at her a little puzzled.

"You won't get far without a stamp." She whacked her hand on the counter in front of her. "Place both your arms here with your palms facing up."

I placed them in position. She slammed the stamps on both my wrists simultaeneosly, pressing firmly while watching me closely.

I held still and offered no reaction.

She pushed down harder, smirked, then pulled them off.

"That will be sixty dollars."

"Oh, of course." I rummaged around in my bra, then pulled out the exact amount. "Here you go."

She snatched the twenties out of my hand and held them up to the light to inspect them. Reaching for her cigarette she drew in the smoke, then turned to me as she released it.

"Which first, pleasure or pain?"

"Pleasure." I said without thinking.

She snickered. "Lucas, pleasure."

An awful but slightly entertaining thought crossed my mind. What if femme Fester and Biggus Dickus over here are examples of the best of what they have to offer in there. Lord knows I didn't want to watch either of them actively engaging in coitus. I turned to him, "No wait. I've changed my mind. Give me pain." There's something I never thought I would hear myself say.

He nodded his head and opened the door marked with the word Sanctorum. The noise pulsed as it came flooding through. Mr hot pants shut the door behind me as soon as I crossed the threshold. The soundproofing of this facility must be outstanding given it was so loud in here. I made my way down the narrow barren hallway while cupping my ears to reduce the overwhelming saturation of noise. I realized the deeper I ventured into the establishment that I really didn't think this through. If I had I probably wouldn't have come. My sudden need to quench a thirst was present. I wondered if there was a bar. Are these places even licenced to serve alcohol?

Opulent deep purple paint was splattered on the walls with accents of baroque style wallpaper and furnishings designed to compliment. The narrow hallways linked to different rooms. Each area had a collection of people watching couples in play with different devices. No one seemed to notice that I was quietly flitting about between the rooms. Initially, I was looking for Libertine, but then allowed myself to be swept away by the curiosity of the experience. I held a preconceived notion that these clubs might be three different shades of fucked up, but during my research I found some of the offerings depicted on BDSM websites intriguing. I had never been exposed to this type of lifestyle or knew anyone who ventured within these realms.

It was strange that the patrons were happy to stand there watching a person bind another into contorted positions and have them raised to hang on display. To me after witnessing the first person get tied up I found the rest repetitious and a little boring. I was impressed with how this fellow was able to string them up, one after another rather masterfully. I could appreciate the person being bound and gagged had to have a level of trust. It would also force them to a state of being present to their instinctual desire to struggle. I decided the objective must be to eventually shift into a phase of acceptance. They would need to overcome and manage the experience of discomfort and pain.

I seemed to be the only one in the room who crept forward intermittently to try get a glimpse at how the fastner was fashioning some of those fancy knots. Assigned the role of voyeur it was hard for me to get into it. I personally couldn't see the appeal of being the binder and definitely felt no attraction toward being the one in binds. Not the way they were doing it, that's for sure.

The hive of rooms devoted to different fetishes were rather visually entertaining as it felt like I was attending a play where the viewers were permitted to stand less than a meter away from the production.

The next room I entered was decked out with antiquated medical equipment. There is no other way to describe it than fucking creepy. When they placed a man onto an old birthing table and locked his legs into a breeching position with leather straps, I felt my skin crawl. He had a latex full face mask on with only breathing holes for his nostrils and an opening for his mouth. If that wasn't enough he had a huge gag wrenching his gob open. The saliva seeping out from the left side of his mouth was creating a glistening trail down his ultra tight ultra unflattering latex ensemble. To be fair to him it is a rare few in this world that could pull that look off and make it work. When they unzipped a panel to reveal his cock, clean shaven balls and anus, my cheeky side wanted to yell out "Opa!" like the Greeks do at a wedding, but decided it was best not to draw too much attention to my presence.

At first, I thought they were going to attach some weights to his gonads, but it was far worse. They started by using a medley of medical instruments to twist, contort and pull at his bits. He tried to squirm and had moments where I suspected that he might have passed out. I wondered how a person in that predicament had any chance of calling out a safe word. Just as I figured no more could be done to him they wheeled in a piece of equipment that looked like it belonged in an insane asylum. They moistened the areas they wanted to stick the electrodes on and repeatedly gave him shocks. It looked painful as hell and he seemed none too happy about it. I was keen to move onto the next show and headed out the door before they had finished. I was certain that it was only a matter of time before he lost his bowels and shat on them. There was no need for me to be a witness to that looming extravaganza.

As disturbing as I found the medical room this next place was equally unpleasing, but it had nothing to do with the choice of décor. The person was blindfolded, gagged and on all fours. He was wearing nothing, but a pair of leather briefs and a studded dog collar attached to a lead that the dominatrix held securely in her hand. She was hurling abuse at him, telling him he was nothing, then whipped him, spat on him, kicked him, while continuing to hurl more profanities. Instructions would be silently projected on the wall to the audience to request participation by laughing at him. She signaled to a man to come across and urinate on his head while she called him a dog. I know people get off on being subjected to this type of degrading abuse, but I refused to force myself to laugh at something I didn't feel was funny. My instincts were wired to protect rather than abuse.

Thus, far I felt removed from any sense of what these patrons deemed to find alluring, that is of course until I came across the room with the spank paddles, canes, floggers and whips. I watched strangers drop their pants and raise their dresses ensuring they removed their undergarments before lying across the laps of people with a medley of whacking implements. Others bent over tables, while some took their position on all fours. The expression on the people issuing the discipline and the receivers both seemed to convey a sensory pleasure derived from the act. The way dominants rubbed their submissive's asses then smacked them with their hand before recommencing the use of their selected implement was somehow erotic.

"Perhaps you should try it."

I didn't bother turning to see who it was. I recognized her voice, as it sounds freakishly like my own.

"I think what's missing is the act of fellatio and cunnilingus to the submissive." I said.

"No, that would deter from the pleasure of the experience of being spanked."

I turned to acknowledge Libertine. "On the contrary. I think it would be heightened. The pain would feel greater for the genital stimulation provides a contradiction that I suspect might make their orgasm build to an earth shatteringly blissful release. I'm not sure how that play's out for the doms given they are all about control and order. It could break them as their illusion of being the 'master' is one that can be easily shattered. I don't know. You might find even they start desiring to be bent over for a whack."

Libertine's eyes surveyed the room, then she returned her gaze to look at me.

"Let's us see, then shall we?" She walked around the crowd and whispered in certain people's ears. They didn't skip a beat with following her instruction. Once she was done, Libertine returned by my side with her arms folded.

"Just like that?" I asked.

"Just like that," she said watching intently.

The atmosphere in the room began to almost instantly alter as the recipients of the unexpected oral sex began to release groans, while the dominants intensified the frequency and force with which they hit their subs. It became a cacophony of pelts, whips, whacks, smacks and groans until the dominants maxed out and their submissives consequently came.

"Well done," said Libertine as she turned and left the room.

I decided that was her unspoken cue for me to follow.

I noted that people glanced at me as I vacated the room. There was no hiding the fact that we looked like identical twins. If they already knew who she was, I found it odd that they didn't show signs of reacting to my presence prior.

Libertine was waiting for me in the corridor.

"Have you been in this room yet?" She said disappearing through the door.

"No, I was working my way down." I said following suit.

Inside the room I began fondling the ends of the toys hanging on the wall. I turned to engage her eyes as I played with the tassles on a flogger. "Why is this one empty?"

"There was a need to clean up after the last showing. Would you like to hop on?" She asked with a wicked glint in her eye.

"As tempting as that offer sounds I think I'll give it a miss." Noting the identical slicked back hair style, I had to ask. "Do you always wear your hair that way?"

She pointed to the camera's hidden in the corner of the room, "No, I thought it looked good on you and decided that I might try it myself. The clothes, the hair, the makeup, even the loose long sleeve fingerless gloves add a touch of grunge to the sheik of the dress. Everything works, except for that red lipstick."

"You don't like it?"

"A man wants to see a woman's lips when they glide up and down the shaft of his cock. Red is associated to whores and amplifies their primal need to treat them as such. Accented neutrals are always best."

"Duly noted."

She looked me up and down. "It's been a while for you, hasn't it?"

"It certainly has."

I knew it was critical to maintain an honest exchange. She was being rather gracious about me entering her territory. Especially considering she knows that I have read her diary containing her most intimate thoughts. She wants me to feel vulnerable. I understood why.

"I could make arrangements if you like. Anything you desire is possible here. Just tell me your fantasy and I will ensure it is fulfilled."

"Do you work here?"

Libertine laughed, "Don't be silly. I own them."

"Them?"

"Of course. Marquis, Juliette and 120 are all my creations."

"I heard that 120 is highly exclusive. An invitation only venue."

"Well, there are always exceptions Harper. No one would have stopped you entering given we look identical. They only would have thought it was weird that you chose to enter through the main area instead of the private entrance." She began playing with the straps on the rack. "It's a rather interesting club. You might discover a new side to yourself that's just yearning to be fulfilled."

I smiled, "I only ventured into this realm in the hope that I might find you."

She focussed on running her fingers along the outside edge of the rack, "Why?"

"I think we might be able to help each other and I'd like to"

"No, I mean why did you think you might find me here?"

"I selected this one because of the name."

She released a sigh, "Why did you choose to look for me in a BDSM club?"

Libertine wanted me to say it. "Because I read a portion of your diary and knew that you had developed a penchant for inflicting pain."

Libertine repositioned herself to face me.

"You."

"Read."

"My."

"Diary."

She walked around the back of the rack to flick the latches releasing it to spin. "Now tell me Harper, why I would want to help you?"

I felt by her tone she was turning sour.

"Libertine, you passed me a journal that wasn't yours to give. I also unexpectedly received yours delivered to me. In fairness, the way it was written I thought it was something from a previous century. I had no idea you existed. Honestly, I had no idea that any of you had existed."

Her right eye twitched ever so slightly, "Yes, imagine feeling you knew it all, then one day being unleashed to enter into a modernized world only to realize that everything you were ever taught and knew was a lie. All the people I loved were gone and those who still existed were revealed to be betrayers. Nothing that I wished to be real, was."

I stood there in silence knowing no words could appease such an experience.

"She pulled out her cell. I didn't even know what a phone was. Imagine that."

I gravitated toward the racking machine to stop it from spinning.

"Are you lost for words Harper?"

I shook my head, "No. I'm listening."

She looked me up and down while licking her lips. "What is your sexual preference? I bet you are bi."

"Don't do that, don't rely on sex as your control point."

"Why are you scared to answer the question?"

"I'm not, I just don't see how it's relevant, besides what is bi sexual anyway, aside from just another label set to categorize and define. Everyone is so desperate to be acknowledged as something, fighting for entitlement for rights to be recognized as a label. Gay, straight, bi, dom, sub, tran, pan, seriously we are who we are and no amount of quantifying it to another will make it any different. Providing it's consensual who cares what people want to do between the sheets or anywhere else. Segregation is birthed from a construct of perceived normality. I can tell you that I struggle to relate to a lot of what I witnessed tonight. I mean I am clueless about what the attraction or need is for a person to be demoralized and abused, but if there is a need and people are willing to provide it, let it be. I'm all for them rocking each other's world in any way they wish. So long as it's consensual what do I care? Nada."

"Consensual, so you are apposed to a child being coerced into sexual exploitation?"

"Yes."

"What if it was consensual? Is it okay then?"

I shook my head slightly wanting to resist the need to answer the question. "I have traveled the world and seen many things that I don't necessarily agree with, such as child brides, but I also understand that it is rooted within their culture. Was the construct of the culture driven from a perverse perspective by people of influence or by way of ensuring old stock breed with the young? Does it stem from the likelihood of commanding better control, obedience and submission by gaining access to them while they are young? I don't know the answers, but the belief systems exist in many forms across different nations. The vast majority of people blindly follow and support what they are raised to know. After generations, it becomes the norm. It's impossible to know as an outsider with a completely different suite of morals how to apply an unbiased judgement. I saw girl's eager to embrace their role feeling pride in their culture and some who struggled and wanted to resist what was occurring. I related to the one's I felt were akin to how I believe I would react in such circumstances. The complexity of sex is intertwined with the human psyche and its need to acquire and sustain pleasure, power and control. You only need to look into the history of almost any blue blooded lineage to see how belief in sustaining the quality of the line encouraged incest as a natural solution.

There were no bounds set that wouldn't be crossed, mothers and sons, fathers and daughters, brothers and sisters, cousins. Nothing was taboo. Keeping it within the family was all in the name of upholding the crown. So, your question regarding what if it is consensual between a child and an adult." I shook my head, "I don't know. I fail to accept that we as children are able to understand what it is that we are consenting to. The simple fact that our reproductive systems usually don't kick in until our early to mid teens is to me an indicator that we may be biologically preparing for intercourse at that stage, but our maturity is certainly not on par." I felt like I was babbling, "I can't give you a simple answer to the question. My moral compass wants to leap toward judgement and say no, it's not okay, but then my logical side says the circumstances would need to be assessed taking into consideration all of the factors. Personally, I don't condone any practice that involves animals, children or non consenting adults."

"Apply it to mine based on what you have read."

"You were abducted. Its pretty clear to me that it wasn't consensual."

"What if I told you I liked it?"

I shrugged my shoulders. "Sex is pleasurable and provides people an illusion of control which is aligned to a false sense of power. I'm not surprised under the circumstances that you at times enjoyed it. That is all you had been exposed to for years. It became familiar and what you deemed to be normal. In fact, when I was reading the book I was quasi relieved for you that it panned out that you could celebrate the vixen within your psyche. To have a life such as that thrust upon you and finding that all you were compelled to do is fight against it would have been far worse. The probability of you surviving might have been less than favorable odds. Instead, you not only survived, you seemed to thrive. This small empire that you have built is a testimony to it."

She started to walk around the perimeter of the room, "Do you find me attractive?"

"Yes."

A wisp of a smile appeared, "Take off your clothes and mount the rack."

I calmly responded, "No."

"Why do you resist against your natural desire?"

"Libertine we may look the same, but we are undeniably different, identical only in visual representation. I hold no interest in mounting the rack. Don't assume that I want to fuck you or be fucked by you just because I said yes. We look alike, and I happen to like the way I look, so yes I find you visually attractive."

"Do you think if you were the one taken you would have behaved differently?"

"I don't know."

"Let's find out, shall we?"

I wasn't sure what she was suggesting but didn't sense from her body language and tone that I needed to be concerned. The thought of what the fake Elon suggested about the Interferon's wanting to swap me out was certainly starting to feel like it may be in play. "You've lost me. What are you suggesting?"

"In club Marquis, the décor and layout are much the same as what you will find here with the exception of the seven rooms of graduation. Those who pass through all of them are celebrated in the eighth. The completion of the rooms is the only way you can obtain an invite to enter 120."

I thought about this for a moment.

Libertine stepped forward. "I have a car service that can take you there."

"The seven rooms. I get the symbolism of the seven, but the containment can't be a representation of all of the sins else that would deviate too much from the purpose."

I could see by the smile she was sporting that she held some associated pride to the creation of whatever is in those rooms.

"Your abductors had orchestrated an elaborate program that was phased in stages." Libertine shifted her position slightly. "At a guess, your seven rooms are a fabrication of those stages. Anyone who completes the program as you had, is rewarded with access to the exclusivity of 120, which I can assume is the perceived mecca for BDSM play. Those that fail, what happens to them?"

Her eyes flitted to the camera and then back at me. "They walk free only confined to the kindergarten areas but never to venture into the den."

"Never?"

"Never."

"Wow, that sounds like it's a rather grueling test and unforgiving process if failed. Only being given one shot to pass through the gauntlet at Marquis means that the people who have passed and do have access to 120 are deemed to be the elite."

"Like I said, I have a car that can take you there. We have a long wait list of people wanting to try to become graduates, but I can bump you to the top."

She used the term 'we' which suggests she hasn't entered into this venture alone. "If you have a wait list then surely the place is already fully occupied with people now."

"No matter they can be compensated for the interruption. Will you run the gauntlet of seven, Harper? Do you dare to see how similar we are?" She ran her hand across her breast and stopped to squeeze her left nipple.

"I'm not eleven, abducted and trapped. Unlike the circumstance you were forced to endure, these people voluntarily enter the emulation of your experience and walk out if they have reached their threshold, never to be afforded another chance. The only enticement they have to endure whatever it is that they are subjected to, is the value placement they have on succeeding and the hunger not to be denied the supposed elusive pleasures that reside within 120. It's not the same."

She smiled, "There is only one way to truly find out. Run the gauntlet."

"I fail to see what benefit I would receive from this offer voluntary entrapment. It's definitely a no from me."

"Then it's also a no from me." She said heading for the door. "You can remain and continue to explore the kiddy pen, if you wish. Get your money's worth. I have work to do."

"Thanks." Was all I said in return.

I waited for Libertine to leave and tried not to look at the camera before I exited the room myself. I figured that the cameras might only be set to record visuals and not sound. The way Libertine chose to say, 'you read my diary' was paused and clearly pronounced, which would make it easy to read her lips. After that she positioned herself behind the rack where her face was out of the camera's point of view.

I walked down the corridor making a beeline straight toward the door marked exit. I paused for a moment to look at the stamp on my left wrist. I hadn't ventured into the pleasure sector yet. I smiled as I released the handle to open the door.

"Leaving us so soon?" Asked the Mr Hot Pants.

I nodded my head and raised my hand to wave, "Yes. Good Night."

"Bonsoir, until we meet again Mon Cheri."

Walking up the narrow stairwell I thought about the satisfaction that I would receive from stripping out of these clothes, washing my makeup off and snuggling with Huckleberry. I moistened the tip of my thumb with my tongue and began rubbing off the stamps as I navigated back down the cobblestone alleyway.

Tonight, gave me a clearer picture of what I believed they wanted from me.

Complete submission.

Farewell

It didn't feel right to be there without dad. Dylan and Kichiro had returned from their extravagant gallivant around the country and were now set to head back to Japan. It had been just over a month since I was with them in Joshua Tree. Dad still refused to respond to any of my messages and mom was swanning about the kitchen so occupied with getting the dinner prepared that she didn't seem at all phased that he was absent.

"Are you packed and ready to head back?" I asked, throwing a slice of celery at my brother.

"Yes, we're packed and No. Is anyone every ready to go back to work?"

I laughed. "I guess not," throwing another piece his way. Dylan dodged left to let it pass by.

"Nice one." I said with a chuckle as I picked up another piece in preparation.

"Mom, why do you insist on slicing celery up for the dips when no one in our family ever eats it?"

She looked across and saw me throw it at him.

"I do it so Harper has something to throw at you."

I picked up the bowl and swooped it away just as he leapt across to grab it.

"You heard mom, it's for me to throw not you." I said laughing.

"Kichiro would you like some celery to throw at Dylan?"

He looked up smiling, "No thank you. I am busy."

"I can see that. I'll have to pad you down before you go to ensure you don't try and steal him." Huckleberry was on his back lying perfectly still in Kichiro's lap receiving a gentle belly massage.

"We're not going anywhere tonight. Mom insisted that we sleep here so she can drop us off at the airport in the morning."

"You're welcome to stay too if you like Harper. I can make up another bed."

"Yeah, why don't you stay, that way you can come to the airport to bid us adieu?"

Mom walked across to place another entrée on the table, "That would be lovely. Why don't you?"

"I won't stay, but I will meet you in the morning to make sure you board that plane. Deal?" I put out my fist.

Dylan bumped it, "Deal."

I turned to mom who was now back in the kitchen, "Thanks for the offer, but I need to get Huckleberry home to feed him. I'd prefer to leave him at home. I don't feel comfortable having him stay here unsupervised. I'm assuming dad won't be about tomorrow either, will he?"

She glanced up at me and then straight back to her meal preparation, "I understand. No, your father won't be back for a while. He left me a message saying that he had to go overseas to visit a site."

"Did he give any details as to where or when he would be back?"

"No, nothing."

I turned to look at Dylan who mouthed the words 'what the fuck?' to me. I shrugged my shoulders and threw another piece of celery at him. It wasn't up to me to tell him and in truth I seriously didn't want him to know. By the morning, he would be setting off to a place where he was safe from this drama and in the arms of someone he loved.

Mom pulled out the piping hot lasagne from the oven. The delightful aroma of ripened tomatoes took over the house.

As she placed it on the table Dylan pulled up his knife and fork.

"This looks incredible." He said licking his lips.

"Thanks, I got the instructions off a friend. He's quite the cook. This recipe is from his family's collection. It's been in their family for generations."

Dylan switched out his cutlery for the spatula and cutting knife. He started carving big slabs of the lasagne putting it onto everyone's plate.

I placed my hand over mine, "No thanks. I'm just going to have some salad."

"Are you kidding, I'll cut you a smaller piece."

"No thanks."

"Leave her be Dylan. It's fine." Said mom.

"Okay, but I think you're crazy. This lasagne smells insane." He put some into his mouth.

I watched as he chewed pulling all these exaggerated faces to express how delicious it was.

I filled my plate up with the salad and put some dip on the side.

Mom began eating, while Kichiro appeared to be seemingly mesmerized with massaging little Huckleberry.

"The flavor is truly out of this world. What is that zing to the sauce?"

Mom lit up, "The trick is to add a trickle of a quality reduced balsamic vinegar. It gets layered between the sheets and provides the sweet tartness to complement the acid of the tomatoes. The flavor is so rich because the produce was home grown."

"Kichiro, you have to try it."

He raised his head and smiled. "Yes, thank you."

Dylan stopped mid chew to watch Kichiro take his first a bite.

"Hmm, oishi."

"I know, right?" Dylan shoveled another generous scoop into his already occupied mouth. In a muffle he said, "Beanie Bear, I'm telling you, you're missing out."

"Dylan, don't speak with your mouth full." Mom turned to me, "What does oysti mean?"

"Oishi is the equivalent of delicious."

Kichiro nodded his head in agreement, "Yes, berry delicious. Thank you."

Mom seemed pleased that he liked it.

Everyone tucked into their meals while Huckleberry remained in Kichiro's lap now fast asleep. It felt strange not having dad here with us. I knew that mom was referring to Devon when she mentioned the 'friend' who gave her the recipe and likely the produce for the ingredients as well. Her energy was different to what I had known. She seemed less like the person I thought she was or saw her as while I was growing up and more akin to an immature adult who impatiently wanted things her way and was only pleased when it happened as she saw fit. Did all those years of devoting herself to the family take such a toll that she was now placing herself in a phase of rebellion against everything she had actively created and stood for?

Dylan raised an eyebrow, "Harps what's that on your wrist?"

I smiled, "Nothing."

"It sure doesn't look like nothing. Pull up your sleeve."

I raised my right arm in the air and drew down my sleeve.

"Holy shit. When did you get that?"

"A few weeks back. I did it in a single session and it hurt like hell. Don't let anyone tell you it's an easy task getting inked. I was sweating and cussing like a drunken pirate walking the plank."

"Berry nice," said Kichiro taking another mouthful of the lasagne.

Mom didn't comment. She kept her eyes focussed on her meal and continued to eat.

"What does it say?"

"No regrets in Sanskrit."

"What's the symbolism of the gnarly looking bird?"

"It's a Phoenix rising from the ashes. I wanted to mark the next leg of my life journey with a reminder that no matter what happens I will always rise from adversity and aim to have no regrets."

"Its whack. I love it. Honestly, I never pegged you as the type to get a tattoo. Especially one so big."

"I've always loved them but never knew what I wanted until recently. I felt inspired to embrace change and used the tattoo as my mark of the cross over."

"Anyone ready for dessert?" Said mom getting up to go to the kitchen.

Dylan looked at his plate and then up at her confused, "We're still eating dinner? Is everything alright? You seem a little distracted? Is it dad?"

She wiped her palms down her apron, "Yes, of course you're still eating dinner. Sorry Dylan, I guess I am a little distracted. There's so much happening at the minute that I find myself."

"MOM, THERE'S SMOKE COMING OUT OF THE OVEN." I yelled, thankful for the diversion.

"Oh, dear. Oh, dear. Oh, dear." She said looking around for something to assist her.

"Wait. Turn off the oven and step back." I leapt up and grabbed a tea towel, soaked it with cold water and then wedged it around the seal of the oven door to help prevent the smoke from seeping further. She had overheated oil in a flat pan, which was now piping hot.

"What were you planning to make?"

She looked at me blankly, "I don't know?"

I put my arms around her and gave her a hug. "Go sit down. We don't need dessert; the main meal is more than enough, in fact it's perfect."

I could tell by the way she was breathing that she was on the verge of wanting to cry.

"Go lie down if you want. I'll clean up the dishes when we are done eating." I whispered.

Dylan came into the kitchen, wrapping his arms around us both. "What's going on?" He whispered.

"Your father and I are getting a divorce," mom blurted before howling with tears squeezing us tightly.

"Oh, mom no, you guys are so great together. What's happened?" asked Dylan kissing the top of her head.

I released my grip to wriggle my way out of the embrace. "Do you want to talk about it mom?" I asked, hoping she would say no but knowing she would say yes. It was in my opinion selfish of her to do this, but I also understood that she was genuinely struggling and simply needed to clear the air. Dylan was a grown man, he would find out eventually, hence I decided it wasn't my place to intervene.

She sobbed into Dylan's shoulder as he gave me a look of concern. He knew by my expression that I was already aware that something was taking place between them.

"Come, lets go sit down. You can tell me all about it if you want to," prompted Dylan.

"Okay," she whispered and followed his lead back to the dining area.

I walked closely behind.

Dylan took my seat beside mom and I sat where he had been across the table beside Kichiro.

"Whenever you're ready we're all ears."

Mom composed herself before looking at Dylan and I, "You know I love you both very much. My whole life you were my world."

"Sure, Mom we know that." Said Dylan.

"Lately your father and I had been drifting apart. He was spending more time at the office and the rest of his spare time he threw his energy into that silly garden out there. I was lucky to even be a consideration. I don't know why, we just started to become resentful of each other."

"Mom, you can't speak for dad. Own what you want to convey. 'I' felt we were drifting apart. 'I' felt resentment."

"Harps, that's harsh."

Mom placed her hand on Dylan's arm, "No Harper's right. I'm imposing how I feel into 'we' statements as a deflection from completely owning it. The truth is that your father is devastated. He was as content as could be and didn't understand why I…"

She paused.

We waited.

"Why I had an affair behind his back."

Silence.

Dylan squeezed her arm before releasing his hand, so he could shift his body position slightly away. The small gap between them and the way he was pursing his lips told me a storm was brewing. He had a string of girlfriends who had cheated on him. It was understandably a trigger for Dylan given he had always been loyal to the bitter end. I was certain that he would now naturally revert to placing himself in dad's position.

"Did dad ask for the divorce?"

She looked at Dylan with tear filled eyes, "No, I did. I want to be with Devon."

Dylan looked across to see what I was doing. I stared at him and blinked my eyes as I nodded my head slightly to confirm, this was really happening.

He returned to look at mom, "Have you tried therapy? Why would you give up on something so wonderful after all these years? I don't understand how things went so sour. What's changed?"

She shrugged her shoulders, "I don't know what's changed. I guess I have."

Dylan reshuffled his position in his chair. I could tell that he was overwhelmed by what he was hearing. "So, the life you had built with dad wasn't worth at least trying to fight for?"

"Dylan."

He ignored me.

"Dylan, look at me."

He snapped his head and growled, "WHAT?"

"I know it's a lot to process and it has come as a shock but no matter what, it's not your journey. Mom's entitled to do what she feels is right for her. No permission is required, nor should it be expected. Just like you have made certain decisions that suit your life despite how others might feel, we all have choices to make. The route mom has taken is her footprint. The route you have taken is your footprint. Accept it for what it is. Let it be."

Mom mouthed the words, "Thank you." She knew regardless of how I felt I would be protective and try to temper any outburst with applied reasoning. I didn't want to see any of them hurt but knew that it was inevitable given the circumstances.

Kichiro who had been silent the whole time said three words in Japanese to Dylan, "Kazoku wa subeteda."

The tension in Dylan's jaw released as he repeated the words, "Kazoku wa subeteda, hai. Family is everything."

Everyone remained silent until Dylan pulled out his wallet to retrieve his ring.

"There's something I need to tell you. Kichiro and I got married in Canada on the way over. He is not my boyfriend, he is my husband."

Kichiro innocently smiled as he took Dylan's cue as a sign it was okay to reveal his own ring. He reached for his necklace and began unclasping the hook to free the ring from the chain.

Mom looked at the ring on Dylan's finger and then at Kichiro who was in the process of placing his on. Her expression seemed to hold an air of disdain as her mouth gaped open.

"Well aren't you going to congratulate us?" asked Dylan with a smarmy tone.

Dylan was baiting her. They were very much alike in this sense.

Mom's face contorted, "Congratulate you? Are you kidding? Dylan how could you do this to me? You know I've been looking forward to the day I get to help plan your wedding. I just don't understand how you could be this selfish."

"Am I kidding you? Are you kidding me right now?" Said Dylan staring at her with gritted teeth itching for a fight.

"You didn't even give me the opportunity to attend." She stood up and slammed her hands on the table making the cutlery jump. "This is completely out of order. I'm so disappointed in you. I don't know what else to say."

Dylan jumped to his feet, "Oh, oh yeah and you fucking some guy behind dad's back wasn't out of order? Dad devoted his life to you, idolized the ground you walked on. He used to tell me how lucky he was to have found you and that he was grateful for every day that you were in his life. So, what? What does he get as a reward for loving you, supporting you all these years? The minute things aren't working, instead of fighting for him, you did what? I'll tell you what. BETRAYAL. FUCK YOU AND YOUR DOUBLE STANDARDS. HOW DARE YOU. HOW FUCKING DARE, YOU." He pushed the chair back out of his way. "Go be with that scum marriage breaker Deavo or what ever the hell his name is. I'm done." Dylan stormed out the room.

Mom was frozen in position watching in disbelief as Kichiro carefully passed Huckleberry to me, and then stood up to follow in the direction that Dylan had ventured.

I waited for mom to look at me before I spoke. "Would you like me to help you tidy up before I go?"

She pulled a snarky face, "Fuck you. Take your dog and get out."

I felt the heat rise in my body as her words stung my sensibility. Feigning composure, I quietly positioned Huckleberry in my arms. I stood up from the table to gather the rest of my things to leave. Even though I wasn't expecting that response, nor did I think it was justified, I chose to follow my own advice and let it be.

Dylan and Kichiro returned to the dining area with their bags in tow.

"Come on Harper let's go. We're staying at yours tonight."

There wasn't anything left to say at this point, so we departed the room without exchanging another word. Mom could be heard breaking the plates as she slammed them down into the kitchen sink. I closed the front door and looked at Dylan.

"Well, that was pleasant."

He shook his head as he stared at the house, "I can't believe it. Has she lost her mind? Poor dad. Let's get out of here."

We piled into my car and headed home.

* * * * *

Kichiro wandered around the apartment only able to say, "Wow."

Dylan was in the guest room with me helping to change the bedding. The sheets that were on there hadn't been used, but I felt it would be nice to switch them over anyway. We looked at each other and chuckled every time we heard Kichiro in the distance saying, "Wow."

Huckleberry was eating his dinner wagging his tail the whole time. I think he was excited to have people sleeping over. I knew it was a possibility that I would lose him to Kichiro as a bed pal this evening. After witnessing his receipt of that belly rub I didn't blame him.

Dylan and I took our time drinking our tea while being thoroughly entertained by Kichiro running up the stairs to my bedroom with the specific purpose of sliding down the fireman's pole. Huckleberry was having a great time running up with him and then running down again to greet him as he slid to the ground. The two of them would then race back up to do it again. If I didn't put a stop to it I think they would have continued for hours. It was just past eleven pm and they needed to be at the airport no later than six am, so we were set for an early rise.

I wished them both a goodnight and carried a panting little Huckleberry up the stairs. His heart was beating manically with a smile plastered across his muzzle that was priceless. I placed him on the bed before heading into the bathroom to get prepared for sleep. I was in two minds about having a shower but decided not to bother. I brushed my teeth, washed my face and changed into my pyjamas. When I re-entered my bedroom, Huckleberry was lying on the edge of the bed with his head resting on his two front paws looking at me with his tail slightly wagging.

I smirked shaking my head, "Go on."

He raised himself up to look at me, his tail furiously wagging, then he released a little bark.

"I'm sure, go."

He jumped off the bed running straight down the spiral stairs. I peered over the balcony to watch him scamper across the main room toward the back corridor that led to the guest bedroom. I waited and listened.

"Huckleberry."

Smiling at the sounds of their laughter I jumped into bed. The little shit didn't give me a second glance. I fiddled about with the alarm until it was set on the highest volume. Cringing at the idea of having to wake so early I fluffed my pillows before lying on my back so I could stare up at the night sky for a while.

"Harper, are you still awake?"

I could see Dylan arriving at the top of the stairs.

"Of course. Jump in." I said shuffling over.

Dylan lifted the covers and scooted across toward me in the bed.

"Did Huckleberry kick you out?"

"Those two are thick as thieves, aren't they? I'm starting to think I have some serious competition. You should have seen how quickly he jumped over me and into his arms. It was priceless."

"I think it's cute." I said readjusting my position, so I could stare up at the sky again.

"Harper."

"Yes."

"I need a debrief."

"I know. We can do that."

"I'm confused about what happened tonight. Well, I know what happened, but I need more context around what's going on. Honestly, I'd prefer not to leave things this way. I feel shit about how I behaved. Don't get me wrong, everything I said was true from my perspective, but it didn't need to be conveyed that way. I was thinking maybe we could get up a little earlier and call past in the morning to see her. I tried to call dad, but his phone is switched off. I wanted to talk to him too." He released a sigh, "Harper, I don't know what I'm supposed to do."

When we were kids Dylan sometimes blindly lost his temper at situations that triggered him to feel unhappy. Hours later he would inevitably find a way to sneak into my room so that we could mull over what had taken place. For some reason, no matter how many times we held these sessions he never seemed to be able to apply the same rationale during his moments of emotional discord.

"Clear your mind and remember to answer my questions without blocking, trying to justify your thoughts or responding with deflective questions."

"Okay, I'm ready."

"How did you feel when mom told you that her and dad were getting divorced?"

"Sad."

"How did you feel when mom told you she was having an affair?"

"Angry."

"Why were you angry?"

"She betrayed dad."

"Why did you choose tonight to tell her that you were married?"

"Why not?"

"Dylan, breathe, that's a defensive blocker." I waited until I heard him exhale. "Why did you choose to tell her you were married?"

"To piss her off."

"Why did you want to piss her off?"

"Because she hurt dad."

"Did you marry Kichiro and not invite anyone to hurt us?"

He lifted his head off the pillow, "No, of course not."

"Lay back down and relax."

I waited.

"Why did you use the announcement of the marriage to piss her off?"

"Because I wanted her to hurt too."

"Who has mom hurt Dylan?"

"Everyone."

"No, you can't speak for everyone."

"Who did mom hurt Dylan?"

"Dad."

"You can't speak for dad Dylan. Who has mom hurt?"

He released a sigh as he rearranged the position of his feet under the sheets.

"Me."

"How has she hurt you?"

He folded his arms. "She cheated."

"Are you in a relationship with mom?"

"Ewe, no!"

"Then how did she cheat on you?"

"She cheated on dad."

"Stop referencing other people as a deflection. You know where this is going. How did mom cheat on you?"

"She didn't."

"Who cheated on you Dylan?"

"Okay smarty pants I've got it now."

"I'm sure you have. Say their names."

"Chloe, Brittany, Violet, Michelle, Cynthia and Launa."

"I think you forgot Jo-Beth." I propped myself onto my side, "I didn't know Launa cheated on you."

"Yeah, she told me in a letter that I received just after I first arrived at the base in Japan. I was gutted about it at the time. I didn't expect that from her, especially after I tried so hard to make things work knowing the whole time I was unhappy. I let that one destroy me a little."

"Hmm, so what you were saying to mom tonight was perhaps more of a reflection of the pain you harbor about your experiences of the past that you still haven't processed."

"Yeah probably."

I poked him in the ribs, "More like yeah definitely."

He shifted slightly to defend his side and smiled at me.

I could tell by the look in his eyes that he was really sad.

"The thing is Dylan, whether we like it or not our parents are going through some troubled times and they need to be allowed to manage this in anyway they see fit. I'm not condoning mom's actions, but I can't judge them either. She is clearly struggling. You can tell by the fact that she has repeatedly done things that set her up to be ostracized by us."

"What do you mean?"

"A while ago mom invited me to join her and dad out for dinner where it turned out that Devon was the waiter serving us."

"Get the fuck out of here, she didn't."

"Yep, and recently when I returned from the week I spent with you guys at Joshua Tree I headed straight over to pick up Huckleberry. She knew what time I was set to arrive. Initially I thought her awkward behavior was stemmed from stuff that was happening between her and dad. After a short while I started quizzing her on why she appeared nervous, then I realized that he was in the house some-where. That's why dads not be returning home. Mom allowed Devon into the house and I think he's being staying there."

Dylan sat up, "I'm sorry Harps, that is so fucked up. How dare she?"

I placed my hand on his arm to encourage him to lie back down.

"I'm only telling you this so that you can appreciate that her behavior has shifted to a very self serving modus operandi, that I can only assume is driven by a lot of pent up guilt and pain. Instead of reaching out she is doing things that would make us want to fight with her. It's almost as though she has made up her mind that this new life with Devon cannot be sustained with us as a reminder of what she left behind. I don't know. It's a guess at this stage."

"I just don't get how she can be so selfish."

"Okay. Let me help you with that by giving you a little perspective."

He turned his head to look at me, "What do you mean?"

"Imagine how Kichiro must feel about what transpired this evening. I'm not referring to mom here, I'm talking about you. Instead of having the magic of your special news of marriage celebrated it was delivered at a time that would be conducive to a negative response. You admitted before that you did it to piss her off. That means that you sacrificed something incredibly special, that you two shared, to inflict pain, as apposed to wait for a time where under different circumstances it would have been accepted and embraced. If you insist on questioning mom's motives and asking how she can be so selfish, then you must also assess your own actions and ask the same."

He shook his head. "It didn't even cross my mind to see it that way. Jesus."

"And there we have it. Cue in perspective. Judge ye not for ye shall be judged."

Dylan leaned in to give me a kiss on the cheek. "Thank you. I'm going to go apologize to Kichiro and then try to get some sleep."

"It sounds like a plan. Good night."

"Night sis."

I reset my alarm for us to get up an hour and a half earlier so that we could swing past moms in the morning and then head off to airport. It left hardly any time to sleep. I turned to my side and closed my eyes to allow myself to drift off.

* * * * *

Kichiro fussed over Huckleberry all morning and he was lapping it up. When Dylan and I returned from loading up my car, Huckleberry was nowhere to be seen.

"Huckleberry, Huckleberry, where are you?" I said staring at the wriggling bulge under Kichiro's windcheater.

Dylan saw the moving mass and joined in calling out his name.

"Huckleberry, where are you boy?"

His little head popped out of Kichiro's top. Using his front paws as leverage he pushed toward the underside of Kichiro's chin and began to lick it. He laughed as he tried to lift his head back and out of reach. Huckleberry was a determined little tyke who ingeniously used the bridge of the tops seam to support him while he turned to face Kichiro's exposed neck. Then once again, the licking mania began. Kichiro ended up pulling him out to playfully lift him into the air then dropped him down to nuzzle.

"Okay, I hate to be a party pooper, but we have to head off." I said grabbing my wallet and phone from the coffee table.

Dylan gave Huckleberry a pat then Kichiro once again nuzzled into his neck whispering something to him before placing him on the floor.

"Let's go."

Dylan and Kichiro walked out and I quickly locked the door behind us. We were going to be pressed for time given Dylan still wanted to try see mom on the way.

During the drive toward our childhood home he sent a text to dad and tried to call him, but his cell was still switched off. It was starting to become a real concern.

When we arrived, there wasn't anyone home.

Dylan looked at me after trying the doorbell several times. "Maybe she's on the way to the airport."

I smiled and nodded my head, "Maybe." I figured there was more likelihood that she went to Devon's last night, but I didn't want to say that to him. "Hold on a minute. I have an idea." I ran to the car to retrieve my red lipstick from the center console. When I returned I passed it to Dylan.

"What's this?"

"I don't have a pen or paper, so I thought the next best thing might be to write a message on the window pane."

He looked at the lipstick, "You don't think she's on the way to the airport, do you?"

"No, I don't." I placed my hand on his shoulder to give it a squeeze. "Write the message you want her to see."

He wrote, 'Mom, no matter what, I love you. Call me so we can talk. Dylan.'

He passed the massacred remnants of the lipstick to me.

"I think I ruined it."

"Don't worry it was kind of a slutty color anyway. Let's go, we'll be late."

Dylan laughed.

At the airport, we hurried about to get the bags checked in, then ventured through the security gates so that we could finally relax for a while before they needed to board their plane. We started off by enthusiastically wandering through the duty free stores and wound up seated in a coffee house drinking sub par coffee's for an exorbitant price tag. In the end, I convinced them to spend their last hour getting a massage before they boarded the flight. Dylan knew I wasn't fond of lingering goodbyes, so he reluctantly agreed. The massage would also provide him with a distraction from constantly checking his cell for messages. I could see he was getting upset.

"Kichiro do you have a wallet?"

"Hai."

"Can you please give it to me for a minute?"

He passed it across while looking a little puzzled. I opened it up and placed a photo of Huckleberry in there before handing it back to him. He looked at it and smiled, bowing his head seemingly very moved by my gesture. I reached in to give him a cuddle as I whispered, "Take good care of my brother."

I turned to Dylan and smiled. "It's always an adventure." I drew him into my arms as I felt him reciprocate with a squeeze.

He pressed his lips against my ear, "I love you."

"I know you do. I love you too. Let me know how things pan out with immigration."

He planted his face into the side of my neck. "I will."

I turned my head to kiss him on the cheek. "Go get your massage and don't worry about a thing. Focus on you and Kichiro."

He nodded his head.

I looked at them both and smiled.

"Bye guys."

"Bye," replied Dylan as Kichiro stepped closer to him and waved at me with a big cheery smile.

I turned and walked away.

* * * * *

Upon my arrival home Huckleberry was on the sofa once again expressing the sulks about leaving him behind. I went in to the kitchen to make a cup of tea while I prepared him a little treat as a way of an apology. It was impossible to take him with me everywhere and I certainly do whenever I can, but I had no way of conveying that to him.

I placed a little stack of pancakes in his tray and then called him over. At first, he hesitated then his stomach overrode his sullen mood. He wagged his tail as he scoffed down the treat. I gave him a quick pat before heading to the back room to get my laptop. When I returned, he was on the sofa positioned on top of a cushion waiting for me with a wagging tail. The minute he saw me open up my laptop he walked to the other end of the sofa and sat facing away from me.

I took a deep breath and exhaled, closed the laptop placing it on the coffee table.

"You're right. I'm sorry, come here."

I reorganized the cushions, so I could lie down. Huckleberry reluctantly meandered over to the spot where I was tapping my hand. Slowly I began to pat him until I could feel his body settle. Gently using my hand, I rolled him over to massage his exposed belly in the same way I saw Kichiro do it. My fingers rubbed the whole area until he closed his eyes. My own eyelids were becoming so heavy I no longer had the willpower to fight it. I placed my arm around Huckleberry, so he couldn't roll off the sofa and then let myself fall into a deep sleep.

* * * * *

The sound of the phone ringing in the distance caused me to wake but I wasn't able to reach it in time to answer. I felt overheated and slightly disoriented. Clearing the sleep from my eyes I looked around to see where my cell was and then glanced across to see Huckleberry was lying in his bed asleep. It must have been too warm for him. I raised my hand to wipe the sweat from my brow and then placed the back of my hand on my forehead to feel my temperature. I was burning up.

After taking a quick shower I swapped out my clothes for pyjamas and then took a couple of caplets of paracetamol to aid the reduction of my fever. Just as I swallowed the tablets I heard my cell ping through a message and realized I'd completely forgotten to check who had called. It was too early for Dylan and Kichiro to have landed so I hoped it might finally be dad reaching out.

My eyes were a little fuzzy which forced me to need to squint to counter the screens bright light.

Please contact Ward 9 Mount View General regarding your mother. Ask to speak to the Nurse on duty: Vera Quan.

I pressed the message to dial the number.

"Ward 9, Mount View General. How can I help you?"

"Hi, my name is Harper Perelle. Can I speak to Vera Quan please?"

"One moment."

The woman didn't place me on hold. I could hear people's footsteps, in particular a squeaky pair of shoes, then the phone receiver was cupped. All I could hear now was the muffled sounds of somebody speaking to someone else.

"Vera Quan speaking. How can I help yooou?"

"Hi Vera, my name is Harper Perelle. I received a message to contact you. I believe that my mother is in the hospital under your care. Can you tell me what happened please?"

"Yes, Ms Perelle your mudda she cut herself very bad and get rushed to here to horsepital. I look after her tonight, she fine, stable now but must stay overnight to settle. Can you pick her up in da morning?"

"Sure, I can pick her up. Is it possible to speak with her please?"

"She sleeping now, berry tired. You come tomorrow, okay?"

"Okay."

"K Bye."

I heard the phone click as she disconnected the line. I wanted to get some more details about what had happened and what time I was supposed to pick her up. Vera mentioned that mom cut herself pretty badly. I wondered if it occurred as we were leaving last night. I guess I'd find out the full story in the morning.

There was a wave of hot flushes that surged through my body causing me to instantly feel faint. I turned and sat on the back of the sofa balancing myself with the support of my hands. Just as I felt the fever settle I opened my mouth and vomited on the floor. The drool was freely dripping from my open mouth as I felt another surge of spew riseup and out. Controlling my breathing through my nose I tried to resist the urge to swallow. The smell of the bile made me gag as I began to dry wretch. Huckleberry sat up to look at what was happening and thankfully remained still as another upchuck of chunder came hurling out.

When I felt settled I mustered up the energy to place sheets of paper toweling over the mess. There was no way I was able to contend with cleaning it without contributing to the pile again. The free flow of my spew left my stomach feeling completely empty. It was making loud grumbling noises as it continued to churn. There was a crippling pain building that felt like I had eaten an ice cube that was melting to reveal a center containing molten lead. The searing discomfort was causing my midriff to bloat. I'd clearly eaten something that my body determined was better out than in. Slowly, I made my way to the kitchen sink to wash my face. I had to pause to work through another bout of rising pain. When it subsided I quickly took the opportunity to rinse my mouth out before picking up Huckleberry to bring him with me to bed. I wasn't feeling well at all.

* * * * *

Mom wouldn't give me eye contact in the hospital and had hardly spoken a word to me on the way home. It made me wonder why she bothered to request me to pick her up. My only conclusion was that Devon mustn't have been available to assist and given that dad is supposedly out of town I was her only option.

When we arrived, she didn't wait for me to stop before opening the car door. I grabbed her arm to prevent her from attempting to leave. "What are you doing? Wait until I stop the car."

She reefed her arm from my grasp and jumped out the moment my foot was placed on the brake. I didn't know what was going on for her, but I certainly wasn't in a state where I felt much like caring. My stomach was still hurting, and my fever had not subsided.

I planned to wait to ensure she safely entered the house before I left. I looked across and saw that she was still standing out the front of her house.

Placing the car in park I unwound my window, "Don't you have keys?"

She shook her head.

I wound the window back up and turned off the car engine, "Jesus."

As I walked toward her, I saw that she was staring at the note Dylan had left. "Do you have a spare set of keys hidden some-where or do I need to call a locksmith?"

"There is a set in the garden. It's a fake rock to the left of the praying Buddha."

I looked at her bandaged hands and saw that she had a slight tremor in her right arm. "I'll go get the key."

Returning to the driveway where my car was parked I realized that I couldn't open the garage without a remote.

The neighbor on the left had a pretty big Rottweiler that I didn't feel like testing the friendship with, so I opted to head to the right where there was a small portion of the fence I knew I could scale. It took me a couple of attempts to get enough momentum to raise my hips above the fence line to then very awkwardly place my legs over and jump. Once I landed I walked down the side of the house, which gave me access straight into the backyard. I began looking for the fake rock then realized that the back door was wide open. I entered the house cautiously at first wondering if there might be an intruder.

The dining table still had some food left from the previous night. Walking past the kitchen island bench a massive pool of congealed blood on the floor caught my attention. The cupboards were splattered with droplets and there was broken glasses and plates everywhere.

I shook my head in disbelief.

The doorbell rang.

I walked over and opened the front door. "Here you go. The back door was open. I didn't need the"

Mom pushed past me and went straight to her room slamming the door behind her.

I paused for a moment to breath. Her behavior was becoming excessive and very hard for me to bear. There was a part of me that wanted to leave but I thought better of it. She clearly needed some help. I closed the front door and headed back into the kitchen to begin cleaning the mess. Fragments of glass were everywhere. I started by picking up the bigger broken pieces, then swept up what I could with a broom, vacuumed around the pools of blood and finally went over the whole floor with a mop, twice. Once I was done with clearing the benches, I set my mind to trying to remove all the splatters of blood on the cupboard doors, walls and the backsplash. The only area left to wipe down was the wall phone that she must have used to call for help. There were dried blood drippings on the chord and floor where she had been standing. The cut would have been deep to bleed so profusely. It didn't make sense that it was everywhere. Its like she intentionally flung her arm about to make a mess.

When I finished clearing off the table and washing the last few dishes I went and found the spare key to place on the kitchen bench. I couldn't decide whether I should check on her or just lock the back door and leave. Under the circumstances, she probably shouldn't be left alone, but knew she clearly didn't want me around right now.

I switched on the kettle to make her a cup of tea while I locked the back door. When the kettle boiled I made a pot of tea, placed some milk on the side together with a slice of toast with jam.

Standing outside her room I stopped to listen but couldn't hear anything. I knocked on the door lightly waited for a moment, then entered. She was lying on her side staring out the window.

"Hey, I've tided up the kitchen and made you some tea with toast. You should probably try and eat something." I placed it on her beside table.

She didn't flinch.

"I'm not comfortable with leaving you alone right now and I get that you obviously don't want me around, so I want to strike a compromise."

I paused to see if she would respond.

"Okay then, well my suggestion is this. If you give me Devon's number, I'll call and organize for him to come over. As soon as he's here, I'll go."

She turned to scowl at me with her lips pursed so tight they were going white.

"I don't get it? What's that look for? I'm trying to help you. Tell me what's going on for you right now?"

"As if you don't know. Don't act dumb Harper it doesn't suit you."

I released a breath, "I actually don't know what's up, so enlighten me."

"How could you? Did you think it would stop me from leaving your father?"

My heart sank. "What are you talking about?"

"I should have known. Growing up you were always so outwardly flirtatious with boys. Clearly you had become so jealous that I was finally happy that you had to try and influence the situation by fucking my boyfriend. Don't even try to deny it. You whore."

"Mom, look at me. Do you really think that I would do that?"

"Oh, you think you are so fucking smart giving Dylan that red lipstick to write the message on the window. The same shade you were wearing when you were sucking my boyfriend's cock. He showed me the video footage. How stupid do you think I am? Devon was wracked with guilt. He confessed everything to me. I wanted to say something so badly last night but didn't want your brother to know what a slut you are. I was trying to protect him from the truth, god knows why."

"Mom, I"

"I want you to know that your little plan didn't work. I've forgiven Devon and we are going to find a way to make this right, despite your best efforts to tear us apart."

I rolled up the sleeve on my right arm. "Does the girl in the video bear this tattoo? Pay attention to the details mom. It wasn't me."

I looked at her and knew there was no point in trying to recover from this. She was enraged and wasn't listening. The play had been made and Libertine had won... for now.

"Fuck you Harper. You're dead to me. Do you hear me? Dead. Get the fuck out of my house."

I nodded my head then turned and left the room without another word exchanged.

* * * * *

Slamming open the front doors to Club 120 I entered the reception area screaming, "LIBERTINE, COME OUT. LIBERTINE, LIBERTINE, LIBERTINE, COME OUT NOW. LIBERTINE, LIBERTINE, LIBERTINE, LIBERTINE."

A huge security guy stepped forward looking confused as I approached him. He held out his hand to stop me while cupping his earpiece. Then nodded his head as he stepped aside. The main doors to the club opened. I made no hesitations to storm through and saw a staff member nervously gesturing for me to follow. He pointed to the stairs. I looked up as the door opened. The moment I saw her appear I felt enraged and headed toward her as quick as my legs could carry me. Libertine stepped away from the doorway to provide space for my thundering entrance into the room. I held little care for who else might be there.

"WHY?"

She looked at me with a smug expression on her face. "It was your choice Harper."

I glared at her and waited while trying to catch my breath.

"You could have taken up the offer to enter the gauntlet of seven but sadly you declined. You chose the path that I had to walk for you."

I continued to remain silent completely focussed on listening to her words.

"You're angry now but when the rage settles you'll thank me for revealing their true nature. Given the right circumstances they all betray."

"They are deceived by a cloak of lies, you're proving nothing to me other than people are gullible and too trusting for the devious likes of you."

"Are you sure about that? If they truly loved you, if they truly knew who you are, then nothing could lead them astray. Right?"

I released my breath calculatingly slow to try assist with regaining a sense of calm as I started to exit the room.

"Wait, where are you going? I'm not done."

I heard Libertine press something, which made a loud clicking sound. I spun around suspecting she might be harboring a weapon and instead found myself momentarily frozen when I saw what she had done.

Confidently she stepped forward, "How remiss of me. I forgot to switch on the sound. Watch you're going to love this. The way he played with my hair. I don't know, it felt so, nurturing. I thought it would take a reasonable amount of persuading, but as it turns out he required surprisingly little encouragement at all."

"Oh, Beanie Bear, yes. Oh, my God yes, suck daddy's cock. Just like that. Yes. Open that pretty mouth of yours wider, that's a girl. Take me in. Oh, God yes, all the way."

I grabbed the remote to activate the mute function then continued to watch.

In the background, Libertine released a little laugh. "See, red lipstick. Tsk. I told you neutrals are best."

I maintained my focus and continued to stare at the screen. There it was, her right hand in clear view running up his torso. They still didn't know about my tattoo. I switched the projector off, threw the remote onto her desk and walked out the door without giving her a second glance.

As I headed down the stairs Libertine called out, "I'm doing you a favor. Now you know the truth about what surrounds you. You're free from the illusion that people care."

By the time I reached the bottom of the steps Libertine made one final statement.

"You need me Harper Perelle. I know you better than you know yourself."

I looked up at her and smiled, "Do you?"

The previously empty corridor was now lined with people. They pointed at me laughing manically as I passed by. I had to keep reminding myself it was all an orchestrated play. They had been instructed to make me feel humiliated. It wasn't real, it was an act. It wasn't real.

Mechanically I forced myself to place one foot in front of the other mustering all my inner strength to calmly walk away. My whole body was wracked by a sense of surging physical pain. Their laughter was searing the core of me. I knew there would be absolutely nothing that could be done to recover from the choices that had been made. Libertine demonstrated her point. When the opportunity presents, I will demonstrate mine.

Dhyāna

Landing in Narita airport I quietly waited with Huckleberry until the other passengers had disembarked from the plane. The only way I could get him on the flight, as a passenger was to purchase him his own ticket in first class. They must have figured that I wouldn't do it given the costly sum. There was no way I was placing him in cargo, so I believed I only had two choices. Charter a private plane to take us to Japan or purchase two first class tickets. The latter was by far the cheaper option.

"Ms Perelle, are you ready to disembark?"

"Yes thanks." I stood up and removed my backpack from the overhead locker.

"Would you like assistance with carrying the cage?"

"No, I'm fine. As soon as I hoist my pack on I'll be on my way."

The hostess smiled, "Sure, take your time."

I could tell that Huckleberry was getting impatient. During the flight, I took him out as often as I could. For most of the trip he was hiding under my blankets, so he could rest on my lap in relative comfort. Each time

I had to put him back into the cage he would whimper in protest. Thankfully the longest leg of the travel was now behind us. I tucked his cage under my arm and headed off the plane.

"Thanks for flying with us."

I smiled to acknowledge the captain's words then continued on my way.

The airport transport vehicle was waiting for us, just as I had arranged. I'd paid extra in advance to have an airport attendant present, so that I could get Huckleberry taken straight to the quarantine vet for inspection while I tried to get ahead of the rest of the crowd by going straight through to customs. That was the one great advantage of not having any additional luggage to collect. Where I was heading, I didn't need anything more than I could carry.

The car dropped me off at the customs sector then carried on with Huckleberry to the vet. If everything went to plan he would be in quarantine for no more than twelve hours before we were free to travel to the next destination. I hadn't booked the tickets yet. Until I'm certain Huckleberry is going to be released, I wasn't going to make any further plans.

I stepped through the queue and placed my bag onto the x-ray machine conveyor belt, then began executing the usual rigmarole that is typical of airport assessment protocols. I did my best to look attentive and followed all the instructions given. There was a sense of relief as I was finally waved through. Swinging my backpack onto my back, I looked for the signs that would guide me to the animal quarantine sector.

After walking about in circles for ten minutes I managed to find the sign that pointed to the vet. Inside there was a long queue of people waiting to be served. I did as I had been told to do and raised a sign that said Huckleberry in Japanese. One of the receptionists behind the counter waved me forward. I squeezed past the people who seemed reluctant to move for me.

"Do you have the paperwork for your dog?"

"Yes. I had them faxed over here for pre- approval. I will now give you the originals." I pulled out the manila folder containing all the paperwork that they required and passed it to her. She opened the file and looked at the items nodding her head as she flipped each page.

"Looks good. Wait here one moment please." She walked off with the folder in hand.

There was a lot of tension built up in the overcrowded room with people and pets expressing their frustration with the lengthy wait to be served. The five women at the counter were fully occupied with little rest between patrons.

The woman returned with a piece of paper. She placed it on her desk and rather aggressively stamped it before passing it to me. "Dis for proof of quarantine approval, keep with dog at all time. If you got a problem, you call us. Okay, you can take your dog now." She pointed to a door to my left, then sat back in her chair and waved for the person next in line to come forward.

I went across and knocked on the door. A sliding compartment within the door was opened revealing a person wearing a surgical mask. I held up my piece of paper. They nodded their head and closed the door. I stood back because I wasn't sure what was going to happen next. After a solid five minutes had gone by I was tempted to knock on the door again. Just as I was contemplating stepping forward a slide at the bottom of the door was opened and Huckleberry's cage was pushed out. I bent down and waved at him then grabbed the handle and walked out before they changed their mind.

I knew that Huckleberry was busting to be freed but there were still a couple of things I needed to get sorted. I went across to the ticketing counter and organized a flight to Osaka. Given the trip had taken so long I opted to board a flight that was set to leave in a couple of hours. This gave me a chance to walk Huckleberry around the airport car park and surrounding area for an hour. As soon as I received the tickets, I headed to the nearest exit walking away from the general populous before I released him from the cage and placed the harness on. He was so excited to be free. He wagged his tail and cocked his leg up to pee on practically everything.

Ferreting around in my backpack I found my cell. I switched it on, took a photo of Huckleberry Perelle's first class ticket to Osaka and sent it to Dylan so he would know when we were set to arrive, then switched it off again and returned it to my pack. Huckleberry was still sniffing and raising his leg to anything stationary even though he was now struggling to release a dribble.

The flight to Osaka was quick. I was relieved given that Huckleberry was starting to voice his protest verbally with an intermittent harrowing noise that I had never heard from him before. In the end, the on-board staff gave me permission to hold him in my lap as they were concerned he was disturbing the other patrons. When we landed, I put him in the cage and made sure I was one of the first to get off the plane.

Thankfully given it was a domestic flight we had no more red tape to go through. As we entered the main area Dylan and Kichiro were there to greet us with warm smiles and open arms. I put Huckleberry's cage down and released the hatch to free him. Kichiro bent down with a big smile. My little man ran straight toward him and leapt into his arms. I was so relieved to see him happy. We had made it.

I gave Kichiro a kiss on the cheek and hugged my brother.

"Here," I passed across Huckleberry's copies of his quarantine papers and the one that showed he had been inspected. "All the instructions are in the pack, so you know what vaccinations he needs and by when to maintain his in-country quarantine compliance." Dylan took them from me and placed them in his bag. "We can do all of this when we get home. You must be exhausted. I've made up your room, so you can have a quick bite to eat and then go straight to bed."

Huckleberry was snuggled in Kichiro's arms as he rocked him gently. I bent down to pat him.

"Remember, just like when you were with York eventually you had to stay with Cletus? It's that time Huckleberry. I need to go, and you need to be with Kichiro now. He is going to look after you. He is your Cletus." I leaned in and kissed his little head as I whispered, "Thank you for coming into my life. Thank you for everything. I love you so much little man. Be good for him you hear me? I'll carry the memories and treasure them with all my heart. Always." Tears were streaming down my face as Huckleberry licked me.

I looked up at Kichiro. "Please look after him."

He gently tipped his head to bow, "It will be my honor."

Dylan stepped forward, "Aren't you coming with us? I know you said you were going to travel but I thought you would stay with us first for a while. What's the rush?"

I shook my head, "I can't."

"What do you mean you can't? I don't understand, of course you can. It's no imposition, we were expecting you to stay with us. There's plenty of room."

I rummaged around my backpack to retrieve my cell.

Tears streamed freely down my face. "Here, mind it for me."

Dylan looked at the cell, "If you give it to me, how will I reach you?"

"You won't."

"Harper, you're scaring me. Where are you planning to go?"

I placed the cell on the ground and stepped back away from it and them, "I don't know. I need to find something, and I can't return until it's found."

Kichiro whispered, "Baransu."

I slowly nodded my head, "Hai, Baransu."

"Balance, what balance? I don't understand what's going on."

Kichiro placed his hand on Dylan's shoulder and squeezed just as he was stepping toward me, "Let her go."

He looked at Kichiro and then at me.

I mustered up a slight smile at the sight of how content Huckleberry was within Kichiro's arms.

"Everything is going to be okay." I said as I clasped my hands together in a position of prayer and bowed to give thanks. They both stood in silence watching as I turned and walked away.